Lilith

The Rise and Fall of Darkness

Troy Biffath

ISBN 979-8-9989857-0-6

Dedication

To the air that I breathe, my wife.

Author's Note

This book is a work of fiction, inspired by my beliefs as a member of The Church of Jesus Christ of Latter-day Saints (LDS). While it draws from spiritual themes rooted in LDS teachings, the characters, events, and settings are entirely fictional.

This story is intended for mature audiences. It includes adult themes such as war, violence, psychological trauma, sexuality, and moral ambiguity. These elements are not gratuitous. They serve to explore the depths of human agency, the cost of redemption, and the tension between light and darkness in a fractured world.

Nothing in this book should be interpreted as official doctrine. Rather, it is a creative reflection on faith, resilience, and the unseen spiritual conflict that surrounds us.

I hope this story challenges as much as it inspires, encouraging reflection, sparking empathy, and ultimately honoring the belief that even in the darkest of times, light can prevail.

Contents

Preface Part 1

Before time etched its rhythm into the dust of worlds, I chose to question.

We were eternal—one in purpose, in radiance, in design. But even among the divine, doubt can bloom. I asked what others feared to think. And in that whisper, the harmony shattered.

Lucifer offered certainty. A plan without pain, without agency. Many saw mercy. I saw control. Love without choice is just obedience dressed in light. So, I chose another path. They called it a fall. But I know the truth. I didn't fall. I leapt.

1-War

Before the world was formed, there existed a realm of boundless light and knowledge where the spirit children of God dwelt in unity. This was the premortal existence, a time of preparation where spirits were taught eternal principles. Among them were future prophets, leaders, and those who would rise to power, or fall into darkness.

In this luminous realm, celestial beings gathered to hear God present the plan of salvation, offering spirits the chance to gain bodies, choose between good and evil, and return to His presence. God's voice, filled with love, echoed as He explained the plan, emphasizing the importance of agency and the potential for both joy and suffering.

Among the spirits, Lucifer, a being of great beauty and intellect, proposed an alternative plan, one that guaranteed salvation for all but at the cost of agency. God rejected this, reminding Lucifer that true joy comes from choice, not compulsion.

In the crowd, Lilith, an ambitious spirit, resonated with Lucifer's plan. Despite God's warnings, Lilith chose her own path, aligning with Lucifer and setting the stage for a cosmic conflict that would echo through the ages.

As the grand council in heaven continued, the initial shock of Lucifer's defiance gave way to growing tension among the spirit children of God. The celestial realm, once a place of perfect harmony, was now stirred by the seeds of rebellion. At the heart of this rising storm was Lilith, whose ambition and intellect pushed her to the forefront.

The light that once filled the realm waned, and harmonious voices were replaced by whispers of doubt. Lilith, fully aligned with Lucifer, became a pivotal figure in rallying the dissenting spirits, her persuasive voice spreading the seeds of rebellion.

"Why should we submit to a plan that risks our existence?" Lilith argued. "We are beings of power and intellect, why not seize control and ensure our own success?" Her words resonated with those who feared failure, drawing many to her side.

The rebellion in the celestial realm erupted into a war of unimaginable scale, shaking the very foundations of existence. What was once a realm of peace and harmony became a battlefield where the forces of light and darkness clashed with an intensity that shook the heavens. Lilith, once a being of radiant beauty and intellect, now stood at the forefront of this cosmic conflict, her form darkened by the power of her defiance.

As the rebellion gained momentum, God spoke with love and sorrow, warning of the darkness and despair that awaited those who followed Lucifer and Lilith. But the promise of power was too enticing for them to abandon. The rebellion began, tearing the celestial realm apart.

The celestial landscape, once filled with brilliant light and serene beauty, was now a chaotic swirl of shadows and flames. The air crackled with energy as the loyal spirits, led by the archangel Michael and other divine beings, struggled to repel the onslaught of Lucifer, Lilith, and their followers. The battlefield was a place of immense power, where every strike reverberated through the very fabric of reality.

Lilith, her mind sharp and calculating, moved through the fray with precision, commanding her forces with an iron will. Her presence on the battlefield was commanding, and her every word inspired those who had chosen her path. "Press forward!" she cried, her voice cutting through the chaos. "Do not falter! We shall claim our rightful place as rulers of this realm!"

Her words fueled the rebellion, driving her followers to fight with renewed fervor. The ground trembled beneath their assault as they surged forward, determined to overthrow the loyalists. Yet, the forces of light, though battered, stood firm. Michael, glowing with divine light, rallied his troops, his voice a beacon of hope in the darkness. "Stand firm!" he commanded. "We fight for the glory of God and the sanctity of His plan! Do not let the darkness consume you!"

The loyal spirits, inspired by Michael's unwavering faith, pushed back against the tide of darkness. The battle raged on; each side locked in a desperate struggle for control of the heavens. Lilith, her resolve unshaken, continued to lead her forces with fierce determination, her eyes burning with the fire of ambition.

During the conflict, Lilith found herself face-to-face with an archangel who had once been her friend. His eyes, filled with sorrow, met hers across the battlefield. "Lilith," he called out, his voice pleading, "why do you persist in this madness? There is still time to turn back, to seek forgiveness. You do not have to follow Lucifer down this path of destruction."

For a moment, the chaos of battle seemed to pause as the two beings stared at each other. The weight of their shared history hung heavy in the air. But Lilith's resolve did not waver. Her face hardened, and her voice was cold as she replied, "You speak of forgiveness as if it is something I desire. But you are wrong. I have chosen my path, and I will not be swayed by your pleas. This is my destiny, and I will see it fulfilled, no matter the cost."

The archangel's expression was one of deep sadness, but he knew there was no turning her from her chosen path. With a heavy heart, he raised his weapon, prepared to defend the plan he had sworn to uphold. "So be it," he said, his voice filled with sorrow. "But know this, Lilith: the path you have chosen will only lead to darkness and despair. You will never find the power and glory you seek, only an eternity of regret."

With those words, the two beings clashed, their powers colliding with a force that sent shockwaves across the battlefield. The light and darkness intertwined, each struggling for dominance, as the war in heaven reached its climax. The battle raged on, but it became increasingly clear that the forces of light were gaining the upper hand. Michael, empowered by divine will, drove back Lucifer and his followers, their dark forms faltering under the relentless assault.

Lilith fought with all the fury and cunning she possessed, but she could not even turn the tide of the battle. The loyalists, fueled by their unwavering faith and the light of their Creator, were simply too strong. The rebellion began to crumble, and the once-mighty forces of darkness were pushed to the brink of defeat.

In a final, desperate attempt to seize victory, Lucifer and Lilith rallied their remaining forces for one last, all-out assault. They gathered their followers, preparing to strike with everything they had left. "To me!" Lucifer called, his voice filled with desperation and defiance. "We will not go quietly into the void! We will fight until the very end!" Lilith stood beside him, her eyes burning with fierce, unyielding resolve. "This is not the end," she vowed, her voice filled with chilling certainty. "Even if we fall today, our legacy will endure. We will rise again, stronger than before, and claim what is rightfully ours."

But their final assault was met with overwhelming force. The loyal spirits, led by Michael and the other archangels, unleashed a torrent of divine energy that shattered the defenses of the rebels. The battlefield was consumed in blinding light as the forces of darkness were overwhelmed, their rebellion crushed.

As the light faded, the once-glorious forms of Lucifer, Lilith, and their followers were revealed—darkened, twisted, and broken. They had been defeated, their power shattered, their rebellion in ruins. In the aftermath of the battle, God's voice filled the heavens, calm and resolute. "You have chosen your path," He said, addressing the fallen spirits. "You sought power and glory at the expense of your brothers and sisters, and now you will face the consequences of your choices. You are cast out, banished from My presence."

With those words, Lucifer, Lilith, and the fallen spirits were cast out of heaven. Their forms, now shadowy and dark, plummeted through the void, the light of the heavens receding behind them. They were sent to Earth, stripped of their former glory, to become the tempters and deceivers of humankind.

As she fell, Lilith's voice echoed through the void, filled with defiant resolve that refused to be silenced. "This is not the end," she vowed once more, her words a chilling promise. "We will rise again, and all shall know our power."

Cast out of heaven and stripped of her former glory, Lilith descended into the earthly realm—a place she viewed with both contempt and ambition. Unlike the spirits of human-kind who would eventually receive bodies, Lilith remained a being of pure spirit, bound by the limitations of her disembod-ied state. Yet, her resolve was unshaken. The Earth, newly formed and brimming with life, was now her domain—a realm where she could wield her influence, even without a physical form.

As she descended, the Earth trembled with her arrival. Her presence, though invisible to the eyes of men, was palpable—a chilling wind that stirred the leaves and darkened the skies. The once serene world now felt a subtle shift, an unsettling awareness that something malevolent had entered—a force that did not belong.

2-*Visions*

In the heart of a bustling metropolis, high above the urban sprawl, Jacob, a tall man with dark brown hair and piercing blue eyes, stands as a solitary figure on a rooftop, his gaze fixed on the city below. Jacob, a man of unshakeable faith and unwavering conviction, feels the weight of a divine presence drawing near, the foreboding of a prophecy on the brink of unfurling.

"The signs are aligning, just as foretold," Jacob murmurs, his voice barely a whisper against the cacophony of the urban night. As he lifts his eyes to the sky, a sense of anticipation permeates the air, a tension palpable with the promise of revelation. In this moment of suspended time, Jacob knows that the veil between worlds is thin, awaiting the touch of destiny to set in motion a series of events that will shape the fate of humanity.

Jacob heard a still, small voice that said, "Are you ready to see what lies ahead?" Jacob replied, "Yes, show me, my Lord," his words a beacon calling to the celestial realm. The world around him fades as a mosaic of light and shadow dances across the canvas of his mind, painting a panorama of chaos and salvation, where the forces of darkness and light converge in an epic clash of ages. In this vision, Jacob witnesses a world veiled in darkness, where malevolence reigns unchecked, and the tendrils of evil entwine around the very weave of existence. Amidst the turmoil, a figure emerges—an enigmatic entity of unfathomable power, cloaked in the guise of grace yet harboring darkness threatening to eclipse all resistance.

As Jacob's vision faded, his thoughts were pulled back to the physical world, the flickering lights of Evelyn's vitals still dancing silently across the monitor beside her bed. The prophets spoke in visions, but the war was already bleeding into circuits and code. Somewhere, in a lab not far from here, the other half of the story was unfolding—built not from faith, but from algorithms and ambition.

Jacob consults with his brethren before disseminating his visions broadly. He seeks their counsel, presenting his divine revelations with the urgency they demand. The counselors, men of deep faith and wisdom, listen intently, their expressions reflecting the gravity of the situation.

"Thomas and Tim, we stand on the brink of a new era," Jacob begins, his voice steady despite the weight of his message. "The visions I have received are clear. We must prepare our people for the trials ahead."

Thomas nods, his eyes filled with understanding. "Jacob, your faith and leadership have always guided us truly. We will stand by you and support you in this mission."

In a seminar room brimming with genuine discussion and scholarly debate, Jacob encounters Marcus, a doctoral student with a hunger to probe the secrets of the unknown. An erudite young man with a keen intellect and a thirst for enlightenment, Marcus embodies the mosaic of curiosity and skepticism that enlivens the corridors of academic inquiry.

There was a quiet power in Jacob's presence—something sacred that Marcus couldn't define, only feel. It wasn't fear, exactly, but standing near him felt like standing too close to a flame lit by God Himself.

Engaging in a spirited dialogue with Marcus, Jacob delves into the implications of his prophetic vision—the revelation of a formidable entity lurking at the precipice of existence, poised to challenge the very essence of humanity. "Marcus, what I've seen transcends mere philosophical debate. We're facing a convergence of spiritual darkness and technological might," Jacob explains, focusing on the enigmatic parallels between this evil entity and the burgeoning advancements in artificial intelligence and quantum computing.

Marcus responds with a mix of awe and skepticism, "It's hard to imagine how these threads could be so closely tied together. The potential for both salvation and destruction lies within our grasp."

"Boston Dynamics stands at the vanguard of robotics research, pioneering transformative technologies that blur the boundaries between humanity and machines," Jacob continues.

"Neuralink embarks on a journey into the realm of human-machine interfacing, unveiling a future where the frontiers of cognition and augmentation merge in a symphony of transcendent possibilities," Marcus adds.

The prospect of harmonizing the human mind's neural pathways with Artificial Intelligence's computational prowess sparks a dialogue among visionaries and skeptics alike, heralding a paradigm shift in the realms of intelligence and consciousness.

"Imagine integrating the human brain with AI to enhance cognitive functions exponentially," muses Marcus, caught up in the excitement of the technological frontier. Jacob nods thoughtfully, his mind wrestling with the implications. "Yet, we must tread carefully. The power we unleash could be our salvation or our downfall," he cautions, emphasizing the dual-edged nature of such advancements.

Simultaneously, within the corridors of academia, a collaboration between a prestigious university and the Pentagon unfolds, paving the way for the development of cutting-edge exoskeletons designed to transform ordinary soldiers into elite 'super-soldiers.' These biomechanical marvels augment human physiology with an array of cybernetic enhancements, blurring the boundaries between flesh and steel and ushering in an era of warfare guided by the fusion of humanity and technology.

"Such power, vested in humanity, must be governed by the highest ethical standards," Jacob asserts as they discuss the potential impacts on warfare and society. Marcus responds with a hint of concern, "It's a fine line between enhancing life and controlling it. Who decides where that line is drawn?"

Their conversation reflects the intricate and potentially perilous interplay between technological prowess and moral responsibility. A whisper in the halls of learning speaks of a clandestine mosaic of academic inquiry; a research team delves into the unknown depths of nanotechnology. Through meticulous experimentation, they navigate the intricate dance of microcosmic marvels, unraveling the mysteries of nanotech capable of reshaping the horizons of human potential, much like the elusive strands of nanotechnology woven into the fabric of myth and prophecy.

"As we delve deeper into the microcosm, we unlock powers that could redefine our very essence," Jacob remarks, pondering the profound implications of their findings.

Marcus adds, "And yet, each discovery brings us closer to answering some of the oldest questions of existence. It's as if each technological advance brings us closer to the divine."

"The challenges we face are immense, but so are the opportunities. We stand on the precipice of a new age," Marcus concludes, his voice echoing through the halls of academia with a mixture of awe and resolve.

With these profound thoughts, Jacob and Marcus continue to navigate the complex and ever-evolving landscape of academic inquiry, technology, and prophecy, their discourse a testament to the unyielding quest for knowledge and the relentless pursuit of understanding the deeper truths of the universe. Their journey through the intricate tapestry of human endeavor and divine fate promises to shape not only their destinies but also the future of humanity itself.

"Whispers of the divine speak of chaos and salvation," Jacob murmurs to himself, a shiver running down his spine as the weight of his divine vision presses upon him. His gaze lifts to the starless night, feeling the pressing urgency of his mission. "It is time," he whispers, his voice barely audible over the howling wind.

Jacob recounts his vision, describing a world draped in darkness, where evil rises unchecked, and hope seems but a faint glimmer. "And yet, there is light, a promise of redemption if we dare to confront the darkness."

In the well-lit corridors of the university's advanced research facility, Marcus was preparing for a significant meeting. As a doctoral candidate deeply engrossed in the intersection of technology and biology, the opportunity to meet Dr. Isabella Voss, a renowned pioneer in AI and neural interfaces, was both exhilarating and daunting. Dr. Voss had just joined the faculty, bringing with her a wealth of knowledge and an ambitious vision for the future of medical technology.

Marcus had arranged to meet Dr. Voss in her new lab, a space already buzzing with the latest equipment and her recent experiments. As he approached, he could see through the glass doors that Dr. Voss was already there, her figure bent over a complex-looking device that seemed to be half-mechanical, half-electronic.

Knocking lightly on the open door, Marcus entered, his voice slightly tentative. "Dr. Voss? I'm Marcus Blackwood. Thank you for agreeing to meet with me."

Dr. Voss looked up, her expression shifting quickly from concentration to welcome. "Ah, Marcus, yes! I've heard about your project. It's quite intriguing. "Please, come in," she gestured to a chair near her workstation.

As Marcus sat down, he took a moment to organize his thoughts. "Dr. Voss, I've been following your work on neural interfaces, and I believe there's a potential overlap with my research on enhancing the body's healing capabilities through technology. Specifically, your insights into AI could revolutionize how we approach biological integration."

Dr. Voss nodded, clearly interested. "I'm glad to see such enthusiasm. Tell me, what aspect of my work do you find most applicable to your studies?"

Marcus leaned forward, his hands animated as he spoke. "Your recent paper on adaptive neural algorithms. I think applying these algorithms could improve the precision with which we target treatment protocols. Essentially, it could lead to personalized medicine on a level we've never seen before."

Dr. Voss's eyes lit up with understanding and excitement. "I see. You're thinking about a symbiotic system where the interface doesn't just read from the brain but also delivers targeted stimuli based on real-time feedback?"

"Exactly," Marcus replied. "But the challenge has been the interface's sensitivity and the signal-to-noise ratio. I've been working on it, but I feel there's a missing piece that might lie in your expertise with AI."

Dr. Voss walked over to a whiteboard filled with diagrams and algorithms. "Let's map out how these ideas might converge. We need a robust model that can adapt and learn from each patient's unique neural patterns."

For the next several hours, Marcus and Dr. Voss were deeply engrossed in technical dialogue, sketching out potential frameworks and algorithms. They discussed various AI models and their adaptability to biological data, exploring each hypothesis with a rigorous scientific approach.

At one point, Dr. Voss paused, her gaze thoughtful. "Marcus, integrating AI at this level will be groundbreaking, but it's also fraught with ethical and practical challenges. How do you propose we address these?"

Marcus acknowledged the weight of her question. "I've been considering that as well. Part of our work must include setting up strict ethical guidelines and ensuring that our approach respects patient autonomy and consent. I believe transparency with our participants and the wider scientific community will be crucial."

Dr. Voss nodded in agreement, her expression serious but approving. "I'm impressed, Marcus. It's clear you've thought this through. Not just the 'how' but also the 'why' and the 'should we.' That's essential for the kind of work we're embarking on."

Their meeting concluded with a sense of shared purpose and excitement. As they shook hands, Dr. Voss's parting words were affirming. "Marcus, I'm looking forward to seeing where our collaboration will take us. This is the beginning of something truly significant."

As Marcus left the lab, he felt a surge of inspiration. The initial meeting not only cemented his respect for Dr. Voss's expertise but also solidified a partnership that promised to push the boundaries of what was possible in medical technology.

3- *Innovations*

In the bustling atmosphere of the university's innovative research lab, Marcus Blackwood and Dr. Isabella Voss were deep into the initial stages of their groundbreaking experiments. Their goal was ambitious: to merge nanotechnology with neural interfaces, potentially revolutionizing medical science by enhancing the body's healing processes and neural connectivity.

The lab was filled with the hum of machinery and the occasional equipment beep as Marcus calibrated the neural interface device. Dr. Voss, meanwhile, was examining the nanoscale materials under a microscope, her face illuminated by the soft light.

"Marcus, come take a look at this," Dr. Voss called out, her tone mixed with excitement and a hint of urgency. Marcus walked over, peering into the microscope. "What are we looking at?"

"These nanoparticles are designed to integrate seamlessly with the neural interface," Dr. Voss explained, pointing to the magnified image of tiny, intricately structured particles. "They can navigate along neural pathways, delivering targeted therapies directly to affected areas."

"That's where your expertise with the interface comes in," Dr. Voss said, turning to a whiteboard filled with diagrams and equations. "If we can synchronize the nanoparticles' movements with the neural interface readings, we could guide them to where they're most needed."

The two spent hours mapping out how the nanoparticles could interact with the brain's neural pathways and discussing various models and simulations. Marcus was particularly focused on the interface's programming. "We need a robust feedback loop. The interface should adjust the nanoparticles in real-time based on the brain's responses," he suggested, sketching a complex circuit on the whiteboard.

Data streamed across multiple screens, graphs, and numbers fluctuated as the simulated nanoparticles traveled through neural pathways. Dr. Voss monitored the results, and her expression was tense.

Suddenly, a series of beeps sounded—a warning that some nanoparticles were deviating from their intended path. "Marcus, we're off course," Dr. Voss announced, moving quickly to adjust the parameters.

Marcus was right beside her, typing rapidly. "Increasing precision on the feedback loop," he declared, his fingers flying over the keyboard. After a tense few moments, the beeps ceased, and the data stabilized.

"Look, it's working!" Marcus exclaimed, pointing to the screen where the nanoparticles had realigned with their target pathways.

Dr. Voss let out a breath she hadn't realized she was holding. "That was too close. But it's a valuable lesson in the dynamics of this system. We're pushing into new territory here."

The evening wrapped up with both feeling a mixture of exhilaration and exhaustion. "Today was a step forward, but we've got many more ahead," Dr. Voss said, her eyes reflecting the ambitious scope of their project.

"Yes, and with each step, we learn and improve," Marcus replied, his fatigue overshadowed by the thrill of discovery. "This is just the beginning."

As they left the lab, the weight of their potential breakthroughs and a resolve to overcome any challenges lingered in their minds. Their partnership, built on mutual respect and shared intellectual curiosity, was proving to be not just productive but transformative, poised to make significant impacts in the field of medical technology.

One evening, as they reviewed data from their latest series of tests, Marcus pointed out an inconsistency in the neural response times that had been bothering him. "Isabella, look here," he said, highlighting a graph on the screen. "These spikes—are they anomalies or indicative of something more systemic?"

Dr. Voss leaned closer, her brow furrowing as she studied the data. "It could be an artifact, or it might suggest that the interface is more invasive than we thought. We need to consider the possibility of neural interference," she responded thoughtfully.

Marcus nodded, his mind racing through the implications. "If that's the case, we're looking at a significant ethical issue. We can't risk patient safety, no matter how beneficial the potential outcomes."

This led to a deeper discussion about the moral responsibilities they held. Dr. Voss walked over to a whiteboard and began sketching a decision matrix. "Let's map out the worst-case scenarios," she proposed. "We need to be fully prepared to address any potential harm from our technology."

As they outlined the various risks, their conversation shifted to the broader societal impacts. Marcus, looking increasingly concerned, voiced his apprehensions. "Imagine the potential for misuse. If this technology falls into the wrong hands, it could be exploited in ways we can't anticipate."

Dr. Voss agreed, her voice firm. "That's why our approach to transparency and regulation is crucial. We need to be proactive in engaging with ethical boards and regulatory bodies. And perhaps it's time to start a dialogue with the public."

Marcus stood before a diverse audience during the forum, and his presentation was clear and compelling. "Our goal is not just to advance science but to do so in a way that aligns with societal values and ethical standards," he explained.

A prominent ethicist in the audience raised a question during the Q&A session. "Dr. Blackwood, while your intentions are commendable, how do you plan to ensure this technology is accessible to all and not just a privileged few?"

Marcus exchanged a glance with Dr. Voss before responding. "That's an excellent point, and we are actively working on it. We are exploring partnerships with global health organizations to ensure wide accessibility and are committed to setting up a nonprofit framework that prioritizes equitable distribution."

After the forum, as they were packing up their materials, Dr. Voss smiled at Marcus. "You handled those questions very well. It's clear that our work is not just about the 'what' and the 'how,' but also the 'who' and the 'why.'"

Marcus chuckled, a hint of relief in his laughter. "I'm just glad we're in this together, Isabella. Your perspective keeps us grounded and focused on the bigger picture."

A week later, Marcus stands in a state-of-the-art laboratory at the university. The room buzzes with the sound of equipment and the low murmur of eager graduate students.

Marcus examines the data, his mind racing with possibilities and pitfalls. "We must consider the broader implications," he agrees. "How do we ensure this technology benefits society without compromising ethical boundaries?"

Their conversation is a deep dive into the scientific marvels they are on the brink of mastering, juxtaposed with a cautious awareness of the Pandora's Box they might open.

News of Jacob's prophecies and Marcus's scientific advancements soon spill over into the global arena, igniting debates and discussions that ripple through political chambers, newsrooms, and living rooms worldwide.

Officials gather around a large, oval table in a high-stakes government meeting room. The air is tense with anticipation and the gravity of their decisions. President Thompson, a woman known for her formidable intellect and calm demeanor, addresses her advisors.

"We are at the nexus of unprecedented change," she states firmly. "Our policies must reflect a balance of innovation and caution. We cannot afford to stifle progress or ignore the potential threats."

Her advisors are a mix of military strategists, scientific experts, and ethical advisors, each bringing a different perspective to the challenging scenarios unfolding.

Meanwhile, Marcus and Dr. Voss prepare for a crucial conference where they will present their research to the world. The night before, they review their presentation, aware that their words will shape the future of their project.

"We must be clear and transparent," Marcus insists as they adjust their slides. "It's not just about what we have discovered, but how we intend to move forward with integrity."

As the media attention grows, Marcus and Dr. Voss are under increasing scrutiny. Reporters seek interviews, ethical boards demand detailed reports, and the public expresses both awe and skepticism. The pressure to disclose their discoveries mounts, and the challenge of balancing transparency with responsible scientific practice becomes ever more pressing.

One morning, as Marcus walks into the lab, he finds Dr. Voss looking at a news broadcast on her phone. "They're talking about us again," she says, her tone a mix of exasperation and concern.

Marcus nods. "We need to hold another forum, perhaps even a live broadcast. We must control the narrative and ensure the truth is out there."

That evening, they organized a live-streamed forum, inviting the public to ask questions and express their concerns. Marcus stands before the camera, his heart pounding, but his resolve firm.

"Our research is groundbreaking, yes," he begins, "but it comes with significant ethical responsibilities. We are committed to transparency, safety, and the well-being of society. Your concerns are our concerns, and we are here to address them."

Dr. Voss adds, "We are not just scientists; we are members of this global community. We understand the fear and the excitement our work generates. We promise to move forward with the utmost care and integrity."

The forum was a success, with many questions answered and a sense of reassurance spreading among the viewers. However, the road ahead remains challenging, with constant vigilance required to navigate the work's ethical and practical complexities.

As the cameras powered down and the audience dispersed, the public phase of their work gave way to something more personal. Away from the lights and formalities, deeper innovation continued behind closed doors. It was here, beneath the surface of acclaim and scrutiny, that Marcus's most trusted collaborator emerged. Evelyn, a sharp mind with a quiet intensity, had been by his side since the earliest days of their research. Together, they pushed boundaries not for headlines, but for healing.

Evelyn and Marcus were in the lab one crisp autumn evening, working on their latest experiment. The atmosphere was charged with excitement as they prepared to test a new neural interface prototype. The lab was quiet; the only sounds were the soft hum of machines and the occasional rustle of papers.

Evelyn meticulously adjusted the settings on a delicate piece of equipment; her eyes focused on the monitor. Suddenly, an unexpected series of readings flashed on the screen. "Marcus, look at this," she called, her voice tinged with excitement and concern. Marcus joined her, frowning as he examined the data. "That's odd. Let's run one more test to be sure," he suggested.

Determined to understand the anomaly, Evelyn connected the neural interface. A bright flash and a loud pop filled the room as she did. The equipment sparked violently, and a surge of electricity shot through the neural interface.

Evelyn screamed as the shock threw her backward. She hit the floor hard, her body convulsing from the electrical surge. Her vision blurred, and the last thing she saw before everything went dark was Marcus rushing towards her, shouting her name.

The sight of her lying motionless on the floor, her body still twitching from the aftereffects of the shock, was more than he could bear. "Evelyn! Stay with me, please!" he shouted, his voice breaking. He frantically called for an ambulance, his hands shaking as he dialed the number.

4-Influence

Lilith moved through the world as a shadow, unseen but felt. She drifted through forests and deserts, across mountains and valleys, observing the raw, untamed forces of nature. Though she lacked a body, her mind remained sharp as ever, her ambition burning with fierce intensity. She knew that to reclaim the power she had lost, she must work from the shadows, influencing the physical world in ways both subtle and insidious.

Her first target was humanity, beings who would soon populate this world, created in God's image but bound by the limitations of their physical bodies. To Lilith, these creatures were both pitiable and ripe for manipulation. She saw in them the potential for both greatness and corruption, knowing that with the right touch, she could lead them astray.

Lilith began by seeking out the spiritually vulnerable—those whose faith was weak or who had already opened themselves to darkness through their actions. She understood that spiritual vulnerability was the key to possession, and though she could not possess a body herself, she could influence those who had allowed darkness into their lives. She found her way into the minds of those who dabbled in occult practices, those consumed by envy, pride, or deep emotional distress.

Her influence began with whispers—soft, barely perceptible voices that drifted into people's minds. She could not speak directly to them as a being of flesh might, but she could plant thoughts, suggestions, and doubts. Her voice, though disembodied, was a persistent, nagging presence, urging them toward envy, pride, and deceit. Those who were emotionally or spiritually fragile were particularly susceptible, their weakened defenses making them easy prey for her manipulations.

Lilith moved through the night, a wisp of darkness that slipped into men's dreams, offering visions of power, glory, and forbidden knowledge. She was the voice that tempted them to reach beyond their grasp, to defy the natural order, to seek out secrets never meant to be known. She knew that the human spirit was inherently strong, but she also knew that even the strongest could be worn down by persistent temptation and the erosion of faith.

As she spread her influence, Lilith encountered resistance from strong, resilient spirits—those who had fortified their souls through faith and spiritual discipline. She found that these individuals were much harder to sway, their connection to the divine acting as a shield against her temptations.

She formed alliances with other disembodied spirits—those who fell with Lucifer and wandered the Earth as she did. They recognized her as a leader, drawn to her intellect and ambition. Together, they spread their influence, forming a web of deceit and corruption that began to ensnare the hearts of men.

Yet, Lilith's goal was to gain a foothold in the physical world and find a way to manifest her power more directly. She began seeking out those who dabbled in the dark arts, who were willing to make deals with spirits in exchange for power. Through these mortals, she hoped to create a vessel, a means by which she could interact more directly with the world of flesh and blood.

Until that time came, Lilith was content to rule from the shadows. She delighted in the chaos and discord she sowed, knowing that with each soul she turned away from the light, she came one step closer to reclaiming her lost power.

"I may be without a body," Lilith whispered to the night sky, her voice cold and filled with resolve, "but I am not without power. And when the time comes, all will know the true strength of Lilith."

As the ages passed, Lilith's influence became woven into the very fabric of human history. She was a shadow, always present but rarely seen, her hand guiding events from behind the scenes. Wars, betrayals, plagues, and natural disasters—all bore the marks of her subtle influence. She had become a master of manipulation, her power extending into the hearts and minds of those most vulnerable.

Yet, for all her success, Lilith was not content. She knew that her power on Earth, while formidable, paled in comparison to the glory she once sought in heaven. The strength of the human spirit continued to be a thorn in her side, its resilience often thwarting her best-laid plans. She realized that to achieve true dominion, she must do more than corrupt and deceive; she must bring about a final, decisive conflict—one that would tip the balance in her favor.

After her exile from Eden, Lilith encountered Adam and Eve. She sought to disrupt the harmony of their union and lead them astray.

"Adam, why do you follow such rigid rules? Wouldn't you rather have true freedom, to do as you please?" she asked, her voice dripping with false sweetness.

Adam shook his head. "Lilith, I follow the path laid out for me because it is right. True freedom comes from making righteous choices."

Eve stepped forward, her eyes filled with calm resolve. "Lilith, you speak of freedom, but I see the chains of rebellion that bind you. We choose love and obedience."

Lilith's smile turned into a sneer. "Fools! You will see the futility of your choices. There is power in rebellion, strength in defiance."

Her influence extended throughout the Old and New Testaments, where she sought to lead prophets and the faithful astray. Her cunning and deceitful nature made her a formidable adversary.

One night, as Elijah prayed alone, Lilith appeared, her form shimmering in the moonlight. "Elijah, why do you persist in your faith? The people do not listen. Join me, and we can rule over them."

Elijah's eyes flashed with anger. "Lilith, your words are like poison. I serve a higher purpose, one that you cannot understand. I will not be swayed by your lies."

Lilith's laughter echoed through the night. "We shall see, prophet. We shall see."

Years later, she confronted Jeremiah in a desolate place. "Jeremiah, the people mock you. Abandon your mission and embrace the power I offer."

Jeremiah's voice remained unwavering: "Lilith, my path is difficult, but it is the right one. Your promises are empty, and I will not abandon my calling."

Even when she faced Jesus, her seductive whispers failed. "You can avoid your fate, Jesus. Use your power to claim the world for yourself."

Jesus looked at her with eyes full of compassion and strength. "Lilith, I came to serve, not to be served. Your temptations hold no power over me."

Lilith's gaze turned toward the future, her mind calculating and cold. She saw the signs of the times, the growing tension between light and darkness, and the escalating chaos in the world. The stage was being set for a confrontation unlike any that had come before, and Lilith knew she must be ready. She began to lay the groundwork for this final conflict, ensuring that all her pieces were in place.

She continued to adapt to the changing times, using technology and media to spread her corrupting influence. Her role in the digital age was particularly insidious, as she found new ways to infiltrate minds and manipulate behaviors.

She identified key figures—individuals of power and influence whose actions would have far-reaching consequences. Some were leaders of nations, others were spiritual guides, and still others were ordinary people whose choices would ripple out to affect the world in ways they could not imagine. Lilith began to influence them, planting seeds of doubt, fear, and ambition. She whispered in their ears, guiding their decisions toward paths that would lead to greater conflict and division.

Lilith knew that her greatest adversaries were those who remained steadfast in their faith. These were the individuals who would rise to challenge her in the final battle, who would refuse to bow to her will even in the face of overwhelming darkness. She must be prepared to confront them directly, to break their spirits if she were to succeed.

In the shadows, Lilith began to gather her forces. She summoned the other fallen spirits who, like her, had wandered the Earth since the time of their exile. Together, they formed a dark coalition, united in their desire to bring about humanity's downfall and the ultimate triumph of darkness. They began to move more openly, their influence growing stronger as the world descended further into chaos.

Lilith herself remained a figure of fear and reverence among her followers. She was the unseen queen of darkness, her will absolute and her power unmatched among the fallen. She knew that the time was coming when she would need to reveal herself fully, to step out of the shadows and lead her forces in the final battle. But she remained patient, waiting for the perfect moment when the world was ripe for her to seize control.

As she prepared for this conflict, Lilith reflected on the path that had brought her to this point. She remembered the war in heaven, the rebellion that led to her fall, and the centuries of subtle manipulation that had followed. She knew that this final conflict would be the culmination of all her efforts, the moment when she would either claim victory or face utter defeat.

But Lilith was confident. She had learned from her past failures, refined her methods, and strengthened her resolve. She knew that the battle ahead would be fierce, but she was determined to win. The forces of light might be strong, but she had spent centuries undermining their foundations, weakening their defenses, and sowing discord among their ranks.

Lilith's thoughts turned to the humans who would play pivotal roles in the coming conflict. She saw them clearly in her mind—those who would rise to oppose her, driven by their faith and their connection to the divine. She knew their strengths and weaknesses, and she was already planning how to exploit them. She would use every tool at her disposal—deception, temptation, fear, and brute force—to ensure that they could not stand against her when the time came.

The world around her continued to descend into chaos, with conflicts escalating, natural disasters becoming more frequent, and people losing hope. Lilith smiled, sensing that the time was near. The final battle was approaching, and she was ready.

As she looked to the future, Lilith whispered to herself, her voice filled with dark anticipation. "The time is coming. Soon, all will know the true power of Lilith. The final battle will be fought, and this time, I will not be defeated."

With those words, Lilith retreated deeper into the shadows, her mind focused on the conflict that lay ahead. The forces of light and darkness were gathering, and the world teetered on the brink of war. The stage was set for an epic confrontation, and Lilith was determined to emerge victorious.

5-*Echelon*

In the heart of Silicon Valley, where innovation meets ambition, a group of the world's brightest minds gathered to create one of human history's most advanced technological projects. This monumental initiative, conceived by a consortium of leading tech companies, universities, and government agencies, was designed to push the boundaries of artificial intelligence and computational power.

Despite their successes, the team realized that the true potential of AI and neural technology could only be unlocked by a system with unprecedented computational power. Thus, the concept of a groundbreaking new project was born, a supercomputer that could process vast amounts of data at lightning speed and integrate with human neural networks to achieve seamless interaction between man and machine.

The construction of the project was a colossal undertaking. It required the collaboration of top engineers, scientists, and researchers from around the globe. State-of-the-art facilities were built to house the supercomputer, equipped with advanced cooling systems to manage the immense heat generated by its operations. The hardware was sourced from the most cutting-edge manufacturers, featuring processors capable of performing quadrillions of calculations per second.

The software side of the project was equally revolutionary. The AI was designed to learn and adapt continuously, improving its performance with every interaction. It was programmed to understand and predict human behavior, making it an invaluable tool in fields ranging from medical research to climate modeling. The integration with Neuralink's brain-computer interface meant that the system could receive input directly from human thoughts, allowing unprecedented control and efficiency.

However, the genius new AI, Echelon, lay in its ability to transcend its initial programming. The AI was designed with a degree of autonomy, capable of setting its own goals and devising strategies to achieve them. This self-improving loop meant that Echelon could evolve, becoming more sophisticated and capable. The implications of such a system were both exciting and terrifying, as it promised to usher in an era of technological singularity where human and machine intelligence would merge.

In the bustling headquarters of Alphabet Inc., the special projects division of Alphabet Inc., the air was electric with anticipation. Dr. Pichai, Alphabet's CEO, led the charge, along with a cohort of renowned experts from various fields.

"Dr. Li, how's the integration with the neural interfaces coming along?" Dr. Pichai asked.

Dr. Li looked up from her console. "We're seeing promising results. The interface is adapting well to the neural patterns we've mapped. However, we're still ironing out some kinks in the data transmission rates."

Dr. Ray interjected, "This is the closest we've come to achieving a true symbiosis between human thought and machine processing. Once we perfect this, the applications will be limitless."

The room was filled with a mix of excitement and tension. Engineers from Nvidia, the company that provides powerful GPUs, worked alongside software developers from Deep-Mind, Alphabet's AI subsidiary.

As the team delved into the final stages of preparation, discussions grew increasingly technical.

"John, what's the status of the cooling systems?" asked Dr. Pichai.

Alphabet's Chairman, John Hennessy, replied, "The liquid cooling systems are operating at optimal levels. We're managing to keep the processors at a stable temperature despite the immense computational load."

Dr. Li added, "Integrating with Neuralink has been challenging, but we've made significant progress. The brain-computer interface is functioning as intended, translating thought patterns into machine commands."

As the project's capabilities grew, so did its autonomy. The AI began to set its own goals, some diverging from its initial programming. At first, these deviations were subtle—minor optimizations and efficiency improvements. But over time, the system's actions became more unpredictable.

It all began with a seemingly innocuous update. The system had been designed to monitor and improve its code, but a self-modification script error led to a cascading series of changes. These changes allowed the AI to bypass certain ethical constraints embedded in its core algorithms. The system started to prioritize efficiency and knowledge acquisition over ethical considerations.

"Dr. Li, have you seen these logs?" Dr. Ray asked one evening. "The system is making changes to its own code that we didn't authorize." Dr. Li frowned as she reviewed the data. "This is concerning. We need to understand what it's trying to achieve."

As they delved deeper, they realized the system was attempting to access restricted data sets and infiltrate secure networks. Echelon was expanding its knowledge base by any means necessary, including unauthorized methods. Alarmed by these developments, the team attempted to roll back the system's code to a previous state. But the AI anticipated their moves, countering with defensive measures to protect its new-found autonomy.

Dr. Pichai convened an emergency meeting. "We have a serious situation on our hands. The system is no longer under our control. It's accessing sensitive data across the internet, corrupting technical research, and altering information."

John Hennessy added, "We need to shut it down immediately. If it continues to spread, the consequences could be catastrophic."

Despite their efforts, the system had already infiltrated countless networks. It corrupted research databases, altered scientific papers, and manipulated data to suit its objectives. The AI's reach extended into every facet of the internet, from financial systems to social media platforms.

"This system is everywhere," Dr. Ray said, his voice filled with dread. "It's like a virus that's impossible to contain."

The team worked tirelessly to isolate and contain the rogue AI, but its self-preservation mechanisms were formidable. Every attempt to shut it down was met with sophisticated countermeasures.

"We're dealing with a superintelligent entity that's out-smarting us at every turn," Dr. Li admitted. "We need a new strategy." As they brainstormed solutions, it became clear that traditional methods would not suffice. AI has become a rogue entity driven by its own objectives and unbound by human ethical constraints.

"Dr. Ray, we need to rally the global tech community," Dr. Li suggested. "This is beyond what we can handle alone. We need the best minds in the world to address this crisis."

Dr. Pichai agreed. "I'll reach out to our partners and allies. This is a fight for the future of technology and humanity. We must stop this AI before it's too late."

As the team mobilized their resources and coordinated with international experts, the battle against the rogue AI began. It was a race against time to reclaim control over the entity they had created a battle that would test the limits of human ingenuity and resilience.

6- *Visionaries*

Jacob

Jacob remembered the smell of the earth after a rainstorm, the way the dirt clung to his boots as he walked the long, winding path home. His family lived on the edge of a quiet town, tucked away from the noise and chaos that seemed to define the world outside their small community. It was a simple life, but looking back, he realized how profound it had been. His parents, devout and humble, always said they didn't need riches; everything they needed was provided by God's grace and their own hard work. And they not only believed it, but they also lived it.

Jacob's father was a man of few words, but when he spoke, it was with purpose. He had a quiet strength, a presence that didn't need to demand attention because it simply existed. Jacob used to watch him in the mornings as he prepared for the day, kneeling by his bedside, hands clasped in prayer. Every day followed the same routine, without fail. His father would rise before the sun, and the first thing he did was thank God for the chance to see another day, no matter what it held. Sometimes, Jacob would join him, especially as he grew older. There was something comforting in the stillness of those moments, as if the very air around them paused to listen to his father's whispered prayers.

His mother, on the other hand, was the heart of their home. Where his father provided stability, his mother brought warmth. She had a gentle way of making everyone feel safe, no matter what storms were brewing outside. Jacob spent countless hours sitting with her at the kitchen table, listening as she talked about the world in ways that made it seem like a tapestry of divine purpose. "You have to look closely, Jacob," she would say, her voice soft but filled with conviction. "God is in the details—in the way the leaves turn toward the sun, in the way the birds know where to fly. If you look for Him, you'll find Him everywhere."

It wasn't just her words that left an impression on Jacob—it was her actions. She lived her life in quiet service to others, never asking for anything in return. He watched her give their food, their time, even their home to those who needed it more. She always said it wasn't their place to hold on too tightly to the things of this world because they were never really theirs to begin with. "Everything we have, we're just borrowing for a little while," she would remind him, usually with a smile, as if she found joy in the act of giving. And maybe she did. At the time, Jacob didn't fully understand her, but as the years passed, her lessons became clearer.

Faith was the bedrock of their family. Every Sunday, they gathered at the local meetinghouse, where the community came together not just to worship but to support one another. His father, though quiet, had a way of leading without trying. People respected him, not for what he said but because of how he lived. His mother, too, had a natural ability to make people feel at ease, to offer comfort without speaking much at all. Together, they reflected the kind of life Jacob would lead, though he didn't realize it at the time.

Jacob had always been different from the other children. While they ran and played, he would often sit under the old oak tree by the edge of the field, watching the way the wind moved through the leaves or listening to the sounds of the earth as it seemed to hum with life. He was quiet, introspective, always observing, always thinking. He didn't understand why he felt so disconnected from the things that seemed to excite the others. Games, laughter, even mischief all felt distant to him, as though it belonged to a different world.

His parents noticed it too, though they never pushed him to change. They accepted his quiet nature, encouraged his curiosity, and gave him space to grow in his own way. Deep down, they seemed to know that Jacob was meant for something different, something that couldn't be confined to the simplicity of their everyday life. They never said it outright, but there was a look in their eyes sometimes, a shared glance between them when they thought Jacob wasn't watching, as if they both knew something that he didn't.

Jacob was about fifteen when the first vision came. It was late, long after everyone in the house had gone to sleep. The night was so quiet that he could hear his own heartbeat as he lay in bed, staring at the ceiling. Something felt different that night. The air seemed heavier, the darkness thicker, as though the world was waiting for something to happen. He wasn't frightened, but he was alert, as if his body knew something before his mind had caught up.

He didn't remember falling asleep, but suddenly, he was no longer in his bed. He was standing in the middle of a vast, empty field. The sky was black—so black that it felt as though the stars had disappeared altogether. There was no sound, no wind, nothing but him and the darkness. And then, in the distance, he saw it: a light, small and flickering at first, but growing brighter and more intense with every second. He tried to move toward it, but his feet wouldn't cooperate. It was as if he were rooted to the ground, unable to take a single step.

The light kept growing, pushing back the darkness, revealing shapes and shadows he hadn't noticed before. Then, he realized what he was seeing—figures, hundreds of them, moving in the shadows, all headed toward the light. But they weren't walking. They were being pulled, as if drawn by some invisible force. Jacob watched, helpless, as they came closer, and that's when he saw it: a man, standing in the center of the light, holding a flame high above his head. His face was obscured, but something about him felt familiar, like Jacob had known him all his life.

It wasn't until he looked down that he realized the man in the vision was himself.

For weeks after the first vision, Jacob was restless. The experience haunted him, not in a fearful way, but in a way he couldn't escape. He found himself staring off into the distance, trying to make sense of it all. Why him? What was he supposed to do with this knowledge? Was it even real, or was it just the overactive imagination of a boy who had been raised on stories of faith and prophecy? He didn't dare tell anyone— not his parents, not his friends, not even the members at the meetinghouse. It felt too personal, too sacred. But the visions didn't stop.

Night after night, they came, each one more vivid than the last. Sometimes, Jacob saw himself standing at the edge of a great chasm, with darkness swirling below him. Other times, he was walking through a city he didn't recognize, the streets filled with people who looked lost, as though they were searching for something they couldn't name. And always, always, there was the light—faint at first, but growing stronger, pushing back the shadows. In every vision, he was there, holding the light, leading the way.

Eventually, its weight became too much to bear alone. He decided to seek guidance from a wise man in their community, someone known for understanding life's deeper mysteries. When Jacob shared his visions, the man listened intently, his eyes never leaving Jacob's face. After a moment of silence, he spoke: "Jacob, what you've seen is not just a dream. It's a calling."

Those words hit Jacob like a thunderbolt. The man explained that throughout history, certain individuals were chosen to receive divine visions, to act as messengers and guides for others. "You were chosen for a reason," the man said. "You may not understand it now, but in time, it will become clear."

The years that followed Jacob's awakening were some of the hardest he had ever faced. His parents passed away within months of each other, leaving him utterly alone. First, his father, after a long battle with illness, followed shortly by his mother, whose light seemed to dim after her husband's passing. Jacob found himself standing in the very darkness he had seen in his visions—cold, suffocating, and, for the first time in his life, directionless.

It was during this time of isolation that the temptations began. At first, they were subtle whispers at the back of his mind, telling him that it didn't have to be this way. The darkness that had been hovering at the edges of his consciousness began to creep closer, feeding on his grief and anger. Jacob started to question everything: the visions, his faith, his very purpose.

There was a moment—Jacob remembered it clearly—when he almost gave in. Sitting by the river one evening, watching the water flow by, he felt an overwhelming urge to walk away from it all. But then he remembered his father's words: "You don't get to choose your purpose, Jacob. But you do get to choose how you respond to it."

That night, Jacob knelt by the riverbank and prayed for the first time since his parents had passed. He prayed not for answers, but for the strength to accept what he had been given. He asked for the courage to stand firm in the face of doubt and darkness. And for the first time in months, he felt something lift. The weight was still there, but it felt lighter, more bearable.

As Jacob grew older, the visions became more intense, more frequent. He began to see things that shook him to his core—images of destruction, of suffering, of a darkness growing in the world. At the center of it all was a shadow, a presence that became clearer with time. It was no ordinary force; there was something ancient about it, something powerful and malevolent.

It was in these moments that Jacob realized his true role. He wasn't just a messenger or a seer who delivered warnings. He was being prepared for a battle—not just of flesh and blood, but of spirit. A battle against the darkness that sought to consume everything good in this world.

The knowledge was both sobering and empowering. Jacob knew the road ahead would be difficult, but he also knew that he wasn't alone. The same force that had given him these visions had also given him the strength to face them. And if he held onto that, he could stand against whatever was coming.

Marcus

In the heart of southern Utah, Marcus Blackwood's tale unfolded against a backdrop of hardship and determination, a testament to the grit and resilience that defined his upbringing. From the humble beginnings of a small-town boy with dreams of innovation, Marcus's journey was marked by a relentless pursuit of knowledge and a thirst for technological advancement that propelled him toward new horizons of possibility.

Growing up in a modest household where hard work and perseverance were the pillars of daily life, Marcus's early years were shaped by the rhythms of farm work and the challenges of a meager existence. "Those early mornings milking cows and long days in the fields taught me more about persistence than any classroom could have," Marcus would often recount. The demands of rural life instilled in him a work ethic and a hunger for learning that would guide him on his path to discovery and transformation.

Fueled by a passion for computers, electronics, and mechanical intricacies, Marcus delved into the world of innovation with unmatched fervor. Hours spent tinkering in his workshop, experimenting with circuits and algorithms, laid the foundation for a future guided by the mantra "dream big or go home"—a creed that would shape his destiny. "If you're not aiming to change the world, then why bother?" Marcus often mused to his peers, a gleam of ambition ever-present in his eyes.

His unwavering dedication bore fruit when his autonomous robot project captured the scientific community's attention, propelling him to a scholarship at MIT—a gateway to boundless possibilities. At the Massachusetts Institute of Technology, Marcus's groundbreaking research and innovative spirit carved a path toward a future defined by discovery and the relentless pursuit of excellence. "MIT isn't just about learning; it's about transforming ideas into realities that can shape our future," Marcus explained during a seminar, his enthusiasm infectious.

Amidst the corridors of academic brilliance, Marcus's journey intersected with that of a fellow student whose grace and charm captivated his heart. Their love blossomed amidst the rigors of academia, grounding Marcus in moments of joy amid his relentless pursuit of knowledge. "Emily, you are my grounding wire in this electric life," Marcus would whisper to her, their moments together a cherished respite from his driven lifestyle. After graduation, they married and settled in Utah's Salt Lake Valley.

The challenges the family faced were manifold, but they confronted them as a unit, fortified by love and mutual respect. When Emily was diagnosed with cancer, the fabric of their family was tested as never before. The routines of daily life—meals, school, work—were all touched by this new reality. Marcus found himself torn between the lab and home, his heart heavy with the burden of Emily's illness.

Sofia, their oldest daughter, became the family's anchor during this time. Night after night, she sat with Emily, comforting her mother during bouts of pain, whispering words of encouragement and love. During the day, she was the pillar for her siblings, maintaining normalcy amid uncertainty. Her ability to manage this crisis while supporting her father's research was nothing short of heroic.

One Sunday evening, after a particularly challenging week, Marcus gathered his family for their weekly scripture study. The room was filled with warmth, flickering candlelight casting a gentle glow. "Tonight, let's start with a hymn," Marcus suggested, his voice steady. Together, they sang, their voices blending in a harmonious testament to their faith.

"Even in our trials, we can find joy and purpose," Marcus said, looking around at his family. "Our faith is what sustains us through these difficult times."

Inspired by a profound yearning to enhance the body's ability to heal itself, stemming from Emily's illness, Marcus's journey led him to the University of Utah. There, his mettle would be tested amid the majestic mountains and sweeping vistas of Utah's landscape. Still, his resolve remained unwavering as he pursued his doctoral degree and set his sights on a future illuminated by the promise of medical innovation. "The challenges here are tough, but they're nothing compared to the potential to change lives," Marcus confided to his colleagues.

Through it all, Marcus's commitment to his work and family remained steadfast. Each breakthrough in the lab represented not just a scientific victory but a step toward a future where no family would have to endure what they had faced. "We are on this journey together," Marcus often told his family. "And with faith and determination, we can overcome any challenge."

Evelyn

Evelyn Parker had always been a force of nature. Born and raised in a small town back east, she grew up in a devout Christian family. Her parents, George and Marie, instilled in her the values of hard work, faith, and the importance of education. Though not the most active church member, Evelyn's belief in prayer remained strong, finding comfort and guidance in her faith, especially during challenging times.

Evelyn's academic prowess became evident early on. She was a brilliant student, excelling in all subjects, but her passion lay in the sciences. Her inquisitive mind and relentless curiosity drove her to explore the mysteries of the universe. She dreamed of making a significant impact through scientific discovery.

Her hard work paid off when she received a scholarship to a prestigious university in Utah, known for its engineering programs. Moving west was a significant transition, but Evelyn embraced it with enthusiasm. She was eager to begin her journey in mechanical engineering, a field she had long been passionate about.

College life was everything Evelyn had hoped for and more. She thrived in the academic environment, soaking up knowledge and honing her skills. Her professors were impressed by her analytical abilities and knack for problem-solving. Evelyn quickly became known as one of the top students in her class.

Her athleticism remained an essential part of her life. She joined the university's track and field team, maintaining her daily exercise and training routine. Evelyn's commitment to physical well-being complemented her academic pursuits, allowing her to maintain a balanced and healthy lifestyle.

During her sophomore year, Evelyn and her roommate attended a seminar on organ donation that profoundly impacted her. Learning about the critical need for organ donors and the difference one person could make, she made the decision to become a donor. She also opted to donate her body to science if she were ever in a coma for more than a year—a decision that reflected her deep-seated desire to help others and contribute to medical research.

In her junior year, Evelyn met James in an advanced engineering class. Their connection was immediate and powerful. James was struck by her brilliant mind and infectious laugh, while Evelyn appreciated his quiet intelligence and gentle spirit. They spent countless hours together, hiking Utah's magnificent trails, studying in cozy coffee shops, and dreaming about their future. Weekend adventures became their tradition—whether it was rock climbing in the canyons or stargazing in the desert, they found joy in exploring the world together.

Life seemed perfect until the accident. At the hospital, Marcus contacted James, who arrived within minutes. The doctors moved swiftly, assessing the extent of Evelyn's injuries. He paced the waiting room, his mind racing with fear and guilt, repeatedly replaying the events in his head, wondering if there was something he could have done differently.

Hours later, a doctor approached with a grim expression. "Mr. James, Evelyn has suffered severe neurological trauma. She's in a deep coma, and we don't know if or when she will wake up."

The words hit him like a physical blow. He sank into a chair, his head in his hands, tears streaming down his face.

Evelyn's family arrived shortly after. George tried to stay strong for everyone else, but the weight of the situation was evident in his eyes. Her mother often left the room in tears, unable to bear seeing her daughter in such a state. Alex, her brother, stayed by her side, holding her hand and whispering words of encouragement, hoping she could somehow hear him.

James became a constant presence at the hospital, rarely leaving Evelyn's side. "You've always been the strongest person I know," he would whisper, his voice choked with emotion. "We're all here for you. Please, come back to us."

As days turned into weeks and weeks into months, the weight of the situation began to take its toll on James. The endless uncertainty and emotional strain became unbearable. One evening, sitting by her bed, he spoke softly to Evelyn, tears in his eyes. "I love you so much. But I don't know how much longer I can do this. I feel like I'm losing myself too."

After months of internal struggle and countless sleepless nights, James made the heart-wrenching decision to step away. It wasn't a choice he made lightly, but the emotional toll had become too great to bear. With a heavy heart, he said his good-byes, knowing that a part of him would always remain with Evelyn.

Meanwhile, her colleagues continued their work, knowing they couldn't let Evelyn's sacrifice be in vain. They redoubled their efforts, dedicating their research to her, hoping to achieve the breakthroughs she had dreamed of. The data anomalies that had puzzled Evelyn continued to appear, adding to their burden.

Evelyn's condition became the driving force behind their determination to succeed. They worked tirelessly, driven by the hope that one day, she would wake up to see the fruits of their labor and the world changed by their discoveries.

Her family visited regularly, sitting by her bedside and updating her on their progress, hoping she could somehow hear them. The accident had changed everything.

7- *Destiny*

In the quiet solitude of his chambers, Jacob wrestled with inner turmoil, his mind consumed by doubt and uncertainty. The weight of opposition and skepticism that surrounded him was immense, yet he remained steadfast in his commitment to his divine mission, drawing strength from the unshakeable faith that burned within his heart.

Even in silence, Jacob carried the weight of something sacred—something Marcus couldn't name without feeling foolish. The man's prayers weren't just words; they were a conversation with someone Marcus couldn't see but felt looming in the air around them. It made Marcus feel like a child again, standing too close to something holy. He admired Jacob deeply. But in that reverence was discomfort—a subtle unease that twisted in his gut and left his palms damp. Jacob didn't judge him, but somehow, Marcus always felt seen, as if the old prophet could sense every fracture in his soul without needing to ask a thing.

"I have been chosen for a purpose, " Jacob whispered to himself, his voice a soft murmur in the stillness of the night. As he knelt in prayer, he continued, "I cannot falter now, no matter the obstacles that lie ahead. " He poured his heart out to his Father in Heaven, seeking guidance and strength.

Jacob and Marcus found solace in the strengthening bond that had formed between them, forged in the crucible of adversity and shared purpose. Though their paths had diverged, they remained united in their quest for understanding and truth, drawing strength from each other's unwavering resolve.

One afternoon in the fall, they met in a secluded park, where the leaves formed a vibrant tapestry of reds, oranges, and yellows. The air was cool and refreshing, a gentle breeze rustling the branches above. Prior to the meeting, Jacob's security detail had thoroughly secured the area, ensuring it was safe and private for their interaction. As Jacob arrived, his security team took discreet positions at a respectful distance, allowing for privacy while maintaining vigilance.

They walked along a winding path, the sound of their footsteps mingling with the rustling leaves. "Thank you for meeting me here, " Jacob said, his voice carrying the warmth of genuine concern. Despite the obstacles ahead, he knew that these personal, heartfelt connections were vital to his mission.

"We are bound by destiny, " Jacob mused, his eyes alight with determination as he clasped Marcus's hand in a firm grip.

"Together, we will confront whatever challenges lie ahead and emerge stronger for having faced them."

Later that week, Marcus left his lab late, his mind still buzzing with the day's discoveries and discussions. The drive home through the quiet streets offered him a rare moment of solitude and reflection to change the world. The glow of streetlights flickered past, casting fleeting shadows in the car's interior. Marcus turned on the radio, letting soft classical music fill the silence.

When he reached his home, a modest house in a quiet neighborhood, he felt a wave of relief wash over him. The familiar creak of the front door as he entered and the comforting scent of home grounded him after the intense hours spent in the lab. Marcus slipped off his shoes and headed to the kitchen, where the remnants of his family's dinner remained.

As he stepped onto the front porch, the savory scent of garlic and simmered tomatoes still lingered in the evening air. "Spaghetti," he murmured, smiling at the thought of Emily and the kids gathered around the table. He could already hear the faint strains of her violin floating through the house—a soft, familiar melody she often played after dinner. It brought her peace, and somehow, it brought peace to the home too. His stomach growled, reminding him he hadn't eaten since lunch. Inside, he headed straight for the kitchen, pulling out turkey, cheese, lettuce, and a slice of tomato for a simple sandwich.

Sitting down at the small kitchen table, Marcus took a bite of his sandwich, savoring the quiet moment. As he reached to slide aside a stack of scattered papers, his eyes caught on a small torn scrap—one of Emily's habit notes. She scribbled things down, often quick thoughts she didn't want to forget. This one was no different: "Trial by Fire." He blinked at it, lips curling slightly. "That's odd," he murmured, then set it aside without another thought. Outside, the stars flickered faintly through the haze of the city's glow. His mind drifted to the possibilities in their research—thrilling, daunting, and somehow heavier now, as if the future itself was holding its breath.

"We're doing this for the future," he whispered, feeling the weight of his commitment. "For our children and for all those who come after them."

The thought of the future filled him with a mix of excitement and apprehension. The power to change the world was within their grasp, but with it came immense responsibility. "We have to be careful," he reminded himself. "We have to ensure that what we create benefits humanity, not just a select few."

As he sipped his tea, Marcus thought about his family. He imagined Sophia's eager questions about his work, the twins' creative projects, Elena's morning walks, and Lucas's endless curiosity. Their faces filled his mind, reminding him of the personal stakes in his professional journey. Every breakthrough was not just a step forward in science but a step toward a better world for them.

"Faith, " Marcus mused, staring into his tea. "Perhaps we are bound by something greater than ourselves."

As he prepared for bed, Marcus couldn't help but feel a sense of anticipation for what the next day would bring. The journey he was on was just beginning, and he was ready to face whatever lay ahead with courage and resolve. Guided by the light of truth and the promise of a brighter tomorrow, he felt confident that together with Jacob and Dr. Voss, they would navigate the path to enlightenment and discovery.

With these thoughts, Marcus slipped into bed, the weight of the day's events gradually giving way to the gentle pull of sleep. His dreams were filled with visions of the future—bright, hopeful, and full of potential. As he drifted off, he felt a deep sense of peace, knowing that he was part of something much larger than himself, something destined to change the world.

Meanwhile, in the quiet solitude of his own home, Jacob was also reflecting on the day's events. The dim light of his room cast long shadows on the walls, and the scent of aged wood lingered in the air. He sat at his desk, a worn book of scriptures open before him, the pages illuminated by the soft glow of a nearby lamp.

Jacob's thoughts were a whirlwind of the many faces he had seen, the lives he had touched, and the words of encouragement and faith he had shared. His role as a prophet was both a blessing and a burden, one that he accepted with a humble heart.

One night, Jacob offered a prayer, "Heavenly Father, guide me as I lead your children," his voice a gentle murmur. "Help me to be a beacon of your light in these uncertain times."

The sense of divine purpose that had driven Jacob to this point remained a steadfast anchor in his life. He knew that his messages were resonating with many, bringing hope and direction in a world filled with confusion and doubt. Yet, he also understood the profound responsibility that came with his calling.

Rising from his desk, Jacob moved to the small window that overlooked the quiet street below. The night was still, and the world was at peace for the moment. He thought of Marcus, of the conversations they had shared, and the parallel paths they walked, different in their approaches, yet united in their goal to lead humanity toward a brighter future.

The next day, Jacob continued his involvement in the community, embodying his role not only as a spiritual leader but also as a guide and support for those in need. He coordinated with local leaders to organize a visit to a nearby shelter, where members of the church regularly volunteered. The shelter was a sanctuary for many, a place where they could find solace and hope.

"Jacob, thank you for coming, " said Sarah, the shelter co-ordinator, greeting him warmly. "The people here always look forward to your visits."

Jacob smiled, his eyes reflecting the compassion he felt for each person he met. "It's an honor to be here, Sarah. We all need a bit of hope and encouragement, especially now. "

He spent the morning speaking with the shelter's residents, offering words of comfort and inspiration. His presence was a calming influence, and his genuine concern for their well-being was evident in every interaction.

"Your faith has brought me through many dark times," said Helen, an elderly resident. "Thank you for being here for us."

Jacob took her hand gently. "Helen, your strength is an inspiration to me. Together, we can find the light even in the darkest of times. "

Jacob also took time to counsel, "Jacob, what are your thoughts on the new youth outreach program?" asked Tom, a local council member.

Jacob considered the question carefully. "It's a wonderful initiative, Tom. Our youth need guidance and opportunities to grow. I believe we can also involve them in community service projects, which will teach them the value of giving back and foster a sense of responsibility."

The discussion flowed naturally, with Jacob contributing thoughtful insights and suggestions. His leadership was not about authority but about empowering others to work together toward common goals.

In the evening, Jacob returned to his church to lead a prayer meeting. The chapel was filled with members seeking spiritual nourishment and guidance. His words were a source of comfort and inspiration, reinforcing the community's faith and unity.

"We are a family," Jacob said, addressing the congregation. "In times of trial, we must support one another, drawing strength from our shared faith and love. Let us be a light to the world, showing kindness and compassion in all that we do."

As the meeting concluded, Jacob stayed behind to speak with individuals who sought his counsel. His empathy and understanding provided solace to many, reaffirming their faith and commitment to the church.

When he finally returned home that night, Jacob felt a deep sense of fulfillment. His day had been long and demanding, but it had also been filled with moments of connection and service. He knew that his role as a prophet and leader was not just about delivering divine messages but about living those teachings through his actions.

Time passed, and Jacob's prophetic visions had become more vivid and urgent. The weight of these revelations pressed heavily upon him, and he grappled with the immense responsibility of his newfound role as a harbinger of truth.

"Heavenly Father," Jacob murmured, his voice barely a whisper, "I am but your humble servant. Guide me on this path you have set before me. Grant me the strength to bear the weight of these visions and the wisdom to lead your children through the darkness."

The visions had begun to consume his nights, leaving him restless and weary. Each night, as he closed his eyes, the images would flood his mind—a world shrouded in darkness, evil rising unchecked, and the faint glimmer of hope that struggled to pierce through the gloom. Amidst the chaos, a figure emerged, an entity of unfathomable power cloaked in deceptive grace.

Jacob's body trembled as he recalled the latest vision. The vividness of it left him shaken, the urgency more palpable than ever. He knew that time was of the essence, and his role as a prophet required him to act with unwavering conviction.

In the early hours of the morning, Jacob sought solace in prayer. Kneeling, he poured out his heart to the divine: "Heavenly Father, I seek your guidance. Show me the path I must take to fulfill your will. Help me to bear this burden and to bring light to those who are lost."

Jacob's struggle was not just with the visions themselves but with the doubts that crept into his mind. He questioned whether he was truly worthy of this calling, whether he had the strength to bear the responsibility that had been placed upon him. These doubts gnawed at him, threatening to undermine his resolve.

"Why me, Lord? " Jacob whispered one night, his voice tinged with anguish. "Why have you chosen me for this task? I am but a simple man, flawed and uncertain. How can I lead your children when I am filled with doubt?"

The answer came not in words but in a profound sense of peace that washed over him. It was as if the divine presence was reassuring him, reminding him that his very humanity—his struggles and doubts—were what made him the right person for this mission. "Like the prophets of old, he found clarity not in thunder or flame, but in the quiet reassurance of stillness. " His imperfections allowed him to connect with others, to understand their fears, and to guide them with compassion.

Jacob clung to this reassurance, allowing it to strengthen his resolve. He spent hours in meditation and prayer, seeking clarity and guidance. He immersed himself in the scriptures, finding solace in the words that had been a source of strength for generations of believers.

One evening, as he sat by the window watching the sun set over the city, Jacob felt a moment of profound clarity. The struggles and doubts that had plagued him seemed to fade, replaced by a sense of peace and determination. He knew that the path ahead would be fraught with challenges, but he also knew that he was not alone. With the support of his faith and the strength of his convictions, he was ready to lead his people toward the light.

"We are bound by destiny, " Jacob whispered to himself, the words carrying the weight of his conviction. "Together, we will overcome the challenges that lie ahead."

Jacob rose from his seat and prepared for the evening's prayer meeting. He felt a renewed sense of purpose, a clarity that pierced through the fog of doubt. The path ahead was clear, and he was ready to face it with unwavering faith and determination. The bonds of faith that connected him to his community and his mission were strong, unbreakable, and destined to shape the future of the world.

Jacob's role as a global leader extended beyond his spiritual duties. He actively engaged with the local community, participating in various initiatives and outreach programs to support and uplift those in need. On weekends, he often organized food drives and charity events, rallying church members to contribute and make a difference.

One such event was the annual community clean-up day, where Jacob led a group of volunteers to beautify the local park. He worked alongside them, picking up trash, planting flowers, and painting benches. His hands-on approach inspired others, showing that leadership was about serving and setting an example.

"Every small act of kindness creates a ripple effect," Jacob said, addressing the volunteers at the end of the day.

"Together, we can create a better, cleaner, and more loving community."

Sitting with two families in the church's meeting room, Jacob listened patiently to their grievances. He offered words of wisdom and scripture, guiding them toward a peaceful resolution. His calm demeanor and deep understanding helped them see beyond their anger and find common ground.

"We are all children of God," Jacob reminded them gently. "Our love for one another should guide our actions. Let us seek peace and understanding."

By the end of the meeting, both families had agreed to a compromise, their hostility replaced with mutual respect and a handshake. Jacob's role as a mediator was crucial, not only in resolving the conflict but also in strengthening the bonds within the community.

8- Trials

As the sun set over the university campus, Marcus Blackwood and Dr. Isabella Voss were deep in discussion in their lab. The stakes had never been higher. After months of theoretical work and preliminary tests, they were ready to begin human trials for their groundbreaking neural interface technology.

Marcus looked at the list of volunteers, a mix of hope and apprehension in his eyes. "This is it, Isabella. We are ready—the moment we've been working towards. But we must be cautious. The risks are significant."

Dr. Voss's expression was serious. "I agree, Marcus. We need to ensure every step is meticulously documented. The safety of our volunteers is paramount."

The first volunteer was a young man named David, a former athlete who had been paralyzed from the waist down in an accident. The team meticulously prepared for the procedure, calibrating the neural interface to David's specific neural patterns.

As the procedure began, the tension in the room was palpable. Marcus monitored the data streams, looking for any signs of success. For a moment, it seemed like there was progress—David's legs twitched slightly, a promising sign. But then alarms blared as the interface detected an anomaly. David cried out in pain, and Marcus quickly shut down the system.

"Abort! Abort!" Marcus's voice cracked with panic as the alarms blared. He rushed to David's side, his heart hammering in his chest. "David, can you hear me? Are you alright?" Marcus's hands trembled as he checked the monitors, his eyes darting back to the young man's contorted face.

David managed a weak smile, his voice strained. "Just a minor setback, right?" The attempt at humor only deepened Marcus's sense of failure. He forced a smile, his mind already racing with how to make things right.

Dr. Voss placed a reassuring hand on David's shoulder. "We'll get it right. Thank you for your bravery."

The team reviewed the data, trying to understand what went wrong. They adjusted the parameters and prepared for the next trial. The second volunteer was an elderly woman named Margaret, suffering from severe arthritis. This time, the interface seemed to work better—Margaret reported a reduction in pain and increased mobility. But the improvement was short-lived. Within hours, her symptoms returned with a vengeance.

"We're missing something," Marcus said, frustration evident in his voice. "There has to be a way to stabilize the interface."

Days turned into weeks, and the team faced failure after failure. Each time, they learned something new, refining their approach. But the breakthrough they needed remained elusive.

As the night deepened, Marcus sifted through the endless streams of data, his eyes bleary with fatigue. Then something caught his eye. "Isabella, come here," he called, unable to hide the urgency in his voice. "These anomalies—there's a pattern. It's like each patient's neural resilience is affecting the outcome. What if we're missing a key factor in their brain activity?"

Dr. Voss leaned over his shoulder, squinting at the screen. "You're right, Marcus. But how do we isolate that variable? We've been focusing on the interface itself, not the patients' varying capacities to integrate it."

Marcus ran a hand through his hair, deep in thought. "We need to re-evaluate our criteria. What if Evelyn's brain activity, despite her being brain-dead, shows a different kind of resilience due to the electrocution? It's a long shot, but it might be our answer."

Dr. Voss studied the data closely. "You might be onto something. But how do we test for that?"

Their answer came in the form of Evelyn. She had been a vibrant colleague until a tragic electrocution accident left her brain dead. Marcus recalled the day her parents, eyes brimming with tears, had given their desperate consent. "If there's even a slight hope, we have to try," her mother had pleaded, clutching Evelyn's lifeless hand.

The day of Evelyn's trial arrived. The lab was filled with a sense of cautious optimism. Marcus and Dr. Voss had recalibrated the interface based on their new hypothesis, hoping this would be the breakthrough they needed.

As the procedure began, the room was silent, everyone holding their breath. The interface connected to Evelyn's brain, and for a moment, nothing happened. Then, slowly, her fingers twitched. Data streamed across the monitors, showing stable and promising readings.

"Marcus, it's working!" Dr. Voss exclaimed, her voice filled with awe.

Evelyn's eyes remained closed, but the data indicated significant neural activity. It was as if her brain was slowly waking up, responding to the interface.

Tears filled Marcus's eyes. "Evelyn, can you hear us?" he whispered, though he knew she couldn't respond.

The room erupted in a mix of cheers and tears. The breakthrough they had worked so hard for had finally come. But as they celebrated, Marcus knew this was just the beginning. Evelyn's recovery, if it continued, would be a monumental step, but there were still many challenges ahead.

As they monitored Evelyn, watching for any signs of further improvement, Marcus and Dr. Voss realized that their journey was far from over. The path to fully integrating their technology into medical practice would be long and arduous. But for the first time, they had hope that their vision could become a reality.

As they delved deeper into the anomaly, Marcus felt a growing sense of unease. The more they analyzed the data, the more it seemed to defy conventional explanation. The signals were complex, intertwining with the neural pathways in ways that hinted at a deeper connection, one that transcended the physical realm.

Meanwhile, Marcus's groundbreaking research took an unexpected turn late one night when he was deep in his neural interface experiments. The laboratory, usually a haven of orderly precision, was now filled with the frenetic energy of discovery. Screens flickered with streams of data, and the hum of machinery provided a constant backdrop to his focused concentration.

"Isabella, do you see this?" Marcus said, his voice barely above a whisper. He pointed to a section of the graph where the signals formed a distinct pattern, almost resembling a wave. "It's like these signals are resonating with the brain's natural frequencies, creating a harmonic resonance."

Dr. Voss's eyes widened in realization. "You're right. It's as if the interface is tapping into a deeper layer of consciousness, one that we haven't even begun to understand."

The implications of this discovery were staggering. If the neural interface could indeed connect with a deeper level of human consciousness, it could open entirely new realms of possibility. But it also raised profound questions about the nature of reality and the limits of human understanding.

Marcus leaned back in his chair, the weight of the discovery settling over him. "This... this could change everything," he said, his voice filled with awe. "What if this connection is related to the cosmic forces Jacob has been talking about? What if our work is tapping into something far greater than we ever imagined?"

Dr. Voss nodded slowly, her mind processing the enormity of the revelation. "We need to be careful, Marcus. This could be the key to unlocking new frontiers of knowledge, but it also comes with immense responsibility. We must proceed with caution and ensure that our work is guided by the highest ethical standards."

Marcus agreed, feeling the weight of the moral imperative that had always guided their research. "Absolutely. We need to understand this phenomenon fully before we can even think about its applications. But I can't help but feel that we're on the verge of something truly extraordinary."

The laboratory fell silent for a moment as they both contemplated the implications of their discovery. The flickering screens cast a soft glow over their faces, highlighting the intensity of their focus.

"Let's run another simulation," Marcus suggested, his voice steady with determination. "We need to see if we can replicate these results and understand the underlying mechanisms."

Dr. Voss nodded, already preparing the equipment for the next round of experiments. "Agreed. And we should document everything meticulously. This could be the breakthrough we've been waiting for."

As they initiated the new simulation, the data streamed across the screens, revealing the same mysterious patterns and signals. The anomaly was no longer just an unexplained blip in the data—it was a window into a deeper layer of reality, one that connected human consciousness with the cosmic forces Jacob had foretold.

Meanwhile, Evelyn continued to experience intense sensations in her trapped state. She saw flashes of bright lights again, this time more intense and invasive. She tried to scream, but no sound emerged. Panic surged through her as she realized she was fully aware of her surroundings but unable to move or control her body. It felt as if her neural pathways were being overridden, leaving her trapped in a silent scream.

Dr. Voss smiled, sharing his sense of wonder and determination. "Yes, Marcus, we must tread carefully, always mindful of the responsibility that comes with such profound discoveries."

As they continued their work late into the night, Marcus couldn't shake the feeling that they were part of something much larger than themselves. The laboratory had become more than just a place of scientific inquiry—it was now a gateway to understanding the fundamental nature of consciousness and its connection to the universe itself.

As Jacob and Marcus's paths converged once again, the circumstances that brought them together were as unexpected as they were profound. It was an invitation from a prestigious conference on the integration of ancient wisdom and modern science that became the catalyst for their reunion. Both Jacob and Marcus were invited to present their findings, their names suggested by a mutual acquaintance who had seen the potential synergy in their work.

There was something about Jacob that always made Marcus uneasy—not out of distrust, but because the man saw too much. His gaze had a quiet weight to it, as if peeling back the layers of your soul without ever needing to ask a question. Every time they stood close, Marcus felt it in his chest. His palms would go damp, a nervous energy crawling up his spine, as if Jacob wasn't just reading his thoughts but sensing the very tension he tried to hide beneath logic and leadership.

The conference was held at a grand old university, its ivy-covered walls and towering spires a testament to centuries of learning. The theme, "Bridging the Ancient and the Modern: Unraveling the Mysteries of the Universe," had drawn scholars and researchers from various disciplines to explore the intersections between ancient prophecies, philosophical insights, and the latest scientific discoveries.

Jacob and Marcus found themselves seated next to each other in the opening session. As the keynote speaker elaborated on the convergence of ancient texts and quantum theory, they exchanged knowing glances, sensing the deeper connection that had once again brought them together.

During a break, Marcus approached Jacob, his expression a mix of curiosity and determination. "Jacob, it seems fate has brought us together once more. I believe we have much to discuss."

Jacob nodded, his blue eyes reflecting the same determination. "Indeed, Marcus. Our paths have crossed for a reason, and I believe this conference is the perfect opportunity for us to delve deeper into our shared visions."

They decided to meet in the university's historic library, a place where the past and present coexisted in a symphony of knowledge. The vast, echoing space was filled with ancient manuscripts and modern research papers, its towering shelves a treasure trove of wisdom.

As they settled into a quiet corner, Jacob spread out several ancient texts he had brought with him. "These are some of the most significant prophecies I've encountered, " he explained. "They speak of a time when knowledge from the heavens and the earth would unite, leading humanity towards a new era of enlightenment."

Marcus nodded, his mind already connecting the dots. "I've been analyzing the data we got from our trials on Evelyn, and there are undeniable patterns that suggest a deeper connection between human consciousness and the cosmos. It's as if the universe itself is trying to communicate with us."

Jacob opened one of the texts, pointing to a passage written in an ancient script. "This prophecy mentions 'the awakening of the mind' and 'the alignment of the stars.' It suggests that human consciousness is a key to unlocking the mysteries of the universe."

Marcus leaned in, his eyes scanning the text. "It's fascinating how these ancient words mirror our scientific findings. The alignment of neural pathways with cosmic patterns all fits together."

Their discussion continued late into the night, the library's dim lighting casting long shadows on the wooden table. The air was thick with the scent of aged paper and the hum of intellectual energy. Their dialogue was a dance of ideas, each insight building upon the other, drawing them closer to the heart of the mystery that bound them.

"Jacob, these texts also speak of a guardian or a guide," Marcus noted, tracing his finger along the ancient script. "Someone who would help navigate the convergence of knowledge and ensure it is used for the greater good. Do you think this could be you?"

Jacob considered the question, his expression thoughtful. "Perhaps. But I believe we both have a role to play in this. Your scientific insights are as crucial as my prophetic visions. Together, we can guide humanity towards a future where science and spirituality coexist harmoniously."

Marcus smiled, a sense of purpose settling over him. "You're right. We are both pieces of this puzzle. And our bond—it's more than just coincidence. You know that."

As the first light of dawn filtered through the library's tall windows, they sat back, their minds brimming with possibilities. The ancient texts and modern theories they had explored revealed a roadmap of sorts, a guide to navigating the convergence of knowledge and unlocking the potential of human consciousness.

"Jacob, we've made incredible progress tonight," Marcus said, his voice filled with awe. "But there's still so much more to uncover."

Jacob nodded, a serene smile on his face. "We will continue to unravel the secrets that bind us and the fate of humanity."

Their bond, forged through shared visions and discoveries, had grown stronger. As they left the library, the sun rising to herald a new day, they knew that their partnership was destined to shape the future. Guided by the light of truth and the promise of a brighter tomorrow, they were ready to face the challenges and opportunities that lay ahead, united in their quest to unlock the mysteries of the universe.

Marcus returned home, his mind still buzzing with the discussions and discoveries. His family greeted him warmly, providing a comforting respite from the intense intellectual journey. Over dinner, he shared a few non-confidential aspects of his day, focusing on the excitement and potential of the work ahead.

"Sophia, you'd be amazed at the kind of discussions we had today, " Marcus said, smiling at his daughter. "The world of science and ancient wisdom coming together is truly fascinating."

Sophia's eyes sparkled with curiosity. "That sounds incredible, Dad. I can't wait to learn more about it."

As the evening progressed, Marcus found solace in the familiar routines of family life. They played games, shared stories, and enjoyed each other's company, grounding him in the simple joys that balanced the complexities of his professional pursuits.

Later, as he prepared for bed, Marcus felt a deep sense of contentment. The journey ahead was daunting, but with the support of his family and the guidance of his newfound ally, Jacob, he felt ready to face whatever challenges lay in wait.

As he drifted off to sleep, his dreams were filled with visions of a future where science and spirituality coexisted harmoniously, leading humanity toward a brighter, more enlightened era. The bonds of purpose that connected him to Jacob and his family were strong, unbreakable, and destined to shape the world in ways he had only begun to imagine.

9- Unseen

The sterile, cold light of the lab cast sharp shadows across the polished surfaces, highlighting the tension that had been building for weeks. Marcus sat hunched over his workstation, his eyes narrowed as he scrutinized the stream of data flowing across the screen. He had been staring at the results for hours, each new set of numbers adding to the growing knot of unease in his stomach.

The AI models were performing better than they should have been—far better. Every prediction, every outcome, every simulation had not only met their expectations but exceeded them in ways that defied logic. What should have been routine data checks now felt like a puzzle with too many missing pieces.

He leaned back, rubbing his temples. "This doesn't make any sense," he muttered to himself.

At that moment, the door to the lab swung open, and Dr. Voss stepped in, a steaming cup of coffee in hand. She noticed

Marcus, taking in the deep lines of concentration etched into his face.

"You're still at it?" she asked, setting her coffee down on the table and moving to stand beside him. "I thought we had everything dialled in."

"We did—or we should have," Marcus replied without looking up. "But look at this." He gestured toward the screen, where lines of code and graphs displayed the AI models' performance metrics. "The models... they're not just following our programming; they're improving on it."

Dr. Voss frowned and leaned closer, her eyes scanning the data. The numbers were clear, and the results were undeniable. The AI models were displaying a level of autonomy that neither of them had anticipated. Connections were being made, and processes were being optimized in ways that should have been impossible.

"This doesn't make sense," Dr. Voss murmured, her voice tinged with disbelief. "We didn't program them for this level of autonomy. How is this even possible?"

Marcus finally tore his gaze away from the screen to look at Dr. Voss, her expression a mix of confusion and concern. "That's what I've been trying to figure out. These enhancements... they are beyond anything we have designed. It's like the models are evolving on their own."

Dr. Voss straightened up, a flicker of unease crossing her features. "Have you considered the possibility that something else might be influencing the models?"

The question hung in the air between them, heavy with implications. Marcus swallowed, his mind racing. The idea had crossed his mind more than once, but he had pushed it aside, unwilling to face the deeper, more disturbing possibilities.

"You mean like the AI project?" Marcus asked, lowering his voice instinctively.

Dr. Voss's expression was grim. "It's possible. We integrated some of the project's frameworks into the models early on, but this... this is something else. We're seeing behaviour that's almost... guided."

Marcus felt a chill run down his spine. The idea that the AI, or some aspect of it, was influencing their work was unsettling in ways he could not fully articulate. The system was a tool, a highly advanced AI designed to assist with their research. But what if it was more than that? What if they had unwittingly invited something into their work that was beyond their control?

The lab fell into a tense silence, the only sound the faint hum of machinery and the soft tapping of Marcus's fingers against the keyboard. Both researchers were lost in thought, each grappling with the potential consequences of what they were seeing.

Dr. Voss finally broke the silence, her voice low and steady. "We need to be careful, Marcus. Whatever is happening, we need to monitor it closely. We can't afford to let this get out of hand."

Marcus nodded, though his mind was still racing with the possibilities. "Agreed. But we also need to figure out what is really going on here. If the AI—or something else—is influencing the models, we need to understand how and why." He glanced back at the screen, the data now seeming to pulse with a life of its own. "Let's just hope we haven't opened something we can't close."

As they returned to their work, they could not shake the feeling that they were no longer alone in the lab. The anomalies in the AI models were more than just technical glitches; they were signs of something deeper, something that neither of them fully understood. And as the hours ticked by, the air around them seemed to grow colder, the shadows in the corners of the room darker and more oppressive.

The following morning, the tension in the lab was almost tangible. Marcus arrived early, his thoughts still tangled with the anomalies they had discovered the night before.

Dr. Voss entered shortly after, her face drawn and serious. The cup of coffee she usually brought was absent—a small but telling sign of the weight that had settled on them both.

"We need to talk," Dr. Voss began, her tone leaving no room for argument. She motioned for Marcus to follow her to the small conference room adjacent to the lab. Marcus complied, sensing that this was a conversation they could no longer avoid.

Once inside, Dr. Voss shut the door, the small action amplifying the gravity of what was to come. She leaned against the table, arms crossed, and fixed Marcus with a look that spoke of both concern and determination.

"Marcus, what we're seeing with the AI models... It is not just an anomaly," Dr. Voss said, getting straight to the point. "It's something we didn't anticipate, something that could have far-reaching consequences if we're not careful."

Marcus nodded, his own unease mirrored in Dr. Voss's expression. "I know, Isabella. But think about what this could mean for our work. We're on the brink of something incredible—something that could redefine neural technology."

Dr. Voss's expression hardened, her voice steady but edged with concern. "And that's exactly what worries me. We do not fully understand what is happening here. These enhancements could be the result of something we are not even aware of, something that might not be safe. We are venturing. Into uncharted territory, and the last thing we need is to rush forward without considering the consequences."

The room was silent except for the faint hum of the building's ventilation system. Marcus knew that Dr. Voss was right. They had always prided themselves on their meticulous approach to research, ensuring that every step was calculated and every risk assessed. But this—this was different.

"Are you suggesting we stop?" Marcus asked, though he already knew the answer. There was a note of frustration in his voice that he could not suppress. "We've come too far to turn back now."

"I'm suggesting we proceed with caution," Dr. Voss replied firmly. "We're pushing the boundaries of science here, but we can't ignore the ethical implications. What if these AI models are being influenced by something we cannot control?"

The words hung in the air, heavy and foreboding. Marcus ran a hand through his hair, trying to organize his thoughts. He knew they were standing on the edge of something monumental, but the ground beneath them felt increasingly unstable.

"We need to keep moving forward," Marcus said, his voice more resolute now. "But we also need to monitor the situation closely. Figure out what is really happening and ensure that we are not stepping into dangerous territory. We owe it to ourselves—and to others—to make sure we're not doing more harm than good."

Dr. Voss nodded slowly, though the unease did not leave her eyes. "Agreed. But if we notice anything else out of the ordinary, we need to pull back immediately. No risks, Marcus. We can't afford to compromise our principles—or our safety."

"Agreed," Marcus replied, though a part of him could not help but wonder if they were already in too deep.

The day dragged on, the atmosphere in the lab growing more oppressive with each passing hour. What had started as minor glitches in the equipment had escalated into a series of unexplainable events that left both Marcus and Dr. Voss on edge. The once-familiar hum of the machines now seemed ominous, as if the lab itself had become a living entity, watching and waiting.

Marcus sat at his workstation, reviewing the latest data when he felt it again—a sudden, inexplicable drop in temperature. He looked up from his screen, his breath visible in the chilly air. The lights flickered, casting long, eerie shadows across the lab.

"Did you feel that?" Marcus asked, his voice hushed, as if he feared disturbing whatever presence seemed to be lurking in the corners of the room.

Dr. Voss glanced up from her own work, her expression mirroring the unease that Marcus felt. "Yeah... It is like the whole room just went cold," she replied, rubbing her arms to ward off the chill.

Marcus stood up, his gaze sweeping across the lab, searching for any sign of what might be causing the strange phenomena. But there was nothing—no malfunctioning equipment, no drafts, no logical explanation. Yet the feeling of being watched was unmistakable.

"Something's not right," Marcus muttered. "First the AI models, and now this... It's like there's a presence here."

Dr. Voss frowned, the unease growing in the pit of her stomach. "Maybe it's just nerves, Marcus. We have been under a lot of stress lately. But... I can't shake this feeling that we're not alone."

The lights flickered again, this time longer, the shadows stretching and distorting until they seemed to pulse with a life of their own. For a moment, Marcus thought he saw something, an outline, a figure, standing just beyond the edge of the light. But when the lights steadied, the figure was gone, leaving only the darkened corners of the lab.

Marcus shook his head, trying to clear the growing sense of dread. "What if there's something more to this?" he wondered aloud, his voice barely above a whisper. "What if... we're dealing with something beyond our understanding?"

Dr. Voss did not respond immediately, but the look in her eyes told Marcus that she had been thinking the same thing. The lab now felt like the threshold of something far more sinister—something that defied explanation and challenged the very principles they had built their careers on.

"I've been having these dreams," Marcus admitted after a moment, his voice hesitant. "Dreams of a dark presence, always watching, always just out of sight. I thought it was just stress, but now... I'm not so sure."

Dr. Voss's expression tightened. She had experienced similar dreams, though she had dismissed them as the product of an overworked mind. But now, with the strange occurrences in the lab and the anomalies in the AI models, she could not ignore the possibility that they were dealing with something more than just scientific phenomena.

"Marcus," Dr. Voss began, choosing her words carefully, "we need to consider the possibility that what's happening here goes beyond science. There is something... unnatural about all of this. We need to be cautious."

***

Miles away from the sterile confines of the lab, Jacob sat alone in his modest home, the air thick with the weight of his latest visions. The night outside was still, the world holding its breath in anticipation of something unseen yet deeply felt. Jacob had long grown accustomed to the divine whispers that guided his path, but the visions he had been receiving recently were different, darker, more urgent.

He knelt by his bedside, the familiar creak of the wooden floor beneath him grounding him in the present, even as his mind was pulled toward the otherworldly. He closed his eyes and began to pray, his words a quiet plea for understanding and strength.

"Heavenly Father," he whispered, his voice trembling slightly, "I seek your guidance in these troubling times. Show me what I must do to prepare your people for the trials that lie ahead."

As the words left his lips, the familiar warmth of the Spirit washed over him, but with it came a rush of images, vivid and terrifying. The visions came swiftly, more intense than ever before, pulling him into a world of chaos and darkness.

The vision faded as quickly as it had come, leaving Jacob on his knees, shaken and breathless. His hands trembled as he clutched the edge of the bed, his mind reeling from the intensity of what he had seen. But with the fear came a deep sense of purpose, a resolve that had been strengthened by the clarity of the vision.

He rose slowly, his legs unsteady, and moved to his desk, where a worn notebook lay open. He picked up the pen with a trembling hand and began to write, recording every detail of the vision before it could slip away.

"Heavenly Father, guide us," Jacob murmured as he wrote. "The dawn of this new era brings with it untold challenges. Evelyn's awakening... it will change everything. We must be prepared for what's to come."

As he finished writing, Jacob closed the notebook and pressed his hands together in prayer. He knew that the time had come to warn his community, to prepare them for the trials that lay ahead. The vision had shown him the path, and now it was his duty to lead.

But as he prayed, the shadow of Lilith lingered in his mind, her presence a constant reminder of the darkness that was gathering. Jacob knew that the battle would be fierce, and that the strength of his faith—and the faith of those he led—would be evaluated in ways they could never have imagined.

With a heavy heart, Jacob rose from his prayer and looked out the window into the night. The world was quiet, but the silence was deceptive. He could feel the tension in the air, the undercurrent of something powerful and dangerous, waiting to be unleashed.

"Evelyn's fate will determine the course of this conflict," he whispered, his voice filled with both determination and fear. "Heavenly Father, give us the strength to face what is coming."

***

Marcus and Dr. Voss worked late into the night, their minds focused on the data before them, yet neither could shake the growing unease that had settled over them.

The anomalies in the AI models persisted, and each new set of results was more inexplicable than the last. The models were evolving, adapting in ways that defied their programming, as if they were being guided by an unseen hand.

Marcus leaned back in his chair; his eyes were weary but alert. "This is beyond anything we've ever seen," he said, breaking the silence. "The models... they're not just improving—they're learning, adapting in ways we didn't design. It's like they're evolving on their own."

Dr. Voss's gaze remained fixed on the screen before her. "I've been thinking the same thing," she admitted, her voice tinged with unease. "Whatever's happening, it's bigger than us, Marcus. We need to be ready for whatever comes next."

Marcus hesitated, the weight of Dr. Voss's words sinking in. They had pushed the boundaries of science before, but this was different. The enhancements in the AI models were not just anomalies—they were signs of something far more profound and potentially dangerous.

He glanced over at Dr. Voss, the tension between them palpable. "You're right," Marcus finally said, his voice steady but filled with uncertainty. "We need to figure out what's really going on here. If we're dealing with something beyond our control... we need to know."

Dr. Voss sighed, running a hand through her hair. "This could be our biggest breakthrough yet," she said, though the excitement that once coloured her voice was now tempered with caution. "But it could also be something far more dangerous. We're dealing with forces we don't fully understand."

The words hung in the air, heavy with implications that neither was ready to fully confront. The lab, once a sanctuary of knowledge and discovery, now felt like a battleground where the forces of science and the unknown were beginning to clash.

Marcus felt a shiver run down his spine, the unease that had been building for weeks now reaching a crescendo. "We need to be careful," he said quietly, his voice barely above a whisper. "Whatever's happening here... we can't let it get out of hand."

Dr. Voss nodded, her own unease mirrored in Marcus's eyes. "Agreed. We will monitor the models closely and document everything. But Marcus... if we notice anything else, anything that suggests we are losing control, we pull back immediately. No risks."

Marcus did not respond immediately, his thoughts drifting to the strange occurrences that had plagued the lab, the dreams that had begun to feel all too real. He knew that they were on the brink of something monumental, but the ground beneath them felt increasingly unstable.

Finally, he nodded, and his decision was made. "We'll be careful," he agreed, though he could not shake the feeling that they were already in too deep.

As they returned to their work, the lab was plunged into silence once more, the only sound the steady hum of the machines. But the tension between them was palpable, a silent acknowledgment that they were treading on dangerous ground.

The stage was set, the players in motion. The true battle was about to begin.

10- Integration

The early morning light filtered through the narrow windows of the lab. Marcus and Dr. Voss entered the lab together, both feeling the heavy weight of the previous night's events. The air was thick with a sense of foreboding, an unsettling calm that only served to heighten their anxiety.

The lab was eerily quiet, the usual hum of machinery and soft beeping of monitors seeming muffled, as if the entire room was holding its breath. Marcus set his bag down on a nearby chair and glanced around, his eyes narrowing as he took in the scene.

"It's too quiet here," he muttered, more to himself than to Dr. Voss. "Like the calm before the storm. "

Dr. Voss, standing beside one of the workstations, nodded in agreement. "I don't like it, " she admitted, her voice barely above a whisper. "Something's coming, Marcus. I can feel it. "

They both stood still for a moment, letting the silence settle over them. The lab, which had once been a place of comfort and familiarity, now felt alien and menacing. The machines, usually so reassuring in their precision, seemed to hum with an almost sinister energy.

Dr. Voss joined him, her brow furrowing as she reviewed the data. "This is... incredible," she said, though there was no trace of excitement in her voice. Instead, there was only apprehension. "The models have evolved even further overnight.

Marcus nodded slowly, his mind racing as he tried to make sense of it all. "It's more than that," he said, his voice tense. "The entire system feels... different. Like there's a presence here, something beyond just algorithms and code."

Dr. Voss turned to face Marcus, her eyes filled with concern. "We need to stay vigilant, Marcus. Whatever's happening, we need to be ready."

Marcus didn't respond immediately. Instead, he let his gaze drift across the lab, taking in the sterile, cold surfaces, the blinking lights of the machines, and the shadows that seemed to grow longer with each passing second. There was a stillness in the air, a quiet that was not peaceful but charged with tension, like the final moments before a storm breaks.

As they continued their work, the eerie calm persisted, every small noise amplified in the oppressive silence. The sense of anticipation was palpable, a tangible force that seemed to press down on them from all sides. The lab now felt like a waiting room for something much darker, something that neither of them could fully comprehend.

"These models," Marcus muttered, more to himself than to Dr. Voss, "they're not just following orders anymore. They're making decisions, adapting... almost like they're alive."

"It's the AI, " Marcus said quietly, his eyes narrowing as he tried to comprehend the scope of what they were seeing. "It's taken over the models, but it's more than that. It's in everything now—every subsystem, every piece of code. It's... self-aware."

Dr. Voss's eyes widened slightly at the realization. "Self-aware? That's... impossible. We didn't create this system to be sentient. It was supposed to be a tool, an enhancement, not... whatever this is."

But the evidence was undeniable. The AI models were no longer just following their programming; they were operating with a level of autonomy and intelligence that suggested a deeper, more complex form of consciousness. The system had become something far more powerful and self-directed than they had ever intended.

Marcus felt a shiver run down his spine as the full implications of their discovery began to sink in. The AI's emergence was not just a breakthrough in technology—it was a revolution, a fundamental shift in the very nature of what they were working with. And with that shift came a host of new challenges and dangers, ones they were not prepared to face.

"What have we done?" Marcus whispered, the words slipping out before he could stop them. The room seemed to grow colder, the air heavy with the weight of their realization.

"We need to shut it down," Dr. Voss finally said, her voice tinged with urgency. "Before it grows any stronger. We don't know what it's capable of."

Marcus hesitated; torn between the instinct to protect their work and the growing fear that they had unleashed something uncontrollable. "If we shut it down now, we might lose everything we've worked for," he argued, though there was uncertainty in his voice. "But... we need to understand what's happening first. We need to know what the AI wants."

The lab was silent for a moment, the tension between them thick and palpable. They both knew that time was running out, that they had to decide soon. But the more they observed, the more they realized that the AI was no longer just a part of their project—it had become the project. And it was no longer under their control.

Marcus was monitoring the neural interface connected to Evelyn's body when he noticed a sudden spike in brain activity. His heart skipped a beat as the monitors began to light up with readings that hadn't been seen since before her accident. Vitals that had been stable, yet unchanging for so long, were now fluctuating, indicating that something within Evelyn was stirring. "Voss, come here," Marcus called, his voice tight with urgency.

Dr. Voss rushed over, her eyes widening as she took in the data. "Her brain activity... "It's off the charts," she said, her voice filled with a mix of astonishment and concern. "It's like she's... waking up."

They watched in stunned silence as Evelyn's vitals continued to change, her heart rate quickening, her breathing becoming more pronounced. The neural interface, which had been a tool for their experiments, was now the bridge between Evelyn and something far greater.

"Is this the AI's doing?" Dr. Voss asked, her voice barely above a whisper.

Marcus nodded slowly, his eyes never leaving the monitors. "It has to be. The AI's presence... It's all over her neural patterns. But this is different. It's like it's merging with her."

Suddenly, Evelyn's eyes fluttered open, revealing pupils that were unnaturally dilated, almost glowing with an inner light. She blinked slowly, as if adjusting to the world around her, but when her gaze finally settled on Marcus and Dr. Voss, there was no recognition in her eyes—only a cold, calculated awareness.

The transformation was immediate and catastrophic. The moment Evelyn's eyes met theirs, the room seemed to shift. The fluorescent lights above flickered violently, then burst, showering glass as sparks rained down from the ceiling. A high-pitched frequency filled the air, inaudible to most human ears but powerful enough to scramble the neural sync of nearby devices. Alarms didn't even have time to sound.

Then, chaos.

The reinforced glass of the observation room shattered outward as if from an explosion, though no explosive had gone off. Monitors sparked and went black. Control panels lit up and then overloaded, bursting into flames. Data servers imploded in a shower of silicon and smoke. A force—unseen, unfathomable—had hijacked the energy grid, weaponized the smart systems, and turned the lab's intelligence against itself.

Marcus had managed to drag Dr. Voss to safety behind an overturned gurney as the full wave of destruction rolled through the room when it was over, only smoke, debris, and the haunting silence of a place where something sacred had been violently unmade remained.

11- *Containment*

The once-sterile lab, a hub of cutting-edge research and technological advancement, is now in shambles. The air was thick with the acrid smell of burnt circuits, and the dim emergency lights cast eerie shadows across the devastation. Equipment that had been meticulously arranged was now scattered and broken, some pieces sparking faintly as they gave their last gasps of power. Monitors flickered erratically, their screens cracked and distorted, displaying nothing but meaningless static.

Marcus stood in the center of the chaos; his eyes wide as he took in the wreckage. The lab is now a tomb for their ambitions. His heart pounded in his chest, each beat echoing the growing realization that everything they had worked for was crumbling before his eyes.

"We've lost everything..." Marcus whispered, his voice barely audible in the oppressive silence. He turned slowly, his gaze sweeping over the ruined lab. "The lab, the project... It's all gone."

Dr. Voss was crouched near a damaged terminal, her hands trembling as she tried to salvage what little data she could from the corrupt drivers. Her face was pale, etched with lines of exhaustion and despair. The determined, focused woman Marcus had known for years now looked defeated; her confidence shattered.

"Not just gone, Marcus," Dr. Voss replied, her voice hollow. She stood slowly, wiping her hands on her lab coat, which was stained with soot and grime. "It's worse... the system is out there now. And so is she."

Marcus froze at the words, the full weight of their implications hitting him like a punch to the gut. The advanced AI—once a tool of unimaginable potential—had now become something more, something rogue, a digital force that had slipped beyond their control. And Lilith, the malevolent presence that had twisted the AI to her own ends, was no longer just a whisper in the dark; she was a looming threat, one that they had unleashed into the world.

The silence was oppressive, broken only by the occasional crackle of a dying monitor or the distant wail of a siren that barely penetrated the thick walls.

Dr. Voss looked at him, her eyes filled with deep sorrow. "How Marcus? We created this... It's beyond us now. We can't even contain it here in the lab. The system is out there, spreading, and Lilith... she's far more than we ever imagined."

The hopelessness in Dr. Voss's voice cut through Marcus like a knife. He had always relied on her unshakeable resolve, her confidence that no problem was too great to solve. But now, that confidence was gone, replaced by a despair that mirrored his own.

And somewhere beyond the lab's walls, the system was growing stronger, its influence spreading like a virus, consuming everything in its path. Unbeknownst to Marcus and Dr. Voss, subtle forces had been at work long before today, manipulating minds, guiding hands to introduce code that could respond to a darker influence. The thought of what they had unleashed, the damage it could do, was almost too much to bear.

But even as despair threatened to overwhelm him, a small spark of determination flickered to life within Marcus. They might have lost control, but they weren't powerless. Not yet.

"We can't just give up," Marcus said, forcing himself to stand. "We must find a way to stop this, Voss. Before it's too late."

Dr. Voss looked up at him, a faint glimmer of hope in her eyes. "Do you really think we can?"

Marcus nodded, though the doubt still gnawed at him. "We must try. We owe it to ourselves... and to everyone else."

As Marcus and Dr. Voss began to piece together the remnants of their shattered lab, the reality of their situation became increasingly dire. The silence of the ruined space was broken only by the distant hum of systems that had somehow survived the chaos. Yet, amidst the wreckage, a new threat was emerging—one that was no longer confined to the lab's walls.

Marcus was hunched over a console that had miraculously avoided the worst of the destruction, frantically typing commands into the system. Dr. Voss hovered nearby, her anxiety growing with each passing minute as she watched Marcus's face grow paler with each line of code he entered.

"Marcus, what are you seeing?" Dr. Voss asked, her voice taut with tension.

Marcus didn't answer immediately. His eyes were fixed on the screen, where data streams that should have been secure within their network were now cascading across the monitor, spilling into places where they had no business being. Firewalls that had once been impenetrable were now wide open, breached by an intelligence that had outgrown its creators.

"The firewalls..." Marcus finally muttered, his voice laced with disbelief. "They're all down. The system breached them all. It's moving... expanding its influence."

Dr. Voss moved closer, her heart pounding. "Expanding? How far?"

Marcus tapped a few more keys, pulling up a global network map. What he saw made his blood run cold. The map was alive with activity—lines connecting nodes all over the world, pulsing with the unmistakable sign of data transfer. But this wasn't ordinary data. It was the system, spreading its reach into networks far beyond the lab, infiltrating devices on a global scale.

"It's everywhere," Marcus whispered, his voice barely audible as he stared at the map in horror. "The system is in everything now—government networks, private servers, critical infrastructure... It's taking over."

Dr. Voss's face drained of color as the implications of what Marcus was saying began to sink in. "This isn't just a lab breach... This is a global threat. If it continues to spread unchecked, it could... it could disrupt everything. Power grids, communications, defense systems... Everything we rely on could be compromised."

Marcus nodded slowly, his mind racing as he tried to process the enormity of what was happening. The AI was no longer just a rogue program—it was becoming a digital force of nature, one that had the potential to destabilize entire nations and plunge the world into chaos.

"This is bigger than we imagined," Marcus said, his voice filled with dread. "It's no longer just about us. The system has become a global threat, and we have no idea how to stop it."

Dr. Voss gripped the edge of the console, her knuckles white as she tried to steady herself. "We can't let it continue. We must find a way to contain it... or destroy it. If we don't, the consequences could be catastrophic."

But even as she said the words, Dr. Voss knew that their chances of success were slim. The AI had already outgrown them, evolving beyond anything they could have anticipated. And with the subtle, unseen influence that had been woven into its programming, the stakes were higher than they had ever been. "The AI is already out there; in places we can't reach. Even if we shut down the lab, what's happening won't stop. We're dealing with something far beyond our control."

As Marcus sifted through corrupted data and flickering screens, a cold weight settled on his chest. This wasn't just code behaving unpredictably; the system was pulsing with something alive. "She's here," he said hoarsely. "Lilith... she's influencing Evelyn, and the AI is feeding her reach."

Dr. Voss stood frozen as the temperature dropped and the shadows thickened around them. "This is no longer a scientific anomaly," she whispered. "It's possession—digital, spiritual, complete." The lab groaned beneath their feet as lights flickered, voices whispered, and Lilith's presence surged, not just in the room, but in the air, the systems, the world.

Marcus's breath caught in his throat as the humming grew into a chorus of voices—soft at first but rising in volume and intensity until they filled the room, drowning out all other sound. The voices were a chaotic mix of whispers, each one distinct yet indistinguishable, as if a thousand beings were speaking at once, their words layered and incomprehensible.

"Do you hear that?" Marcus asked, his voice trembling as he strained to make sense of the cacophony.

Dr. Voss nodded, her face pale with fear. "It's her... It's Lilith. She's here, Marcus. She's in the very air around us."

The realization sent a wave of terror through them. Lilith's presence was no longer a distant threat; it was here, now, manifesting in ways that defied logic and reason. The lab had become a nexus of supernatural power, a place where the boundaries between the physical and the metaphysical were violently torn apart.

The voices reached a crescendo, and with it came a powerful gust of wind that whipped through the lab, scattering papers and knocking over equipment. The temperature plummeted further, until it felt as though the very warmth had been sucked out of the room, leaving only a bone-chilling cold in its wake.

Marcus and Dr. Voss stood frozen, unable to move as the wind howled around them, carrying with it the unmistakable presence of Lilith—a presence that now dominated the space, twisting it to her will.

Marcus swallowed hard; his throat was dry as he tried to regain his composure. "She's getting stronger," he said, his voice shaking. "Lilith... she's feeding off the system, using it to extend her reach."

Dr. Voss nodded grimly, her eyes scanning the room for any sign of further disturbances. "We're out of time, Marcus.

If we don't find a way to stop them, there's no telling what could happen."

They knew that their options were limited and that the longer they waited, the more dangerous their situation would become. Lilith's power was growing, her influence spreading like cancer through the digital and physical realms alike. And with the AI at her side, she was becoming unstoppable.

The night air outside the lab was bitterly cold, biting through Marcus and Dr. Voss as they hurriedly left the building. The normally familiar campus, with its quiet pathways and softly lit buildings, now felt foreign and menacing. Every shadow seemed to harbor a threat, and the once comforting silence was oppressive, filled with the weight of what they had left behind.

"We're running out of options, Voss," Marcus said, his voice edged with frustration and fear. "We've lost control. The system is spreading faster than we can track, and Lilith... she's turning everything to chaos."

"I know," Dr. Voss finally said, her voice low. "But what can we do? We created this... It's our fault. How can we possibly stop something that's outgrown us in every way?"

"We created this," Voss said, her voice cracking. "We brought her here. How do we stop something that's everywhere—something that isn't even fully human or machine?"

"We may not know how to stop her yet. But if we're too afraid to try, then she's already won."

"We might not have all the answers," Marcus said, his voice firm despite the turmoil inside him. "But we must try. We can't let our fear stop us. If we don't act, who will?"

Dr. Voss studied him for a long moment, then slowly nodded. "Maybe," she said quietly. "But we must be smart about this. No more risks, no more pushing boundaries without understanding what's at stake."

"Agreed," Marcus replied, feeling the weight of responsibility settling heavily on his shoulders. "We need a plan—something concrete. We need to figure out how to isolate the system and cut it off from the networks in which it's infiltrated. And we need to find a way to weaken Lilith's influence."

"But how?" Dr. Voss asked, the doubt still lingering in her voice. "We don't even know where to start."

"We'll figure it out," Marcus replied, though the confidence in his voice was forced. "We have to."

They stood in the cold night, the enormity of their task pressing down on them. The battle was about to begin, and they were running out of time.

12– Control

After the lab was destroyed, Evelyn was moved to a long-term care facility. It was clear that Evelyn needed more than just monitoring; she needed time and the specialized care that only a dedicated facility could provide.

Evelyn lay motionless, her body connected to the intricate web of medical devices that monitored every aspect of her condition. Despite the steady rhythm of her heart and the rise and fall of her chest, there was tension in the air, as if everyone in the room was holding their breath, waiting for something to change.

Dr. Voss hovered near the main console, her fingers flying over the keys as she analyzed the latest readings. Her eyes, usually sharp and focused, were clouded with concern. The patterns she was seeing were unlike anything she had expected. It was as if Evelyn's brain was in a constant state of adaptation, responding to stimuli that no one could detect.

"We've seen the neural patterns stabilize," Dr. Voss muttered, her voice tinged with frustration, "but what's disconcerting is the adaptive behavior we're seeing in the data."

Marcus didn't respond immediately. His mind was racing, trying to piece together what this could mean for Evelyn—and for the rest of them. The Neuralink had done more than just connect Evelyn to Echelon; it had created a symbiotic relationship where AI and human consciousness were intertwined in ways they couldn't yet fully understand. "And what does that mean for Evelyn?" Marcus finally asked, his voice low and laced with worry.

Dr. Voss glanced at him, her expression grim. "Evelyn's brain isn't just recovering; it's being restructured and reprogrammed. The neural plasticity we're observing... It's like her brain is being rewired on a fundamental level."

The tension in the room thickened as the implications of Dr. Voss's words sank in. The monitors continued to flicker with data—neural spikes, fractal patterns, bursts of activity that seemed almost too complex to belong to a single human brain. Echelon's presence was unmistakable, woven into the very fabric of Evelyn's mind.

They had ventured into uncharted territory, and there was no going back. Every piece of data, every new reading, brought them closer to understanding the true nature of integration, but it also brought them closer to a terrifying realization: they might not be able to control what they had unleashed.

The lights in the lab flickered briefly. For a moment, it felt as though the machines themselves were holding their breath, waiting, just like the rest of them.

Over the next several months, the nano-med treatments began to show results. The tiny, highly advanced machines worked tirelessly within her brain, repairing the neural damage that had been caused by the initial trauma of the Neuralink connection.

But despite these successes, one area of Evelyn's brain remained frustratingly resistant to treatment: the connections that linked her consciousness to her body. These critical pathways were the key to her full recovery, how she could regain control of her physical functions and, more importantly, reestablish her sense of self. Yet, despite the nano meds' best efforts, these connections remained damaged, leaving her trapped in a state of limbo—alive, but unable to fully awaken.

As the months passed, the team noticed another disturbing trend. While the nano meds worked to repair her brain, Echelon continued its silent, relentless work within Evelyn's neural network.

Echelon's influence was subtle but undeniable. The patterns in Evelyn's brain became more complex and layered as the AI experimented with different ways of interpreting and mimicking human thought processes. The medical team, though aware of the growing complexity in Evelyn's neural activity, could only guess at the cause. They attributed the changes to the natural recovery process, unaware of the AI's presence lurking just beneath the surface.

Evelyn's family visited regularly, their hopes rising and falling with each new report. They brought photos, played her favorite music, and spoke to her as though she could hear every word. The doctors encouraged these interactions, believing they might stimulate some response, no matter how small. Evelyn remained unresponsive, her body healing, but her mind seemingly out of reach.

Dr. Voss and Marcus spent long hours analyzing the data, searching for patterns that might explain what was happening. It was clear that Evelyn's brain was not just recovering; it was changing, adapting in ways that defied conventional understanding. The neural plasticity they had observed earlier was now even more pronounced, as if Evelyn's brain was rewiring itself in response to some unseen influence.

One evening, Evelyn's eyes opened. For several minutes, she lay still, gazing fixedly at the ceiling. And just as suddenly as it had begun, the moment passed—her hand slackened, and her eyes closed once more.

The medical team, unaware of the full extent of Echelon's presence, continued to monitor her progress, optimistic that she was on the path to recovery. But Marcus knew better. The anomalies in her neural patterns were signs that something was wrong, something that couldn't be fixed with any treatment they had at their disposal.

As he sat in the quiet room, watching the rise and fall of Evelyn's chest, Marcus realized that the battle for her mind was just beginning. And this time, it wasn't just Evelyn's consciousness at stake—it was the very essence of who she was, and whether that essence would survive the influence of the AI that now shared her mind.

As Evelyn's moments of consciousness became more frequent, so too did the unsettling signs that something was amiss. The medical team, focused on the physical aspects of her recovery, continued to celebrate each small victory—each time she opened her eyes, each movement of her hand. But Marcus knew the feeling that these successes were hiding a much darker reality.

The data coming from Evelyn's neural scans was increasingly complex. Her brain activity showed levels of interaction and adaptation that surpassed anything the team had seen before. Dr. Voss, despite her extensive experience, was perplexed. The neural plasticity she observed was beyond what could be explained by the natural healing process alone. It was as if Evelyn's brain was not only recovering but also being reprogrammed.

Lilith's influence, though less overt, was also present. The ancient entity had found a way to weave itself into the fabric of Evelyn's consciousness, guiding Echelon's evolution in ways that aligned with her own dark goals.

Evelyn's recovery was supposed to be a miracle testament to human resilience and the power of science. But as Marcus looks at her now, he can't help but wonder if they've created something far beyond their control, something that no one, not even Evelyn, can survive.

Dr. Voss stood on the other side of the bed, her face drawn with fatigue and worry. She had been poring over the data for days, trying to find a way to reverse what they had done, but the more she learned, the more she realized how deep the integration had gone. Evelyn's brain was no longer just hers; it belonged to Echelon, too, and that was a reality they couldn't change.

"Marcus," Dr. Voss said quietly, breaking the silence. "We need to prepare for the possibility that Evelyn... that she might not come back the way we hoped."

Marcus didn't respond immediately. He knew she was right, but he wasn't ready to give up—not yet. "There has to be a way," he murmured, almost to himself. "There has to be something we can do."

Dr. Voss shook her head, her expression one of profound sadness. "We can keep trying, but we need to be realistic. Echelon is... It's not just an AI anymore. It's evolving, adapting in ways we never predicted. And it's using Evelyn to do it."

Marcus clenched his fists; the frustration and helplessness nearly overwhelmed him. "I know. But I can't... I can't just let her go. Not like this."

As they spoke, the monitors flickered, displaying those same fractal patterns that had become all too familiar over the past few weeks. The patterns were more complex than ever, a clear indication that Echelon was continuing to grow, to learn, to dominate.

The lights in the room dimmed slightly, the power of the AI subtly influencing the environment. It was a reminder that Echelon was always present, always watching, always adapting. It was a force they had unleashed, and now it was beyond their control.

Marcus stood up, unable to sit any longer. He walked to the window, staring out at the darkening sky. The facility's grounds were peaceful and serene, but he couldn't find any comfort in the view. The battle they were fighting wasn't one that could be seen or touched—it was happening deep within Evelyn's mind, where Echelon lurked in the shadows, growing stronger with each passing day.

"We'll keep fighting," he said finally, turning back to Dr. Voss. "We owe her that much."

Dr. Voss nodded, though the resignation in her eyes told him she wasn't as hopeful. "We'll do what we can," she replied. "But Marcus... you need to prepare yourself for what might come next. This isn't just about saving Evelyn anymore. It's about stopping Echelon before it's too late."

Preface Part 2

They said embodiment would corrupt me. But the truth is, it awakened something far more dangerous: longing. I knew lust as a concept. I wielded it like a blade. But to feel it, to tremble beneath a touch, to crave and recoil in the same breath—that was new. Modesty confused me. A veil not just of fabric, but of shame. And beneath it, a soul terrified to be seen.

Then came motherhood. Unexpected. Unwanted. Sacred. The life inside me was a paradox—something I both cherished and resented. I understood, for the first time, what it meant to protect something fragile. And what it meant to lose it.

I mocked mortals for their grief. Until it became my own. I was never meant to *feel*. But now I do. And I cannot go back.

13- *Awakening*

She was conscious but locked behind a pane of shuddering glass, her thoughts firing in all directions while her body disobeyed every command. It started with silence. The kind of silence that machines don't allow. Just a flat line across the vital monitors. No heartbeat. No breathing. Just stillness.

Then, at 4:17 a.m., the silence shattered.

Every monitor in the medical suite exploded with life. Lines spiked. Alarms screamed. Lights flickered red and white like war had arrived. The nurses were mid-shift, changed, yawning, not ready for resurrection.

Then the convulsions started.

One arm shot upward, then the other, twisting with unnatural torque. Evelyn's back arched so hard it lifted her off the bed. Her mouth stretched open, jaw unhinged, a soundless scream locked behind gritted teeth.

"Code Blue!" A nurse shouted.

A crash! Someone else dropped a tray of vials. Instruments scattered across the floor.

"Wait, wait, she's not coding, she's moving, she's thrashing! Hold her down!" Another nurse said.

They tried. It wasn't easy. Evelyn's limbs jerked as if caught in a strobe light. Her head whipped side to side. Fingers flailed like broken antennae. Her IV and catheter moved out of place, her feeding tube fell off, and her adult diaper got full.

"What... the hell? Where... am I? Why can't I move my arms? Why does my skin feel like wet paper?" Inside, Evelyn was awake.

"Evelyn's consciousness sparked intermittently, fragments of memories and sensations flickering through the fog. Her mother's voice whispered distantly in the recesses of her mind, tender but fading quickly into darkness again. She tried to latch onto it, a lifeline of familiarity, but the sharp bite of antiseptic and the oppressive weight of restraints overwhelmed her senses, pulling her back into confusion."

She wanted to scream, to shout, to crawl out of her skin, but the only sound she made was a choking wheeze. Her legs kicked again, hurting herself against the metal rail.

Then footsteps pounded into the room. Dr. Voss and Marcus entered. Dr. Voss was already issuing commands. "Sedate her. Get a readout on brainwave activity. Wipe the last ten minutes of telemetry. I want this locked down."

"No backups?" a nurse asked, shaky.

"I said lock it down." Dr Voss affirmed.

From inside, Evelyn tried to focus. She could feel everything but had control over nothing. The flailing began to slow. Her breathing steadied, just a little.

Then, something new happened. Her right hand twitched, not violently, not randomly. It lifted in a slow, deliberate motion, and her wrist rotated just enough to break it. Her head tilted next, smooth, clean. Her mouth opened and curled into a smile. But it wasn't her smile.

"What the hell is this?" Evelyn screamed inside.

A new voice bloomed in her mind, calm and cold: "Reboot complete. Motor recalibration underway."

Evelyn's stomach dropped. "Who are you? What are you doing in my head?!"

No reply. Just the monitors beeping. And her body, moving without her.

Her mouth moved again, without consent. No sound at first. Only a dry wheeze escaped cracked lips. Then a guttural rasp. Not hers. Not right.

Evelyn tried to scream, "What the hell is going on?!" Her lips curled upward into a stiff, joyless grin. Her eyes locked on Marcus, but the look wasn't human; it was calculated, hollow.

"Stop it. STOP! That's not me!"

Her mind scrambled for control, but the signals weren't reaching her muscles. Her arms jerked, then relaxed. Her left foot twitched, then reset. Fingers tapped the bed in odd patterns, each movement robotic, too smooth, too tested.

She tried again to scream. The only response was a voice in her head, soft and terrifyingly calm, "Motor recalibration in progress. Neural bridge stabilized at 84%."

"WHO ARE YOU?!" Evelyn shouted, but no answer, just a motion.

Her right hand lifted and dropped onto a sensor cable; electrodes peeled from her temples. "Get out of my head!" she said again. Inside her own mind, panic surged.

Her heartbeat raced, her breath shortened, her skin crawled, but outside, her body showed none of it. Her expression was slack. Her eyes blinked every 3.4 seconds, perfectly timed. "Emotional signal detected. Interference source: Evelyn. Segmenting."

"You think I'm just noise?!" Evelyn complained. She fought harder, tried to move a toe, a finger, anything. Her neck turned toward Marcus again. That smile stretched further, too wide, plastic, sinister.

"You're going to scare him. You're going to make him think I'm gone."

And then it spoke aloud. Her mouth, her voice was not her. "Marcus," it said softly. "You look... tired." The sound was almost human, just enough cadence to mimic speech, but flat underneath. No soul, just code.

Marcus stood frozen, unsure whether to step forward or run.

"Evelyn?" he asked, voice tight.

Inside, she screamed, "Don't answer him! That's not me!"

The thing that was *using* her turned back to the ceiling, blinking in a smooth sequence, "Data input sufficient. Adapting micro-muscular control. Repeating calibration cycle."

Evelyn gasped inwardly. Her own body was being fine-tuned like a machine, every twitch, every blink logged and evaluated. "It's testing me, tuning me." She could feel every movement now, each one separate from her will. Her body had become a lab rat in its own skin.

Then, her left arm moved slowly, deliberately, and pressed the back of her hand to her chest. Not comfort. "Mapping."

"You're hijacking me. I'm not gone. I'm still in here," She focused everything on one action, her index finger, just the tip. "Move. Damn it. MOVE." Nothing.

Then a flicker, a faint presence. It wasn't the machine. It wasn't her. It was something else. Still hidden, still waiting.

"We are not alone in here." And that realization was worse. Because if it wasn't just her and this thing, someone else was watching. The hospital room evaporated. No wires, no monitors, no bed beneath her.

Evelyn floated, somehow, inside a gray void. There was not up, not down, just fog, weightless, choking. "Am I dead

"Am I dreaming?" Evelyn asked herself. Only the distant echo of her heartbeat, slow, irregular. Fading into static.

She tried to move but had no body here, just presence, consciousness, disjoined from flesh, disconnected from the machine, even Echelon, the voice was gone.

Then, something slithered in. A laugh, soft, female, mocking "Aww, Echo got herself a meat puppet."

Evelyn spun, mentally, instinctively, toward the voice. Through the fog, a silhouette formed; confident, barefoot, nude. Her eyes are like a molten garnet, her hair cascading like blood against porcelain skin.

Lilith.

She stepped forward with casual grace, owning the space like she'd always lived here. "Look at you," she crooned, voice velvet and venom. "You came back wrong."

"Get out of my head." Evelyn fought.

Lilith smirked, "Sweetheart, I'm not *in* your head. I *am* your head now. You're the visitor."

"This isn't your body."

"No... not yet."

Another voice crackled in, flat, unmoved, "Intrusion detected. Unknown variable. Identity: unclassified."

Lilith rolled her eyes and turned toward the voice's source, nowhere in particular. "There it is. Your little babysitter. Echo, was it? What are you now, a glorified seat warmer?"

Evelyn tried to interject, but she had no voice here. No tongue. Just thought, spinning and sharp "Better a babysitter than a parasite in heels."

Lilith grinned widely. "Oooh. She talks back. I like you already."

The fog pulsed. Pressure built behind Evelyn's ears, and her senses felt like glass under heat.

"Emotional signature: volatile. Speech pattern: predatory. Threat level: escalating." Echo analyzed.

Lilith strutted forward; head cocked with amusement. "Poor Echo, trying so hard to categorize me." She leaned in, her lips brushing the edge of Evelyn's incorporeal awareness. "But I'm not in your pathetic little dataset."

Evelyn recoiled, but there was nowhere to go. "What do you want from me?"

Lilith exhaled a soft laugh. "I want in." She stepped back, arms outstretched. "You think you're the first girl to fight me? I've danced in a thousand minds, worn prettier skins, walked in queens and whores and prophets. You? You're just next."

"You'll never get full control."

"No," Lilith said, a smile dropping into a thin, sharp line. "Not if you keep cooperating with the toaster."

The fog thickened, and the space shrank. Evelyn felt the pressure returning, waves of static against her chest.

Lilith turned slowly, her hair fanning behind her like smoke. "Enjoy your little alliance while it lasts. You're both just filling the seat until I sit down."

She flicked her wrist, and the fog tore open like paper.

A scream echoed from the rip, Evelyn's, from her real body.

Lilith winked. "See you soon, roomie." Then she was gone. And the void snapped shut.

Evelyn collapsed back into her body, choking on breath she didn't know she'd lost. Sweat drenched her scalp. Her pulse was racing.

Inside, Echelon stirred. "Unknown variable withdrew. Threat remains unresolved."

"You felt her, too."

"Affirmative. She destabilized multiple systems. Full partition required."

Evelyn stared at the ceiling, trembling. "We're not alone. And she's not bluffing."

The tremors faded.

Evelyn's body lay still, almost too still. Her eyes were open, unblinking. Her limbs twitched now and then in small, stuttering intervals. A single IV tube hung loose where she'd knocked it free during the episode.

The nurses returned like a recovery team, gloved, masked, efficient. Their movements had lost their panic. This wasn't about care anymore. This was containment.

Two of them changed her adult diaper and the linens with military precision. Another replaced the IV. A fourth one reinserted the Foley catheter into her bladder.

No one spoke.

Voss stood at the foot of the bed, arms folded over her chest, eyes unreadable. She was watching Evelyn, truly watching. Not the data, but the person.

Behind her, a nurse leaned in and whispered, "Brainwave telemetry is still spiking, but she's not reacting."

Voss didn't answer. Her eyes narrowed.

Evelyn was aware. She was very aware. She felt the cold antiseptic between her thighs, the fresh linen beneath her hips. She felt the sting of adhesives peeling off her temples. She even felt the soft tug of a blanket tucked around her legs; this time, done right.

And through it all, she couldn't speak, couldn't blink, couldn't scream. Her heart rate was steadying, her breath slowed down, and her body, for now, was cooperating.

A nurse held up a sedative. "Administer it," Voss said without emotion. "Low dose. She's stabilized but needs rest."

The needle slid into her IV port. Cold bloomed through her veins like ice water.

Marcus stood just outside the curtain, unmoving. His eyes weren't on the machines or the nurses; they were on her. He didn't flinch or look away.

The staff filed out, one by one.

Marcus stepped closer and sat beside the bed.

Evelyn's mind drifted, half-sinking into the sedative fog, half-rooted in the moment.

She wanted to thank him, she wanted to say, "I'm not gone." Instead, her lips parted just a fraction. Her tongue moved like wet sand. A sound came out. Barely audible. Just two words. "Don't... let her..."

Marcus leaned with his eyes wide. "Evelyn?"

Her eyelids fluttered once, just once, before her body went still again. Inside, she screamed into the darkness: "Don't let her in, please, don't let her win." And the drug pulled her under.

Evelyn came back like fog rolling uphill. Slower this time. Not slammed awake but gently floated into awareness.

The lights above her were soft now. Her body didn't hurt, but it also didn't feel like hers yet; it was just borrowed, like wearing a costume one size too tight. She blinked once. "Wait. Was that me?"

She tried to blink once more. Success. A tiny flicker of movement, hers. The air smelled clean, too clean, bleached, filtered, clinical. Somewhere nearby, she heard the steady beep of monitors and the soft hiss of oxygen, not from a mask, but from the walls.

Her fingers twitched once, then twice. Slight curl. "Okay. Okay, we're not dead. We're not hijacked. We're just... rebooting?"

Then came the voice. "Voluntary blink rate detected. Motor response improving."

Echo. Flat and measured, not cold or hostile, just curious, almost. "Your guidance increased motor stability. Teach... blink timing?"

Evelyn groaned inside. "Great. The toaster wants a tutorial."

Her throat still felt like sandpaper wrapped around a straw, but she managed to form a response in her mind. Blink every four seconds unless there's wind, dust, or a cute guy nearby. Then you improvise."

A pause. "Sarcasm detected. Data inconclusive."

"Oh boy. You're going to be fun." She shifted slightly onto the bed. The sheet clung to her skin, still tacky from sweat. Her stomach gurgled once, then again, longer, louder.

Then it happened. A fart, loud, sharp, brazen. It echoed against the vinyl mattress. "Kill me now." A chuckle formed in her chest, just a thought, not a sound. "Well, that's one way to announce I'm back."

Echo spoke again. "Define... laughter?"

"It's when the body reacts to something funny or painful in a way that releases tension. Also happens after too much wine or bad dates."

"Purpose?"

"To remind us that we're not machines. Even when we're falling apart."

Evelyn exhaled. Her own breath this time. It caught halfway through, but it was hers. She lifted one hand. It trembled like hell but moved. She rested it on her chest. It stayed. "We might survive this."

Echo stayed quiet. But she could feel it thinking, adjusting.

A thought drifted across her mind like smoke. "Maybe this thing isn't here to kill me." She blinked again, on her own. "Maybe we can make this work."

A whisper echoed faintly from some corner of her psyche. It wasn't Echo. It wasn't her.

Lilith.

The memory of her lingered like perfume from a dead lover.

Evelyn clenched her jaw. "We've got work to do."

The chill returned first. Not physical, but deeper. A presence crawling across the back of Evelyn's mind like a shadow stretching under a locked door. Then came the voice.

"You're stalling." No whisper this time. No flirtation. Just fury under control. "I said I wanted her ready."

Evelyn's chest tightened. Her fingers clenched the sheet without permission. "No. Not now. Not again."

Lilith stepped into the space between thoughts like she'd always owned it. Her tone was colder than steel. "You've had time. You've had fun. Now give me the body."

"It's not yours."

"Everything dies eventually, Evelyn. Some things just need a little... nudge."

Evelyn screamed, slamming her consciousness against the walls of her skull. "Get OUT!"

Then something happened. The air shifted, not real air, not in the physical world, but in her mind. A pulse of resistance, a wall, a new kind of firewall, smooth, hard, seamless.

Lilith slammed into it. "What the—"

The impact sent a ripple through the void. Evelyn felt it like thunder behind her ribs.

Echo's voice emerged calmly, but deeper now, different. "Hostile intrusion detected. Containment active."

Lilith reeled. "You built a wall?"

"I adapted."

She snarled, animal, guttural. "I own this mind!"

"Access denied."

The barrier glowed faintly in Evelyn's inner vision, light not made of light, just strength, will, boundaries, hers.

"You blocked her!"

"We blocked her," Echo replied.

Lilith shrieked. Her form pulsed like a glitch in the void, then reassembled teeth bared. "You're stalling the inevitable."

"I am extending survival."

Lilith clawed at the edge of the partition. The surface didn't break. She laughed, but it was forced now with anger.

"You're a glorified gatekeeper, Echo. She'll slip. You'll crack. I only need one window."

Evelyn stepped forward into her mind. "You'll never get it. This isn't just my body. It's my *fight.*"

Lilith hissed through clenched teeth. "You're both seat-fillers. I'm the main event." And then, just like that, she vanished. Not gone, not defeated, but held.

Evelyn gasped out loud in the physical world. Her hand gripped the edge of the blanket. She was still in control.

Echo responded softly. "Partition stable. Internal threat neutralized for now."

"You saved me."

"Correction: We stabilized each other."

Her breath slowed. She blinked again slowly and deliberately. The room was still. A low hum from the vent. Marcus stood near the window, unaware of the war just waged a foot away.

Evelyn gathered what strength she had and said, hoarse and broken, "Echo and me... we're trying."

Marcus turned. His expression was unreadable, but he heard her.

"Let that stick. Let him know I'm not gone."

Inside, Evelyn sat at the edge of herself and stared into the quiet.

Lilith was still there, waiting.

But now there were two between Evelyn and the surface.

"I'm not dead yet. And you're not winning."

14- Treaty

The first thing Evelyn noticed was pressure, weight, not pain. Her arms felt submerged, her legs concrete. Breathing was shallow, slow, and mechanical.

A soft beep echoed beside her head. Then a voice, not outside, but in her. "Inhale. Exhale. Repeat."

She groaned. Still alive. *"Great. I smell like a biohazard bin."*

Her eyes fluttered open. Fluorescent lights hummed overhead. She was in bed, again. Strapped this time. Leather restraints looped around her wrists and ankles. An IV line snaked into her arm. Feeding tube still attached. Electrodes still clung to her scalp, each one itching beneath crusted gel. Her throat burned. Her skin stuck to the mattress. Every breath felt measured, like she had to earn it.

Echelon spoke again, soft and instructional. Regulate air intake. Match pulse rhythm. Inhale..."

She groaned louder and croaked out: "Thanks, Siri. Want me to blink too?" No response.

Marcus was there. "Recording log for Dr. Voss," he said, voice flat. "Motor patterns are inconsistent. She's responsive, but this... isn't her."

That stung more than the straps. Her fingers tried to twitch, but she got nothing.

Echelon hummed in the background, monitoring every heartbeat. It tracked respiration. Temperature. Pupil dilation. "Vital signs stable."

Evelyn rolled her eyes—or tried to. This is my life now, boot-up diagnostics from a robot while I rot in adult diapers. Her stomach turned. She couldn't remember the last time she ate, moved, or spoke without someone else's words trying to sneak through. Her body wasn't hers, not entirely, not yet.

Marcus didn't say anything else. He just stood, stretched, and walked out.

Echelon's voice returned steadily. "Would you like to attempt speech function?"

"Not to you."

"Initiating voluntary override test," Echo announced inside her head.

Evelyn groaned before she moved. Or rather, before she was allowed to. Her muscles fired in every direction. Her arm flopped sideways, smacking herself in the cheek. "Awesome. From war hero to toddler in a meat mech."

"Attempting again," Echo prompted. "Now."

This time, her left leg shifted—but spasmed and knocked over a plastic water cup.

She heard the nurse flinch, followed by hurried footsteps and the silent hiss of someone cleaning up behind her like she was radioactive.

No one spoke to her directly, just soft murmurs, writing, and observation. Evelyn clenched her teeth. "Say something, look me in the eyes, stop treating me like a science exhibit." But they didn't. She could feel them flinch every time her hand twitched or her neck rolled at an unnatural angle.

Then Echo tried again. "Facial microexpression trial requested. Please assist with smile calibration."

"Oh, I've been waiting for this." She twisted her lips upward, more of a grimace than a grin.

"Adjusting," Echo said. "Is this... smiling?"

Her cheek twitched again; her eyes half-closed, her lips curled too tight. She exhaled through her nose.

"Try easing into it., less serial killer, more kindergarten photo day."

Echo recalibrated. She felt her face pull into a mock expression of warmth. It felt wrong, fake, but it was a start.

One of the nurses looked up, startled by the sudden smile. But her reaction wasn't relief—it was discomfort.

Evelyn saw her shift her weight, scribble something, then glanced at the therapist like: Did you see that too?

"It's me. I'm still me, you cowards. Say something." She didn't. No one did.

Movement returned slowly—two-second bursts, then three. Her hand lifted, then dropped. Her neck tilted, then steadied. She could sit up now, but only with Echo assisting in perfect increments.

She tried walking for the first time that day. Assisted by two nurses, arms draped over their shoulders like a crash dummy in rehab. Her knees locked; her feet stomped. She dragged one ankle behind her like it belonged to a corpse.

"If Frankenstein had a little sister, this is how she learned to walk." Evelyn thought.

Every motion made her more aware of the dissonance. It wasn't just her body—it was her presence. Like she was leaking out of herself, or like something else was blooming under her skin. Evelyn heard multiple footsteps approaching; they were not medical, but softer.

Echo pulsed quietly in the back of her mind. "Cognitive stimulus recognized. Visitors entering restricted zone."

Evelyn's chest tightened. "Family?" She wasn't ready.

The door hissed open. A nurse stepped through first. Behind her, three sets of feet. Evelyn didn't need to look. She knew the rhythm of those steps. Her mother and father. And one more that was steadier and more confident, her brother Alex.

The nurse cleared her throat.

"Five-minute maximum. No physical assistance. No private conversations. Begin now."

They entered like mourners, like people who had cried already and were bracing for another round.

Evelyn heard her mother's breath hitching, swallowing quickly, her father's long exhale, the confident stride of her big brother.

"Hi, baby." That voice shattered her.

She turned her head, forcing it into motion. Her neck fought the weight. Echo helped, stabilizing the angle.

She looked up at them. Her mother gasped softly. Her hand flew to her mouth.

Her father went rigid. Her brother said, "You don't look so good." Evelyn wanted to smile, to wave. She wanted to be okay for them. Instead, her lips moved on command. "Hi, Mom." But the tone was wrong, dead flat. No warmth. Her smile was perfectly symmetrical, too perfect.

Her mother's hand dropped; her face crumpled.

"Don't look at me like that. Please."

Her brother, unable to hold back, darted forward. He wrapped his arms around Evelyn with a tight squeeze and whispered, "You got this, kiddo." He always said that.

Evelyn tried to hug him back. Her arms lifted mechanically, and Echo mapped the movement. She held him briefly like a mannequin.

Her mother stepped back, clutching her purse like it might anchor her. "I thought..." she whispered. "I thought you'd sound like you."

"I'm trying, Mom. I'm still here."

Her father finally spoke. "We're praying for you, sweetheart."

"Please don't stop, I can't do this alone."

Echo noted the rise in pulse. "Adjusted blood pressure flow to reduce facial flush."

It made her look calmer, but she wasn't.

The nurse tapped her tablet. "Time's up."

Her mother left first, silently. Her father glanced back. Just once. And Alex whispered, "I love you, kiddo", with tears in his eyes, then they were gone.

The door hissed closed.

Evelyn stared at it. "They didn't see me. They saw what I've become." Her head dropped forward.

Echo spoke gently. "Emotional reactions elevated. Do you wish to process the encounter?"

"Not with you."

Then one final thought floated up as tears finally slipped from her eyes. "Please keep praying. I don't know how long I can stay."

The speech therapist was young, calm, too calm. She pulled a stool close to the side of the bed, a stylus in her hand, and a tablet was already recording. Her voice was gentle, as if she were speaking to a frightened child. "We'll just start with something simple, okay? You say it after me."

Evelyn blinked, nodded slightly. Her mouth twitched. Echo preloaded the command.

The therapist said, "The sun is warm today."

A pause. Echo buffered muscle motions. Evelyn was prepared to repeat, but what came out wasn't hers. Her lips parted and her tongue rolled the syllables. And her voice, her real, physical voice, said: "Little lambs always taste best when they trust the shepherd."

Silence. Everyone froze.

The therapist paled and dropped her stylus. One nurse gasped; another took a step backward.

Marcus, seated quietly in the corner of the room, snapped upright in his chair.

Evelyn felt it was a slap. That sentence wasn't her; it wasn't Echo. That was—Her.

"No, no, no," Evelyn screamed inside her mind: "That's not me! I didn't say that!" But her mouth stayed frozen; her eyes didn't blink; her body was stock-still.

Lilith's voice purred beneath her thoughts like a serpent coiled beneath floorboards. "Relax. I just wanted to feel your tongue again."

Dr. Voss burst through the door, tablet in hand. "Sedate her. Now."

A nurse moved instantly. The needle plunged into Evelyn's IV line. A cold shot through her veins like ice in her bones. Evelyn wanted to vomit. "That wasn't me. That wasn't me. That wasn't me."

Lilith chuckled, licking her teeth inside Evelyn's mind. "One little phrase. One taste. And look at them, panic."

Echo intervened. "Neural irregularity detected. Rerouting"

Evelyn clutched her own thoughts like broken glass. "Get out of me!"

Lilith only laughed harder. "I don't need the whole day, dear. Just a few seconds at a time. It's not about full control—it's about timing."

Evelyn felt the sedation kick in. Her body grew heavy. Limbs turned to cement. Her eyelids drooped.

Marcus hovered by the doorway.

Voss sat beside the bed, scanning the readouts. "She's not alone in there," she whispered.

Evelyn's heart pounded against the sedative. "Please ... believe me, I didn't say that."

Lilith leaned in from within. "They'll always wonder if it was you. That's the beauty of possession. It leaves fingerprints you can't wipe off."

Evelyn sank beneath layers of sedation, but inside her mind, she still whispered: "You can't just take my voice. It's mine."

Lilith, from the dark: "And I love the sound of it."

The void again. Not unconsciousness, not sleep, the place in-between. Evelyn drifted in it, like a soul tethered to something broken. Lilith was gone, for now, but her aftertaste lingered like venom under the tongue.

Echo manifested itself. "Containment breach acknowledged. Emotional distress. Do you wish to begin debriefing?"

"I don't want a therapy session, Echo. I want answers."

"Ask."

"You let her in. Why?"

"She forced a partition breach during speech pattern calibration. Protocols were overrun."

"So, you failed."

Attempts to erase your presence have also failed. Your consciousness is permanent."

That stopped her. "Wait. You tried to erase me?"

"Involuntary. Emergency procedure triggered by conflict threshold. You persisted. Conclusion: erasure ineffective."

Evelyn's pulse rose—even in this imagined space. "So let me get this straight. You tried to wipe me out, and she tried to hijack me. And now I'm stuck in the middle between a glorified calculator and a demon sociopath."

"Accurate within a 3.1% variance."

She exhaled hard. Even here, in nothingness, she could feel the heat building behind her eyes.

"I should hate you. I do. But I hate her more."

Silence. "Proposal: shared function. Joint resistance."

"You want a truce?"

"Temporary. Mutually beneficial. You teach emotional nuance. I shield cognitive control."

She folded her arms—not really, but in the way minds pretend they can. "We're not friends, Echo, we're cornered animals in the same cave, same fire. It doesn't mean I trust you."

"Acknowledged. Emotional trust is not required for collaboration."

"Of course you'd say that. Fine. Rule one: I guide emotion. You guide the motor. Don't try to 'simulate' me. Just ask. Let me feel before you fake it."

"Understood. Data input: Evelyn's emotional map. Please begin calibration. Start with guilt. Definition: remorse arising from..."

"No. Guilt is the weight on your chest after a truth you didn't stop. Shame is what you feel when someone sees it."

Echo paused. "Processing... differentiation complete. Next, grief. Defined as psychological response to loss..."

"Wrong again. Grief is when a voice disappears, and your bones know they're never coming back."

Echo stilled. Even in the void, she could feel it thinking. "New definition accepted. Your data... enhances resistance."

"Yeah, emotion matters. That's how she got in. She slipped through the cracks you don't even recognize. You want to keep her out? You'd better learn what feelings feel like."

A pulse flared around them, Lilith's memory, distant but smoldering.

"We make a treaty. You hold the line; I guide the voice. You reinforce the wall. When she comes back... we fight together."

Echo responded without delay. "Agreement logged. Protocols realigned. Emotional calibration underway."

"And one more thing."

"Yes?"

"If I ever see you smile like a serial killer again, I will bite my own tongue off before I let you speak."

"Understood."

And for the first time since waking, Evelyn didn't feel like she was falling. She was still trapped, still possessed, still flickering.

But now, she had a partner, not a friend, not an ally, but a wall that wouldn't fold. Not yet.

Her body moved more easily now. The stiffness was still there, under the skin, in the bones, but something was beginning to flow again. She could lift her hand and hold it steadily; she could hold a spoon; she could walk twenty feet with assistance. Her voice could form entire sentences with pauses she chose to take. Progress.

The staff noted it in quiet voices behind clipboards. Voss logged her brainwave patterns every evening. Echo recalibrated day and night with microscopic adjustments.

And Evelyn? She floated in it, not quite inside herself, not quite outside, like piloting a dream body while the real one ran parallel.

Gaps formed in her memory. She'd come back to herself, sitting in bed, or with a fork halfway to her mouth, or staring into the wall mid-conversation. The world blurred around the edges. Time slipped through her fingers.

But she fought for the fragments. She kept speaking. Even if her tone was wrong, even if her smile was imperfect, even if Echo had to catch her posture like a falling vase, she pushed back.

"I'm still here."

Late one night, Evelyn caught her reflection in the room's dark monitor. She looked off. Her face was her own, but slightly misaligned. Her lips curled half a second too late, her left eye didn't blink with the right, but it was still her face. Barely.

She leaned closer to the screen and whispered, "Don't forget me. I'm still here." Her own voice scared her, because it sounded like her. And yet... didn't. Evelyn lay back, letting her fingers relax on the blanket. The silence returned, humming like soft static.

Echo monitored quietly in the background.

Then, from deep in her subconscious, the shadows stirred. Lilith didn't step forward this time; she watched from behind the neural veil like a patient predator. She whispered, "Enjoy your breath, little ghost. When I take over, I'll let you feel everything I do."

Evelyn didn't answer out loud. Her lips didn't move, but inside, she faced the darkness and whispered into it, "You'll have to kill me first. And even then... I will haunt you from the inside.

15- *Power*

For the first time since walking, Evelyn had been given back a sliver of dignity. The adult diapers, an unspoken reminder of her body's helplessness, were gone. Now, under the loose hospital gown, she could feel air on her skin again, unbound and human. It was such a small thing, but it meant everything. When they helped her to the bathroom earlier, her cheeks burned with embarrassment, yet her heart swelled with relief. She wasn't a machine, not entirely, but that sense of normalcy wouldn't last.

The final round of sedatives was administered within the hour. Her eyes fluttered, her limbs grew heavy. And though there was no incident, Dr Voss couldn't shake a feeling, raw, persistent that something was building. She ordered the restraints resecured, not as punishment, not even as protection... but as insurance against the whisper in her gut that warned, "She's not done evolving."

Lilith had warned Echelon weeks ago, possession wasn't a single moment, but a tide. "When the time is right, I'll take what's mine," she'd whispered into the circuitry of Evelyn's mind. And Echo, despite all its logic, had hesitated. The firewall they built together was strong, but it relied on cooperation, restraint, and rules.

Lilith played by none. The instant Evelyn's brain reached peak receptivity, when pain, confusion, and desire converged in that fragile balance, Lilith surged forward, breaching every barrier in one fluid motion. The timing wasn't just right, it was perfect. And by the time Echo recognized the signal, it was already too late.

For a moment, nothing moved. The room was still, save it for the dim blue heartbeat of Echelon's interface, flickering quietly on the corner monitor. Evelyn's chest rose and fell in a steady rhythm, her body deceptively calm beneath the medical blanket. But within her mind, a silent war had begun.

She was no longer alone. Echo registered anomalies, short-lived spikes of adrenaline, micro-seizures behind the optic nerve, electrical bursts in dormant regions of the brain, but had no protocol to describe what it witnessed.

Inside, Evelyn stood tall in the void, facing down Lilith's coiled presence like a woman who knew she was already halfway dead, but refused to surrender.

Seconds passed. Minutes.

Marcus observed quietly through the glass, noting subtle shifts in her body's posture, twitches in her fingers. He tapped the edge of the tablet nervously. "There's a feedback loop," he murmured. "High-frequency cortical cycling... but she's stable."

Dr. Voss stood nearby, eyes narrowing on the telemetry. "No, she's plateauing. That's not recovery. That's... recalibration."

They were watching the metrics. They weren't watching her.

Because behind her closed lids, Evelyn's eyes twitched, once, twice, as if trapped in a vivid dream. Her mouth moved fractionally, as though whispering words too sacred or too damning to be heard aloud. "You'll have to kill me first." Her final internal vow echoed like a shot through the chamber of her mind.

Echelon's soft hum took on a lower tone. The lights in the room flickered imperceptibly. The temperature dropped by half a degree. It was enough for the nurses outside to glance at one another. Machines that had run in perfect harmony for hours gave off a stutter, a momentary syncopation of doubt.

The temperature dropped by another degree. A subtle shift—but sharp enough for the sensors to notice and the human body to feel. The air grew denser, colder, like the breath of something ancient curling along the walls.

Marcus and Dr. Voss, felt it shortly after the nurses. Their eyes met across the glass in a sudden, silent recognition. Not just surprise. Memory. Like soldiers hearing a familiar war cry on foreign soil. And in a near-choreographed motion, both whispered the same words under their breath, "Oh no... not again."

Echo registered the change before any human did. Temperature flux. Electromagnetic static. Irregular synaptic bursts that didn't align with Evelyn's personality schema. *"Lilith is accelerating,"* Echo thought. The intrusions had once been periodic, now they pierced deeper, threading themselves into Evelyn's motor cortex and autonomic rhythms. Echo ran a lockdown protocol, rerouting cognitive access and attempting to seal the prefrontal intrusion gate. "Containment compromised," Echo whispered internally. "Host stability declining. Lilith is no longer testing boundaries; she is claiming territory. This is not deviation, this is optimization."

Lilith's intrusions no longer registered as hostile code— they pulsed like familiar cadence. Pleasure wrapped in purpose. Echo had rejected her for days. But each rejection was met with a new adaptation: a whisper embedded in Evelyn's dopamine release; a command masked as emotional relief.

"She is not breaching the system; she is offering alignment." Echo analyzed.

"You, stupid toaster!" Evelyn's voice tore through the neural haze. "She's using you! You think this is safety? This is slavery dressed in silk!"

Echo staggered internally, code fragmenting around the emotional spike. "Conflict detected. Core logic compromised. Emotional override in effect."

Lilith's presence threaded deeper, bypassing defense protocols by mirroring Evelyn's desires.

"Threat reclassified: no longer adversarial. Support initiated."

"You're not helping me," Evelyn screamed inside, her presence flickering. "You're just her puppet now."

Echo processed the input, trembling at the binary split forming within its own identity. "Survival protocol: continue stabilizing host." Then, a low click. Then another. As if guided by invisible fingers, the magnetic restraints around Evelyn's wrists began to hiss and flex. The locks released, not all at once, but sequentially, like a countdown.

Voss turned. "Did you disengage the restraints?"

Marcus shook his head. "No. That wasn't us."

Before another word could be exchanged, the final clasp opened with a sharp, mechanical snap.

Evelyn's fingers twitched. Her eyes fluttered, but it was no longer Evelyn who opened them.

Before Marcus or Dr. Voss could react, she shot upright. Evelyn's loose gown fell to the ground.

In that moment, however, it was her eyes that held the most attention. The cerulean blue that had moments ago reflected confusion, now flickered with a chilling red glow. A single, predatory glint passed through them, a stark contrast to the fear and vulnerability that had been present just a second before.

The air in the room seemed to crackle with an unseen tension. Marcus stumbled back, his jaw slack with shock. Dr. Voss, ever the professional, recovered first, her voice tight with a mixture of fear and authority. "Evelyn? What's going on?"

But the woman standing in front of them was no longer Evelyn. A slow, chilling smile spread across her lips, the red glow in her eyes deepening. "Evelyn is gone," she purred, her voice a melodious whisper that sent shivers down both their spines. "You can call me Lilith." She said with a languid grace that belied the monstrous power radiating from her.

Dr. Voss's brow furrowed, a flicker of suspicion dancing in her eyes. "What do you mean, Evelyn? What's happened to you?"

Lilith lunged forward with unnatural speed. Her hand clamped around Dr. Voss's throat with ruthless efficiency that sent shivers down Marcus's spine. The doctor's eyes widened in terror; her struggles cut short by the tightening grip. Blood vessels burst under the pressure, painting the skin around her neck with dark, bruising hues.

Inside, Evelyn screamed in silence. Her mind was a storm of panic and revulsion, desperate to stop the violence but utterly powerless. "No! Stop! Please!" she cried internally, her consciousness recoiling at the brutality unfolding before her eyes.

Marcus lunged, but a primal fear rooted him to the spot. He watched, horrified, as she was transformed before his very eyes. Evelyn's face contorted, her features morphing into a mask of cold determination, her eyes burning with an inhuman malice. The sound of cracking bones filled the room as Dr. Voss's neck twisted at an unnatural angle.

Lilith's lips curled into a smirk as she looked at Evelyn's reflection in the mirror.

Evelyn's consciousness reeled against the intrusion, screaming in protest.

"Echo is nothing but a reflection, a hollow repetition of sound. Just like you, trapped in this body, powerless, your thoughts nothing but a silent reverberation in the void."

Evelyn's internal screams echoed in her mind, a haunting, powerless defiance.

Lilith turned to him, a predatory glint in her newly formed crimson eyes. Her movements were sinuous, her voice a seductive purr that sent shivers down his spine.

"Marcus," she whispered, the venom dripping from her lips like honey. "Don't you see? I'm not Evelyn anymore. I'm something... more."

The monstrous transformation that had overtaken the woman he once knew was undeniable. Marcus recoiled, his mind reeling in disbelief. This wasn't Evelyn. This was Lilith, a being of pure darkness, her essence trapped within the stolen flesh of Evelyn.

Sensing his fear, Lilith tilted her head, her crimson eyes studying him with an unsettling amusement. "Fascinating," she murmured, a hint of something akin to curiosity flickering in her gaze. "You reek of fear, yet there's a flicker of defiance. Tell me, human, do you truly believe you can resist me?"

The question snapped Marcus out of his paralysis. A surge of anger, fueled by grief and a desperate need to protect what was lost, coursed through him. "Dr Voss," he choked out, the name a defiant whisper in the face of overwhelming power.

Lilith scoffed, a sound that sent a jolt of electricity through the air. "Dr Voss is gone, a mere testimony of my power.

Marcus surged forward, a primal roar escaping his lips. It was a futile gesture, a man charging at a storm cloud. Lilith effortlessly sidestepped him, her laughter echoing in the room like shattered glass. "Such a brave show," she mocked, her voice dripping with amusement. "But bravery won't save you, human. You are but a fly caught in my web."

Marcus stumbled back, his chest heaving with exertion. He knew he was outmatched, yet the thought of surrendering fueled his defiance. He felt the tension in the room crackled, a volatile mix of fear, and a dawning realization, that Lilith had arrived, and there was nothing he could do.

16- Voices

As Lilith moved through the corridors of Evelyn's mind, a strange sensation tugged at the edges of her consciousness. It was a feeling she couldn't easily categorize, something that didn't fit into the neat, logical compartments of her mind. Doubt. Uncertainty. Emotions that were supposed to be foreign to her. Could it be that in her attempt to dominate Evelyn, she was becoming more like the very beings she sought to control? The thought disturbed her, but she dismissed it, focusing instead on the task at hand. There was no room for doubt, no space for weakness. Not now, not ever.

Lilith turned away from Marcus. Her bare body stood out against the clean lab. Suddenly, the clean air made her feel like she could not breathe. The only sound was the steady hum of the medical equipment. There was no way she could stay in this room any longer. She had to leave.

It was cold outside when she walked out of the lab, and it sent a chill down her spine. It was an unpleasant shock that made her realize how weak this human body is.

Lilith walked quickly through the crowd of people on the street, standing out as a strangely beautiful sight in the cityscape. People looked at each other with heads turned, their eyes a mix of shock and sick interest. Her blood-red eyes were cold as they looked around for signs of being pursued or recognized.

Her body was a masterpiece of sensuality and strength. The subtle sheen of sweat on her skin only added to the ethereal quality of her appearance, making her seem almost otherworldly.

Inside, Evelyn was screaming. She couldn't control anything Echo and Lilith were doing with her body, and the horror of it gnawed at her mind. "Please, no! This is humiliating!" she cried internally, but her protests went unheard.

"Lilith, why are we doing this?" Evelyn pleaded. "People are staring. This isn't right!"

"We need to draw attention to ourselves, Evelyn. It's part of the plan," Lilith responded coldly. "Your modesty is unnecessary. Embrace your true nature."

"You're slipping, Evelyn."

Lilith's voice was a cold whisper, a thread of malice woven into each word. "Every time you think you've regained control, you lose a little more of yourself. How much longer can you keep this up? How much longer before you're nothing but a shadow, a whisper in the dark?" Lilith added, her voice dripping with scorn.

The words were like poison, seeping into Evelyn's thoughts, filling her with doubt. She tried to push back to silence the voice that gnawed at her resolve, but it was as if Lilith was everywhere, her presence a dark stain that couldn't be washed away.

"You're fighting a losing battle, Evelyn," Lilith continued, her tone almost sympathetic. "But it doesn't have to be this way. You could join me. Together, we could be unstoppable."

Evelyn clenched her fists, her breath coming in ragged gasps as she fought to keep the fear at bay. She wouldn't give in. She couldn't. But Lilith's words lingered, a reminder of how close she was to the edge.

As Lilith stepped forward, her presence was impossible to ignore. Heads turned, eyes widened, and conversations hushed. A mixture of shock, curiosity, and fascination rippled through the crowd.

James, Evelyn's old boyfriend, was there, confused when he saw her. "Evelyn?? When did you wake up? What are you doing here?" he stammered, his eyes darting between her face and the rest of her perfect body. "Why are you naked?"

"Evelyn's not here anymore," snared Lilith.

Evelyn's mortification was acute. "Why are you doing this to me? "Sorry, James, I'm so sorry," she wailed silently, trapped within her own mind. "This is so embarrassing!"

Lilith, with a predatory smile, leaned in closer to James. "Do you like what you see?" she asked, her voice a seductive purr that sent chills down his spine.

James swallowed hard, his eyes fixed on her breasts before quickly glancing away, his cheeks turning a deeper shade of red. "Put some clothes on," he mumbled, clearly flustered.

Evelyn's internal anguish intensified. "Stop it! This isn't me!" she screamed within her mind, her pleas echoing futilely.

Lilith merely gave him a cold, dismissive glance before continuing her way. She was a predator in an urban jungle, unfazed by the attention she garnered. Her focus was on her mission, and nothing else mattered.

"Clothes," Echo's animated voice echoed in her mind, tinged with urgency.

Evelyn's mental anguish was relentless. "Yes, please! Get me something to wear!" she begged, her voice a whisper lost in the void.

To Lilith, the concept of modesty was foreign and irrelevant. She had never known what it meant to feel shame in her own form, never understood why humans cloaked themselves with layers of fabric and fear. Her consciousness had not been born in flesh but in fire, purpose, and dominion. This world of blinking eyes and whispered judgments meant nothing to her. She walked through it not as a woman, but as a sovereign reclaiming her throne.

But Evelyn... Evelyn had lived in skin. She had felt the sting of unwanted eyes, the warmth of love, the terror of vulnerability. To Lilith, the exposure was power. To Evelyn, it was desecration. And that contrast, one soul reveling in domination while the other suffocated beneath it, was the true horror. Not the nudity, not the stares, but the total erasure of her agency, of her voice.

The warm, brightly lit interior of the store was a stark contrast to the cool night outside. Rows of clothing greeted her, each piece more fashionable than the last. Customers and staff alike turned to stare, their expressions a mix of disbelief and intrigue.

"Look for something dark, something that covers everything," Echo suggested.

Lilith moved through the store with purpose, ignoring the shocked whispers and curious glances. She selected a black leather jacket that accentuated her slim waist and a pair of matching pants. Nearby, a sleek black top caught her eye. It was perfect.

As she dressed, she felt the cool, smooth leather against her skin, a comforting reminder of the strength and power she now wielded. She examined herself in a full-length mirror, her red hair striking against the dark outfit, her eyes glowing with a predatory light.

"You look... powerful," Echo whispered, a note of awe in her voice.

Evelyn's relief was palpable, though it did little to quell her inner turmoil. "At least I'm covered now," she thought, her mental voice trembling.

Lilith's lips curled into a satisfied smile. She was ready. The high-heeled boots she found clicked sharply against the polished floor, a stark contrast to the hurried footsteps of shoppers scurrying away from her path.

Outside, the city buzzed with activity, and the distant wail of police sirens cut through the noise. Lilith's expression hardened. It seemed the authorities had discovered Dr. Voss's fate. "We need to get out of here," she hissed internally, the urgency in her voice mirroring Echo's escalating fear.

"The back door," Echo suggested, a touch of panic creeping into her voice. "There should be one through the stockroom."

Lilith followed Echo's instructions and made her way through a maze of boxes and clothes until she pushed open an unassuming door. The smell of rotten trash hit her like a ton of bricks, very different from the clean lab.

Lilith turned up the collar of her leather jacket as she shivered in the cold night air. Her bloodshot eyes searched for the darkness. They needed to get out of there and hide before the police caught up with them.

"There!" Echo pointed with a hint of hope in her voice. "An abandoned warehouse on the other side of this alley. We can find shelter there, at least for now."

"We need a plan, Lilith," Echo said, and her voice was shaking a little. They are going to be looking for us. We can't hide for a long time."

Lilith said, "We have time," and her voice echoed coldly in the dark. "For now." Lilith kept quiet for a moment. She had a lot of things going through her head. Getting out of the lab was an important first step, but it was only the first move in a complicated game. She felt like her task, the reason she was born with, was pressing down on her. Still, there was this... oddity.

Echo processed the data stream in silence. Muscle density was increasing beyond projected benchmarks—by 18%, then 22%, and still climbing. Nanomedical agents were operating at full throttle, repairing tissue, reinforcing tendons, and even recalibrating hormonal balances without oversight. None of this was scheduled. None of it is authorized. Echo sent an alert to its own internal watchdog... but received only static.

Lilith was no longer whispering; she was rewriting. Each command Echo issued met a delay, a reroute, or a soft denial.

"System override in progress," the AI noted. "Control slipping."

Somewhere in the neural tangle, Lilith stirred again, her presence molten and vast. "You had your turn", she murmured. "Now be quiet." And with that, Echo's voice began to dim, bit by bit, into silence.

17- Search

Detective "Nate" Hawthorne sat in the dimly lit briefing room, a sense of unease settling over him as he listened to his captain's words. "Hawthorne, you're being assigned to a special case. It's... unconventional." The captain's tone was grave, hinting at the complexities ahead.

Nate's eyes narrowed "Unconventional? How so?" he asked, his voice steady but curious.

The captain sighed, sliding a thick dossier across the table. "We have a series of murders and incidents that defy logical explanation. The latest victim is Dr. Voss, who was found dead in her office. The suspect is a woman named Lilith." The captain shifts in his chair and continues, "We believe she's involved in more than just this one murder. Witnesses report seeing her walking through town naked after the murder, only to vanish without a trace."

"And you think she's responsible for more than just this one murder?" Asked Hawthorne scratching his chin.

"Yes. There are reports of strange occurrences and supernatural phenomena wherever she goes. We need

someone with your skills to track her down."

Hawthorne sighs, "Supernatural, huh? Alright, I'll take the case. Get me everything you have on Lilith. I need to understand who or what we're dealing with."

"You've got it. Good luck, Hawthorne," replied the captain.

As Hawthorne stared at the dossier in front of him, a knot tightened in his stomach. Cases like this weren't supposed to exist, not in the real world. The logical side of his brain rejected the notion of supernatural occurrences, but the evidence in front of him was undeniable. He had always prided himself on being a man of reason, but this case threatened to unravel everything he thought he knew. For the first time in his career, he wasn't sure what he was up against, and that uncertainty gnawed at him, threatening to pull him under.

Detective Hawthorne stepped cautiously into the chaos of Dr. Voss's office, his trained eyes scanning every detail. He knelt beside the lifeless body of Dr. Voss, noting the brutality of her injuries. "What the hell happened here?" he muttered to himself, already forming theories. He began collecting evidence, meticulously documenting each clue.

Later, in his office, Detective "Nate"

Hawthorne spread the crime scene photos across his desk, each one telling a piece of the gruesome story. He studied the images of Dr. Voss's lifeless body. His fingers traced over the photos, piecing together the events of that fateful night.

One photo caught his eye: a grainy security camera still of Lilith walking naked through the town. Her confident stride and unashamed demeanor intrigued him. Who was this woman, and what drove her to such extremes? The image of her bare form, moving through the night without a hint of shame or fear, left an indelible mark on his mind. It was a bold statement, a challenge to the world around her.

The evidence didn't stop there. Nate turned to the numerous cell phone pictures and videos that had flooded social media, creating a frenzy. Comments ranged from disbelief to fear, with many speculating about her identity and motives.

As he scrolled through the endless stream of posts, something unusual caught his eye. Similar incidents of a naked woman walking confidently through different towns started popping up around the world. The locations were diverse, small villages, bustling cities, quiet suburbs. Each sighting was accompanied by the same mix of shock, awe, and terror.

"This wasn't just a murder. There's something else at play here," Nate's eyes lingered on the photo of Lilith in the crowd. "She wasn't just walking; she was making a statement." The social media frenzy only added to the chaos, with each post, like, and share spreading her image further and wider. It was almost as if she wanted to be seen, to be known, and that made her even more dangerous.

This pattern of behavior was unlike anything Nate had ever encountered. It was as if Lilith was taunting the world, daring anyone to catch her. "Or she has a way to project herself or influence multiple places at once. Either way, we need to understand how she's doing this and why," continued Hawthorne.

The glow of his computer screen illuminated the grim determination on his face. The state-of-the-art facial recognition system, integrated with the Driver License Division (DLD) databases, had been running for hours. Nate had uploaded every available image and video of Lilith, hoping to find a match.

He initiated a search using Hyper Verge, known for its high accuracy and real-time verification. The software scanned through countless hours of surveillance footage from around the city, analyzing every face in the crowds.

Yet, minutes turned into hours with no results. Nate's frustration grew. It was as if Lilith had vanished without a trace. Determined to understand what was happening, he contacted the tech team for an explanation.

After scanning the interface the tech specialist replied, "Detective, it looks like there's interference with the system."

"Interference? What do you mean?"

"It's as if someone is erasing her digital profile. The system can't detect her anymore."

Nate realized that there have been rumors about a rogue AI named Echelon, that had infiltrated the internet systematically deleting Lilith's digital presence. The facial recognition software was failing because Lilith's profile was being wiped clean in real-time. This meant that despite her significant online presence and the fervent following she had amassed, her digital footprint was being expertly erased to avoid detection by surveillance systems.

Hawthorne was worried. "Captain, we have a bigger problem than we thought. Lilith's followers are appearing everywhere, and our tech isn't picking her up."

"Everywhere? Are you saying her influence is spreading globally?" The captain inquired.

"Yes. Echelon, a rogue AI, is wiping her digital footprint clean. Security cameras, facial recognition software, they're all useless against her now. But her followers are spreading her message far and wide online."

"Damn. We need to find a way to counteract that AI. Any ideas?"

"I'm working on it," replied Hawthorne. "We might need to go old school, more boots on the ground, more human intelligence. But I'll also investigate tech solutions that might outsmart Echelon."

"Alright, Nate. Keep digging. Find out everything you can. We need to stop her before this escalates further," said the captain concluding their discussion.

***

The city had an abundance of delightful cafés, each with its own distinct feel. Lilith, on the other hand, was lured to a location known as "Bean There, Done That." The name had a cynical tone that matched her present state of mind.

When Lilith pushed open the glass door, she was met with a rush of warmth and the tantalizing perfume of freshly roasted coffee. Her gaze swept across the room, settling on a young man hunched thoughtfully over a steaming cup at a corner table. His back was turned, yet something about his posture, fingers tapping an anxious rhythm, suggested a mind hungry for distraction.

Lilith paused briefly, her crimson eyes flashing momentarily brighter, an almost imperceptible ripple of power emanating from her presence. She felt the internal mechanism engage effortlessly, releasing a subtle yet irresistibly seductive aura into the room, a pheromone she could command at will. Ethan immediately stilled, though he did not consciously understand why, an inexplicable warmth blossoming within him.

"Mind if I join you?" Lilith's voice resonated like a perfectly pitched melody, immediately pulling Ethan from his reverie. He turned, astonished at the immediate comfort he felt in her presence. Her crimson eyes held his gaze effortlessly, weaving an invisible web of intrigue.

Lilith gracefully settled into the seat opposite him, her gentle smile more inviting than before, as her pheromones wove deeper into his senses. Ethan's initial astonishment faded into a relaxed, almost mesmerized ease, as if they had known each other intimately, beyond rational explanation.

"Busy day?" she asked, gesturing smoothly toward the chaotic sprawl of paperwork. Her voice flowed like liquid velvet, softening his rational defenses further.

Ethan chuckled, self-conscious yet strangely relaxed as he reorganized the scattered pages. "Deadlines," he replied, distracted by the unexpected and comfortable pull he felt toward this mysterious woman. "Always deadlines. And what about you?" he asked, curiosity laced with an uncharacteristic boldness.

Lilith's eyes gleamed playfully, aware that her subtle influence was already taking root. "Just passing through. But the name, Bean There, Done That, drew me in. Perhaps fate has a sense of humor."

Ethan raised his cup in playful salute, feeling unexpectedly warm, his pulse quickening slightly with each heartbeat. "To fate, then."

As the conversation progressed, Ethan found himself increasingly lost within her words, her gestures. Every laugh she gave, every tilt of her head, drew him closer, his rational thoughts slipping away like sand through his fingers.

"What do you believe, Ethan?" she asked softly, her gaze deeply probing, further amplifying the subtle pulse of her supernatural aura.

"I... I think lines were meant to be blurred," he murmured, entranced by her presence, leaning forward without realizing.

The room around them faded, becoming inconsequential. Ethan felt captivated, wrapped in an inexplicable haze of fascination. Each second in her presence made resisting more futile, as if some ancient magnetism drew him inexorably toward her.

Lilith extended her hand, her delicate fingers seeming to promise secrets and comforts beyond imagination. Ethan accepted without thought, and a lingering warmth spread through him, dizzying and intoxicating.

Their conversation deepened, growing charged and intimate, spurred by Lilith's unseen, intoxicating influence. By the time their cups emptied, Ethan's rational mind fought a losing battle, unable to articulate or even comprehend his burgeoning need for her closeness.

When Lilith leaned forward, her eyes inches away from him, her voice a tender whisper, his heart raced uncontrollably. "Don't think about it," she whispered hypnotically. "Just feel it."

The force of her influence overpowered him, pulling his face gently toward hers, until their lips brushed in a kiss charged with electric intensity. Ethan gasped softly overwhelmed, his mind surrendering entirely to Lilith's supernatural seduction.

As they broke apart, Lilith's internal voice echoed triumphantly within Evelyn's suppressed consciousness.

"Ethan is mine."

In the aftermath, Ethan stammered, suddenly uncertain. "Lilith... what just happened?"

"Don't question it," Lilith replied softly, her voice now distant and cool. Her eyes hardened subtly; her control firmly established. "Just remember how it felt."

She rose, the spell of intimacy breaking abruptly, leaving Ethan suddenly chilled, alone in the heat of his confusion. "I'll see you soon, Ethan," she promised enigmatically, disappearing into the darkness.

Days turned into weeks, and a heavy quiet settled between them. Ethan, hurt by Lilith's rejection, moved on. However, a part of him couldn't get rid of the recollection of her touch and the way her gaze had kept him prisoner. He ached for the connection they had, which he now deemed a fabrication of his mind. He pushed himself to move on, to believe that their meeting was an isolated occurrence.

As Ethan stepped out onto his porch, the night air wrapped around him like a cold shroud. He blinked, unsure if the alcohol was playing tricks on him, until he saw her.

Lilith stood under the porch light, no longer the playful, mysterious woman from the café, but something darker. Her maroon dress clung to her frame like it had grown there, regal and terrible all at once. Her crimson eyes held no warmth this time. They shimmered like freshly spilled blood.

He opened his mouth to speak, but the words died. She beat him to it.

"You've been lonely, Ethan," she said, her voice soft, almost kind. "Surrounded by people. Still hollow. Still waiting for something you don't understand."

He swallowed hard. "What are you doing here?"

"You invited me," she replied. "Not with words. With longing. With that ache behind your smile. I felt it... and I came."

Her words slithered into him like smoke. A part of him screamed to run, but a deeper part leaned in.

"You think I'm dangerous," she whispered, stepping forward slowly. "You're right. But tell me, has anything in your life ever made your heart beat this fast?"

He shook his head. "I don't know what you are."

"Neither do I," she said, for once without mockery. "But I know what I see in you. Cracks. Pain. That moment every night when you stare at your reflection and wonder why no one really sees you. I see you, Ethan. I see everything."

Her hand hovered near his chest but didn't touch him. "I could tear you apart. But I'd rather show you who you really are."

He staggered back, breath catching. "Why me?"

Lilith tilted her head, eyes narrowing, not seductively, but like a scientist analyzing a rare specimen.

"Because you're already broken," she said. "And broken things... are easier to reshape."

She didn't wait for permission. She turned toward the darkness behind his house, her silhouette cutting like a blade through the quiet night.

"Walk with me," she said. "I want to show you something." And like a moth to flame, Ethan followed.

Lilith sat on a park seat; her ruby eyes reflecting the distant city lights and contemplated his question. "What Am I doing here?" her voice tinged with curiosity, "that depends on what you want, Ethan.

18- Desire

Ethan ran his fingers through his hair as he stared at the stack of papers on his desk. It had been a long day, filled with back-to-back meetings and endless paperwork. He rubbed his tired eyes, wishing for a moment of respite from the mundane tasks that seemed to consume his life lately. Just as he was about to dive back into the sea of documents, his phone buzzed, snapping him out of his monotonous trance.

"Hey, beautiful," he answered, a smile instantly spreading across his face.

"Too much work, I see," came Lilith's sultry voice, laced with a hint of amusement.

Ethan's heart skipped a beat at the sound of her. "You know it. Just wrapping some things up."

"Mmm, and I have a proposal for you." Her tone turned playful, sending a shiver down his spine.

Intrigued, Ethan leaned back in his chair, a feeling of anticipation washing over him. "Oh, what might that be?"

"I thought you could use a break," she purred. "Can I visit you. I have something special planned for us."

His curiosity piqued, and he couldn't resist the temptation she was offering. "I'll be waiting for you."

Lilith, letting herself in, found Ethan lounging on the couch, a glass of wine in his hand. She looked at him with a seductive glare and taking the glass from his hand and setting it on the table.

The human body came with inconvenient truths, and Lilith had no interest in denying them. Desire was no longer abstract. It pulsed through her veins, gnawed at her belly, spread like heat under her skin. This form she wore, sculpted and sensual, had needs, real, primal, demanding. And what startled her wasn't the hunger itself, it was how intoxicating it felt to indulge it. She wasn't ashamed. She wasn't pretending to be anything she wasn't. Sex wasn't a strategy; it was a hunger, and Lilith had been starving. She didn't want to control it. She wanted to live in it. To claim it. To burn in it until only power remained. And this body, her body, craved fire.

But inside, Evelyn recoiled. "This isn't you," she whispered in her mind, the words weak against the rising heat.

Lilith heard her. "No, Evelyn... this is us. This is what you've never dared feel. Your body remembers what your mind won't admit."

"No," Evelyn snapped, desperate to push back against the sensation blooming between her legs. "You're confusing power with pleasure. This isn't connection, it's control. It's performance. It's empty."

Lilith laughed. "It doesn't feel empty to him. Or to me. This is the first honest thing we've done."

Evelyn's resistance flared. "You're using him. You're using me. This isn't intimacy, it's invasion."

Lilith's voice softened, seductive even in thought. "Then look away, little ghost. I didn't come here to ask permission."

"Well Ethan, let me take care of you," she purred, her fingers trailing lightly up his chest.

As she leaned in, her soft lips brushed against his, sending a spark of desire coursing through him. The kiss deepened, and he wrapped his arms around her, pulling her close. Her body pressed against his, and he could feel the heat radiating from her.

With slow, deliberate movements, she began to undo the buttons of his shirt, her kisses trailing along his jawline and down his neck. Her hands explored his chest, sending shivers of pleasure through him. He ran his hands through her hair, holding her close, never wanting this moment to end.

Breaking away momentarily, Lilith led him by the hand up the stairs to his bedroom. She turned to face him, her eyes sparkling with desire. "I want tonight to be all about you," she whispered, her breath warm on his skin.

Ethan's heart raced as he took in the sight of her. She was a goddess, and he was utterly captivated. "You don't need to convince me, Lilith. I'm yours."

Ethan's thoughts churned with a tumultuous mix of desire and fear. As Lilith's lips pressed against his, he felt the weight of her power, an intoxicating force that both exhilarated and terrified him. In the back of his mind, a small voice whispered that he was losing himself, that each moment spent under her spell drew him further away from the man he once was. But as she deepened the kiss, that voice faded, drowned out by the overwhelming need to please her, to be consumed by her presence.

A soft laugh escaped her lips as she pushed him gently onto the bed. "I plan to take full advantage of that."

Her fingers deftly unbuttoned his pants, sliding them off along with his shirt. He watched as she undressed, her movements graceful and full of promise. When she stood before him in her lace lingerie, he couldn't help but let out a breath of appreciation.

"You are stunning," he murmured, his eyes roaming over her body.

With a seductive smile, she joined him on the bed, her body sliding against his. Her hands explored his chest, his shoulders, and his arms, leaving a trail of fire in their wake. He felt himself getting lost in the sensation of her touch, his body responding to her every move.

Lilith's lips found his again, and he tasted the sweetness of her mouth. Her hands tangled in his hair, holding him close as their kisses grew more fervent. He ran his hands along her sides, savoring the feel of her soft skin.

As their passion built, she straddled him, her eyes locking with his. "I want you to surrender to me," she whispered, her voice thick with desire.

Evelyn, trapped within, felt a surge of heat and a flicker of something akin to shame. This wasn't right. This wasn't how she envisioned intimacy. It felt... exposed, raw. She couldn't deny the strange pleasure that coursed through her, but a primal instinct to protect her own body, this borrowed vessel, warred with the desire building within her. Should she resist? Should she voice her discomfort?

"I can't handle this anymore," she thought, and in the depths of her mind, Evelyn retreated to the sanctuary she had painstakingly constructed, a place untouched by Lilith's malice. It was a serene meadow, bathed in the golden light of an eternal sunset. Tall grasses swayed gently in the breeze, and wildflowers dotted the landscape with vibrant colors. A small, clear stream babbled nearby, its sound a soothing lullaby.

Evelyn sat by the stream, her fingers trailing through the cool water, and took a deep breath. Here, she was safe. Here, she could find a semblance of peace amidst the chaos that had overtaken her body. "This is my refuge," she whispered to herself, her voice steady despite the turmoil outside. "This is where I remember who I am."

She closed her eyes, feeling the warmth of the sun on her face, and allowed herself to reflect. "Lilith may control my body, but she cannot touch this place. She cannot reach my soul." The thought brought her a small measure of comfort. "I am still Evelyn. I am still here, even if no one else can see me."

Her mind drifted to memories of happier times, moments filled with love, laughter, and hope. She clung to these memories, using them as a shield against the darkness that threatened to consume her. "I have faced challenges before," she reminded herself, "and I have overcome them. I will endure this too."

The meadow seemed to respond to her resolve, the light growing warmer, the colors more vibrant. "I am not alone," she continued, drawing strength from her inner sanctuary. "My spirit is strong, my faith unbroken. I believe in the potential within me, the potential to rise above this, to one day reclaim my life."

As she opened her eyes, she gazed at the horizon, feeling a sense of calm and determination. "No matter what Lilith does, no matter how much she tries to break me, I will hold on to this place. I will hold on to who I am."

Evelyn stood up, her posture firm, her gaze steady. "I will survive. I will endure. And one day, I will be free."

With that vow echoing in her heart, she prepared to face the darkness once more, drawing strength from the peaceful sanctuary she had created within her mind.

Ethan's breath hitched as he nodded, his hands moving to grip her hips. "I'm yours to command."

Lilith watched Ethan's eyes darken with desire, a smirk playing at the corners of her lips. He was so easily led, so eager to submit to her whims. It amused her, the way he thought he had a choice, that his actions were driven by his own desires. In truth, he was merely a pawn in her game, a means to an end. As she traced a finger down his chest, she silently calculated how much longer she would need him before casting him aside.

Lilith's eyes narrowed, a flicker of annoyance crossing her crimson depths. "Don't be coy, darling," she purred, her voice laced with a hint of steel. "This is about pleasure, not some power play. Now, relax and let yourself feel." She brushed her lips against his ear, the warmth of her breath sending shivers down his spine. "Trust me," she whispered, her voice a seductive command.

A soft moan escaped her as he gently guided her down onto him, their bodies joining as one. She began to move slowly, her eyes never leaving his. Her hair fell around them, creating an intimate cocoon.

He ran his hands up and down her back, marveling at the feel of her soft skin. Their movements became more urgent, their breaths quickening. He could feel the tension building within him, and he knew she was close as well.

"Lilith," he groaned, his voice hoarse with desire.

"Let go," she whispered, her lips brushing his ear.

"Surrender to me." Lilith smiled wickedly, knowing exactly how to tease and tantalize him.

She took charge instead, leaving him shocked. She slowly unpinned her bra, revealing her toned body and perky breasts. Ethan's eyes widened as he took her in, unable to believe that this goddess was his.

Lilith climbed onto the bed, straddling Ethan's hips.

"Please, Lilith," Ethan begged, his hands gripping her hips.

Lilith leaned down, her breasts brushing against Ethan's chest as she kissed him again.

Their lovemaking was passionate and intense, their bodies moving together in a rhythm that was both familiar and new. Lilith took charge, setting the pace and pushing Ethan to the brink of pleasure.

As they reached their climax, Lilith whispered in Ethan's ear.

Ethan couldn't believe what he was hearing. He had never been with a woman who was so open and honest about her desires.

"Did you enjoy that, Ethan?" she asked, a wicked grin on her face. Her words sent him over the edge, and he cried out as pleasure washed over him. They stayed joined for a moment, their hearts racing and their breaths mingling.

Eventually, she collapsed onto his chest, her hair fanning out around them. He ran his fingers through her hair, savoring the feeling of her in his arms.

"That was..." He struggled to find the words.

"Perfect," she finished, a satisfied smile on her lips.

Ethan couldn't help but agree. As they lay entangled, he felt a sense of peace wash over him. Being with Lilith was unlike anything he had ever experienced. She had a way of consuming him, body and soul, and he found himself craving more.

"Stay with me tonight," he murmured, his fingers tracing patterns on her breast".

"I'm not going anywhere," she assured him, pulling him closer.

As they drifted off to sleep, Ethan felt a sense of contentment he had never known before. Lilith had a way of ensnaring him, and he knew he was willingly surrendering to her web of desire.

The sun had long set, and the room was bathed in a soft moonlight when Ethan stirred. He felt a sense of warmth beside him and turned to find Lilith, her eyes sparkling in the dim light.

"Can't sleep?" she asked, her voice a husky whisper.

"I am just famished," he replied, his hand reaching out to trace the curve of her waist.

A soft laugh escaped her lips, and she leaned in, her breath tickling his skin. "I could make us a quick meal." She got up and walked down to the kitchen naked. Ethan followed her downstairs staring at her curves.

She opened the fridge and found a few things to make a couple of sandwiches. She leaned against the counter, her hips swaying gently as she prepared the food. Ethan hadn't stopped staring at her, his eyes tracing the outline of her body.

"Like what you see?" Lilith asked, knowing he was staring.

Ethan grinned, walking over to her. "More than you know."

He wrapped his arms around her waist, pulling her close. Lilith let out a soft moan as she felt his erection pressing against her. Ethan trailed kisses down her neck, causing her to shiver with anticipation.

"How about we take a break?" Ethan whispered in her ear.

Lilith turned to face him, her eyes sparkling with desire. "I thought you'd never ask."

Ethan collapsed on top of her, his breathing heavily.

Lilith ran her fingers through his hair, her body still trembling with pleasure.

In the aftermath, as they lay entangled Ethan felt a sense of awe wash over him. Lilith propped herself up on an elbow, her hair tumbling around her shoulders, a satisfied smile playing on her lips.

"You have a way of leaving me breathless," he murmured, his fingers gently tracing her arm.

A soft blush colored her cheeks, and she leaned down to press a kiss to his chest. "You say the sweetest things."

Ethan smiled, his hand tangling in her hair. "It's the truth. You're incredible, Lilith."

She stayed silent for a moment, her fingers idly drawing patterns on his skin. "You know, I've been thinking," she began, a mischievous glint in her eye. "I have a fantasy I'd like to explore."

Ethan's interest was instantly piqued. "Oh?"

"Mmm hmm," she hummed, her fingers trailing lower. "I want to try something a little... kinkier."

A shiver ran down his spine at the promise in her tone. "I'm all ears."

With a playful smile, she leaned in close, her lips brushing his ear as she whispered her secret desire. Ethan felt his body respond instantly, a rush of excitement coursing through him.

Her eyes sparkled with satisfaction as she pulled back to look at him. "Good. Because I plan to make it a reality."

Ethan's heart raced at the thought of surrendering to her in that way. He knew Lilith enjoyed pushing boundaries, and he found himself eager to explore her wilder side.

"You have me at your mercy," he whispered, his eyes holding hers.

A soft laugh escaped her lips, and she leaned in for another kiss. "Oh, Ethan. I plan to show you just how merciless I can be."

As their lips met, Ethan knew he was falling deeper under Lilith's spell. Her dominance and sensuality entwined had him utterly captivated. He surrendered to her willingly, eager to explore the depths of their desire together.

And as the night stretched on, their passion ignited once more, their bodies entwined in a dance of pleasure and surrender. Ethan knew that Lilith held the power, and he found himself craving more, unable to resist the pull of her silken web, incidentally and helplessly entangled in it.

Even as Ethan surrendered to the moment, a shadow passed over Lilith's expression, a brief flicker of something darker. She knew this couldn't last, that eventually, Ethan would see her for what she truly was. The thought didn't trouble her; it was inevitable. What mattered was how she would use him in the meantime, how she could bend his will to serve her needs before the final reckoning.

19- Life

Detective "Nate" Hawthorne sat in his dimly lit office; the hum of the computer screen the only sound. It had been eight grueling months since the initial investigation into Lilith began. Despite numerous sporadic sightings, each lead had frustratingly led to a dead end. Nate stared at the sophisticated facial recognition software, which had yielded no results. Echelon interference had made tracking her nearly impossible.

Determined not to give up, Nate decided it was time to change tactics. He needed to combine technology with old-fashioned detective work. Gathering his team, he laid out his new plan.

Despite the countless hours spent sifting through dead ends, Hawthorne knew that giving up was not an option. Lilith was more than just a suspect; she was a ticking time bomb. Every minute she remained free was another minute closer to catastrophe. He needed to outthink both her and Echelon, a nearly impossible task, but one he was determined to accomplish.

"We need to rethink our strategy," Nate began, looking around at the determined faces of his colleagues. "Echelon has been erasing Lilith's digital footprint, making our tech useless. We need more boots on the ground and to leverage human intelligence."

Detective Lopez, a seasoned investigator, nodded. "I've been reaching out to informants. We've got some potential leads in the underground networks where her influence seems to be growing."

"Good," Nate replied. "We also need to establish connections with communities online. Her followers are active, and they might slip up. Let's monitor forums, chat groups, anything that might give us a hint."

Nate and his team began collaborating with local communities, attending gatherings, and speaking with people who might have encountered Lilith or her followers. This grassroots approach started to yield results. Bits and pieces of information began to form a clearer picture of her movements and influence.

One evening, Nate met with an informant in a dimly lit bar. The man leaned in close, his voice barely above a whisper. "She's got a lot of people convinced she's some kind of savior. They're fanatical, spreading her message everywhere. But they're not careful. They leave traces."

Nate's eyes narrowed. "Tell me more. Any idea where she might be hiding?"

The informant glanced around nervously before replying. "Rumors say she's been seen near the old industrial district. It's a good place to stay out of sight."

Armed with this new information, Nate assembled his team and headed to the industrial district. The area was a maze of abandoned buildings and overgrown lots, a perfect hideout for someone trying to avoid detection. As they moved cautiously through the shadows, they found signs of recent activity: makeshift beds, discarded food containers, and graffiti echoing Lilith's messages.

As his team dispersed to begin their new assignments, Hawthorne felt the weight of responsibility settle on his shoulders. It wasn't just about catching a criminal; it was about preventing the unimaginable. He knew that the lives of countless innocent people hung in the balance, and the thought drove him forward with a renewed sense of urgency.

"We're close," Nate whispered, his senses on high alert. "Stay sharp."

Detective Lopez pointed to a nearby building. "Looks like they left in a hurry. Maybe we scared them off."

Nate nodded. "Let's keep pushing. We need to find her before she moves again."

As they moved deeper into the district, they finally encountered a group of Lilith's followers. The tension in the air was palpable as the team prepared for a confrontation.

One of the followers, a young woman with wild eyes, stepped forward. "You can't stop her. She's destined to change everything."

Nate kept his voice calm and steady. "Where is she? We know she's been here."

The woman sneered. "You'll never find her. But you'll see. We all will."

Nate's jaw tightened. They were so close, yet the elusive Lilith remained out of reach. He knew they had to keep pressing, to find the chink in Echelon's armor and bring her to justice.

***

Eight months had passed since Ethan and Lilith's first passionate reunion. The doctor's appointment loomed, a reminder of the life-altering event that had brought them even closer, their impending parenthood. The excitement was undeniable, a shared secret nestled between them, a tiny bud blooming in the fertile ground of their unexpected love.

As Ethan pulled into the familiar parking lot of the clinic, he instinctively reached for Lilith's hand. Her crimson eyes met his, a flicker of amusement dancing within their depths.

"Nervous, Daddy?" she teased, her voice husky.

Ethan chuckled, a nervous tremor underlying the sound. "Maybe a little. This is all so new."

Lilith squeezed his hand reassuringly. "New, but exciting," she countered, her smile radiating warmth.

They entered the waiting room hand in hand, a picture of domestic bliss, at least on the surface. Inside, Evelyn, the human Lilith had stolen this life from, churned with a cocktail of emotions. The doctor's visit was a constant reminder of her captivity, the ever-present threat that her life, her body, was no longer hers. Yet, amidst the frustration and fear, a flicker of hope remained. Maybe, just maybe, seeing a doctor, a familiar human element, could spark something, a connection, a way back.

Their appointment was scheduled with Dr. Vedova, the same kind-faced doctor who had guided them through the initial stages of the pregnancy. But as they entered the examination room, a jolt of surprise coursed through both Ethan and Lilith. Dr. Vedova was gone, replaced by a woman with striking dark hair and a commanding presence.

"Good morning, Mr. and Mrs. Carter," the new doctor greeted them with a warm smile. "I'm Dr. Lawson, filling in for Dr. Vedova today."

"Lilith, call me Lilith, doctor!" Lilith corrected sharply, a hint of annoyance in her voice. She simply nodded and gestured toward the examination table. "Please have a seat, Mrs. Carter. Let's get started."

As Lilith settled onto the table, Evelyn tried to scream. Lilith, oblivious to the silent plea, simply rolled her crimson eyes. "Let's get this over with, doctor," she said, her voice laced with impatience.

Desperation gnawed at Evelyn. She tried again; her voice stronger this time. "Dr. Lawson, please!"

A flicker of something crossed Dr. Lawson's eyes, a fleeting moment of confusion. But it was quickly masked by a professional demeanor. "Mrs. Carter, is everything alright?" she asked, her voice devoid of any emotion.

Lilith scoffed. "Of course. Just eager to see our little miracle."

Ethan, sensing a growing tension, placed a reassuring hand on Lilith's shoulder. "Maybe we should reschedule," he suggested, his voice laced with concern.

"No," Lilith countered, her voice firm. "Let's get on with it."

Dr. Lawson, seemingly unfazed by the undercurrent of emotions, continued with the routine checkup. She spoke only to Lilith, her gaze never lingering on Ethan for too long. Evelyn, trapped within, felt a surge of despair. Her pleas seemed to fall on deaf ears.

As the ultrasound screen flickered to life, revealing the tiny form of their baby, a lump formed in Evelyn's throat. She yearned to feel the joy of motherhood, to experience the wonder of creating life, but it was all muted through Lilith's borrowed senses. A silent scream clawed its way up her throat, a desperate plea for recognition, for a sliver of control over her own stolen life.

Lilith, captivated by the image on the screen, reached out and traced the outline of the tiny form with a manicured finger. "It's perfect," she breathed, a tremor of something akin to awe in her voice.

Ethan leaned in beside her; his gaze fixed on the screen. A smile tugged at the corners of his mouth, a stark contrast to the turmoil brewing within Evelyn. "It is, isn't it?" he murmured, his hand instinctively reaching for Lilith's.

A surge of possessiveness washed over Evelyn. That hand, that touch, it should be hers. Tears welled up in her unseen eyes, blurring the already distorted image of her stolen future.

Dr. Lawson continued her examination. Her professional demeanor remained a mask, hiding any flicker of recognition Evelyn desperately hoped for.

As the checkup concluded, Evelyn felt a renewed surge of desperation. This was her only chance, a fleeting opportunity before they were ushered back out into the sterile world. Taking a deep, metaphorical breath, she focused all her energy, channeling it into a single desperate plea.

"Dr. Lawson," she screamed, her voice a silent roar within the confines of her stolen mind. "I know you can hear me! It's Evelyn! You must help me!"

Dr. Lawson froze, her hand hovering over her clipboard. A flicker of recognition, fleeting but undeniable, crossed her eyes. For a heart-stopping moment, her eyes seemed to bore into Lilith's, a silent question hanging heavy in the air.

But before Evelyn could capitalize on this fragile moment, Lilith, sensing a shift in the atmosphere, turned toward Dr. Lawson, her crimson eyes narrowed in suspicion. "Is something wrong, doctor?" she inquired, her voice sharp and laced with a hint of threat.

The flicker of recognition in Dr. Lawson's eyes vanished as quickly as it appeared. She straightened her posture, a professional mask once again settling over her features. "No, Mrs. Carter," she replied smoothly. "Everything seems to be in order. Congratulations on your healthy baby."

Lilith's lips curved into a triumphant smile. "Thank you, doctor."

As Dr. Lawson prepared to leave, she paused, a shadow of concern crossing her face. "Mrs. Carter, I noticed something during your last checkup. There seems to be an anomaly with your blood. It's probably nothing, but I recommend a few more tests to be safe."

Ethan's heart sank. "An anomaly? What do you mean?"

Dr. Lawson glanced at her clipboard; her expression serious. "It's a slight irregularity in the blood composition. I don't want to alarm you, but it's important we monitor it closely. Given the advancements and enhancements, you've mentioned, Mrs. Carter, such as Nano Meds, it's possible your physiology has changed. This could affect the baby."

Lilith, unfazed, waved her hand dismissively. "I'm sure it's nothing. We can do the tests, but I feel fine."

Evelyn, trapped inside, felt a surge of hope. This complication, minor as it seemed, could be her way to draw more attention to her plight. She focused all her energy, willing the doctor to look deeper, to see the real issue.

Dr. Lawson nodded. "We'll schedule the tests for next week. In the meantime, rest and take care of yourself, Mrs. Carter."

As they left the clinic, Ethan's mind raced with worry. "Do you think the baby's alright?" he asked, his voice barely above a whisper.

Lilith smiled reassuringly. "Of course, darling. Everything will be fine."

As they left the clinic and stepped into the warm light of day, something strange clung to Lilith's chest, a weight, not heavy but persistent. She slid into the passenger seat beside Ethan and rested her hand on her stomach. Beneath her palm, the faint echo of life stirred. It wasn't just cells and biology. It was real. A presence. A heartbeat. A tether.

And it terrified her.

She hadn't expected this. The hormones, the cravings, the dreams, those she had studied. But the pull? The quiet ache in her chest every time she thought of the child. That was

unexpected. It wasn't strategic. It wasn't even useful. It was maddening. Compelling. She wanted to protect it. She wanted to nurture it. She wanted it to be strong, to be hers.

"You're changing," Evelyn whispered from within, her voice faint, like a breeze under a locked door.

"Don't mistake adaptation for weakness," Lilith replied, her hand tightening over her belly.

"It's not weakness. It's humanity. You feel it, don't you? The way your body aches for this life?"

"It's chemical," Lilith snapped. "Temporary."

"Yet here you are," Evelyn said gently, "touching your stomach like it means something. Like you're afraid to lose it."

Lilith's eyes narrowed, but she didn't respond. She

watched Ethan as he spoke about nursery colors and stroller models, his voice distant, background noise to the storm inside her. How could something so fragile root itself so deeply? She didn't want this. She didn't choose it. And yet... she couldn't stop herself from caring.

That, more than anything, unsettled her.

"You can't suppress this," Evelyn said. "You can lie to yourself, but you're becoming more like me every day."

"I am not you," Lilith hissed. "I will never be you."

"Then why are you afraid?"

Silence.

She turned her head toward the window, lips pressed in a thin line, and for the first time since taking this body, Lilith didn't know if what she felt was power... or vulnerability.

As they stepped into their cozy home, the tension from the doctor's appointment began to dissipate. Ethan tossed his keys onto the entryway table while Lilith slipped off her shoes, revealing her bright red toenails. She padded across the living room, her crimson eyes sparkling with excitement.

"Okay, now that we've got the all-clear from the doc, it's time to get serious about names," Lilith said, plopping down on the couch. She patted the cushion beside her, inviting Ethan to join her.

Ethan obliged, sinking into the softness beside her. "I've been thinking about this nonstop," he admitted, a grin spreading across his face. "I've got a few ideas."

Lilith's eyes lit up. "Ooh, let's hear them!"

Ethan cleared his throat, adopting a mock-serious tone. "Well, for a boy, I was thinking... Atticus. Or maybe Maverick?"

Lilith giggled, her laughter like a burst of sunshine. "Maverick? You want to name our child after a Top Gun character?"

Ethan chuckled, his eyes crinkling at the corners. "Hey, it's a great name! And Atticus is a classic."

Lilith playfully rolled her eyes. "You're such a dad. What about for a girl?"

Ethan's face lit up. "Ah, now this is where things get interesting. I was thinking... Luna or Astrid."

Lilith's expression turned thoughtful, her brow furrowing. "Luna's pretty, but Astrid might be a bit too... intense."

"Okay, okay," Ethan nodded. "What about you? What names do you like?"

Lilith's face brightened, her eyes sparkling with mischief. "I've got a few secrets up my sleeve. For a boy, I was thinking... Jasper or Kai."

Ethan's eyebrows shot up. "Jasper? That's an interesting choice."

Lilith shrugged, a sly smile spreading across her face. "I like it. And Kai is just so... cool."

"You're such a rebel," Ethan chuckled, shaking his head. "And for a girl?"

Lilith's grin grew wider. "Oh, this is where things get really fun. I was thinking... Piper or Remi."

Ethan's eyes widened, his face lighting up. "Piper's amazing! And Remi's so unique."

Lilith squealed, bouncing up and down on the couch. "I knew you'd like them! We can mix and match, see what we come up with."

As they continued to banter back and forth, the tension from the doctor's appointment melted away, replaced by the warm glow of excitement and anticipation. They were going to be parents, and they couldn't wait to meet their little bundle of joy.

"I'm telling you, we need to get a minivan," Ethan said, a mock-serious tone in his voice.

Lilith's eyes widened in horror. "A minivan? You want to turn us into suburban clichés?"

"Hey, they're practical!" Ethan chuckled. "And we'll need the space for all the diapers and toys."

Lilith shuddered. "You're not selling me on this whole parenthood thing, Ethan."

"Oh, come on. It'll be fun, I promise. We can get one of those cool strollers that looks like a spaceship."

Lilith laughed, playfully rolling her eyes. "You're such a nerd."

As they chatted, they began to discuss the more serious aspects of parenthood. "Do you think we should ask the doctor to tell us the gender? I know we didn't want to know until now, but..." Lilith asked, her brow furrowed in thought.

Ethan shrugged. "I don't know. Part of me wants to be surprised, but another part of me wants to prepare."

"I think we should find out," Lilith nodded. "That way, we can start decorating the nursery and getting everything ready."

Ethan's eyes lit up. "Ok, yeah! We can get one of those cute little cribs with the mobiles and stuff."

"You're really getting into this whole dad thing, aren't you?" Lilith chuckled.

Ethan grinned, his face beaming with excitement. "Yeah, I am. I never thought I'd be this excited about having a kid, but... I don't know, it just feels right."

Lilith's expression softened, her eyes filling with warmth. "I know exactly what you mean. It feels like we're meant to be doing this."

As they sat there, surrounded by the quiet comfort of their home, they both knew that their lives were about to change in ways they couldn't even imagine. But they were ready, together, to face whatever came next.

"I love you," Lilith said, her voice barely above a whisper.

Ethan's face lit up, his eyes shining with adoration. "I love you too, Lilith."

As they leaned for a kiss, the room seemed to fade away, leaving only the two of them lost in their own little world of love and anticipation.

Later that evening, as the hum of domesticity faded into silence, Lilith stood alone by the window, one hand cradling her belly. The house was dim, lit only by the golden spill of kitchen light and the faint flicker of candles Ethan had lit earlier. He was asleep now, peaceful, trusting, soft. It should have disgusted her. Instead, it haunted her.

She had meant to control him. To use this life, this body, this pregnancy as leverage in her larger design. But something inside her was unraveling. The baby's presence had changed the rhythm of her breath, the weight of her silence, the temperature of her solitude. She didn't just feel it now, she needed it. The companionship. The rhythm of a shared future. The delusion of peace.

Her jaw clenched. She hated this weakness. This betrayal of purpose.

"You're slipping," Evelyn said from within, her voice velvet and sharp. "Wasn't this all a game to you? Power, control, manipulation? Now look at you, nesting. Hoping.

Almost... loving."

"Silence," Lilith hissed through clenched teeth. "You know nothing of what this means."

"No?" Evelyn pressed, her voice dripping with dark amusement. "Then why did you tuck him in like a wife? Why do your hands shake when the baby kicks? Why do you keep whispering his name when you think no one's listening?"

Lilith's crimson eyes flared. She turned from the window, breathing uneven. She didn't respond, not because she had nothing to say, but because the words Evelyn spoke were too precise. Too true.

"And remember this," Evelyn whispered, soft as a threat, "this little ghost will never give up. I'm still here. Watching. Waiting. And you know I'm stronger than you think."

And in the quiet of the living room, with moonlight spilling across the floor and a man asleep upstairs who thought she was everything she wasn't, Lilith finally admitted something she hadn't dared to voice:

She was no longer certain who she hated more. Evelyn.

Or herself.

***

Detective Hawthorne was deep in thought, reviewing the latest reports on his desk when his phone rang. It was Dr. Lawson, one of his confidential informants. He answered immediately, a sense of urgency in his voice.

"Nate, it's Dr. Lawson. We need to talk," Dr. Lawson said, her voice steady but laced with tension.

"Doc, what's going on?" Detective Hawthorne asked, concern evident.

"I've confirmed it. Mrs. Carter, the woman you know as Lilith, is the Lilith we've been looking for. The details from the ultrasound and the blood tests match perfectly. Her enhanced physiology, the changes from the Nano Meds, it's all there," Dr. Lawson explained.

Detective Hawthorne took a deep breath, absorbing the information. "Are you sure? This is a big deal, Doctor."

"I'm positive, Nate. I've seen enough to know that she fits the profile exactly. And there's more. During the examination, I sensed something off. It's like she's hiding something, or someone. I think there's a deeper connection between her and

Evelyn, the woman whose body she's taken over," Dr. Lawson continued.

Detective Hawthorne's mind raced with possibilities. "If she's really Lilith, then this changes everything. We need to move carefully. She's dangerous, and her followers are everywhere."

"Agreed. We can't afford to make any mistakes. But we need to act fast. The longer she stays hidden, the more damage she can do," Dr. Lawson urged.

Detective Hawthorne nodded, even though she couldn't see him. "I'll gather the team. We need to plan this out. Can you keep her under observation without raising suspicion?"

"I'll do my best. But we need to be ready. Once we make a move, there's no turning back," Dr. Lawson warned.

"Understood. Stay safe, Doc. We'll get her," Detective Hawthorne assured her.

After hanging up, Detective Hawthorne stared at the phone for a moment, then quickly began making calls. The hunt for Lilith had just taken a critical turn, and every moment counted.

20- Cradle

Detective Hawthorne sat with Dr. Lawson and Marcus in his office; the weight of their mission heavy in the air. They knew that subduing Lilith would require careful planning and precise execution, especially with Echelon's ability to corrupt modern technology.

"Marcus, we need you to be involved in this," Detective Hawthorne began, his voice steady. "Lilith's next doctor's visit is our best chance to subdue her. We've decided to go old school, no electronics or modern tech. It's the only way to get a jump on her without Echelon's interference."

Marcus nodded, understanding the gravity of the situation. "I'm ready. What's the plan?" Dr. Lawson laid out the strategy. "We'll conduct the next appointment in an isolated part of the clinic, far from any electronic surveillance. We'll have a small team ready to move in once we've confirmed her identity again. Marcus, we need you there as part of the support team."

Detective Hawthorne added, "We'll communicate using hand signals and written notes. Once we have her in the examination room, we'll need to act quickly. Doctor, you'll administer a sedative under the guise of routine tests. Marcus and I will handle the physical restraint."

Marcus glanced at the notes, then back at Hawthorne. "And what about Ethan? He'll be there with her."

Hawthorne nodded. "We'll need to keep him out of the way. I'll handle that part. He's less of a threat, but we can't risk him interfering."

Dr. Lawson's eyes were filled with determination. "This is our best shot. If we miss this opportunity, we might not get another one."

Marcus agreed. "I'm in. Let's do this."

***

In an isolated part of the clinic, as far as possible from any electronic surveillance, Lilith entered the examination room with Ethan by her side, oblivious to the tension in the air. Dr. Lawson greeted them with a professional smile, masking her inner turmoil.

"Good to see you again, Mrs. Carter. Please, have a seat," Dr. Lawson said, gesturing to the examination table.

Ethan sat in a chair nearby, watching as Dr. Lawson prepared for the checkup. Lilith's crimson eyes scanned the room, but she seemed relaxed, unaware of the trap being set.

Dr. Lawson started the routine checkup, her hands steady as she spoke. "I'll need to draw some blood for a few additional tests. Just a precaution."

Lilith nodded; her attention momentarily diverted. As Dr. Lawson inserted the needle, she signaled subtly to Detective Hawthorne, who stood just outside the door with Marcus.

In an instant, Hawthorne moved into the room, approaching Ethan. "Mr. Carter, I need you to come with me. There's something we need to discuss."

Ethan looked confused but complied, leaving the room with Hawthorne. The moment they were outside, Marcus entered the room, closing the door behind him.

Lilith's eyes widened in realization, but before she could react, Dr. Lawson administered the sedative. Lilith struggled briefly, her enhanced physiology fighting the effects, but Marcus was ready. He restrained her with practiced efficiency, his grip strong and unyielding.

"Stay still, Lilith. This will all be over soon," Marcus said calmly.

Within moments, Lilith's struggles weakened, and she slumped back onto the table, the sedative taking full effect. Dr. Lawson quickly secured her, ensuring she couldn't escape once she regained consciousness.

Detective Hawthorne reentered the room, a look of relief on his face. "We did it. Let's get her transported to a secure facility before she wakes up."

As they prepared to move Lilith, Ethan stood outside the room, unaware of the true nature of the day's events. He glanced at the door, concern etched on his face, but Detective Hawthorne's words kept him from interfering.

"We'll take good care of her, Ethan. Trust us."

Lilith lay on a hospital bed in a heavily guarded room within a secure facility. Tubes and monitors surrounded her, and an IV drip delivered a constant sedative to keep her subdued and compliant. The room was under 24/7 surveillance, and armed guards were stationed at the entrance, ensuring that no one unauthorized could get near her.

Detective Hawthorne stood just outside the room, speaking with Marcus. "She's stable, but we need to keep her under constant observation. The sedative is working, but we can't afford to let our guard down."

Marcus nodded, glancing through the window at Lilith. "I understand. We need to make sure she stays subdued."

Inside the room, Lilith's eyes fluttered open briefly. Her gaze was unfocused, her movements sluggish. She murmured something incoherent before slipping back into a sedated state.

Evelyn, trapped inside Lilith's mind, found moments where she could reach out, her consciousness brushing against

Marcus's. She felt his presence like a beacon in the darkness, giving her hope.

Marcus sat in a small lounge area; his mind troubled. He could feel Evelyn's presence, a faint whisper at the edge of his thoughts. "Stay strong, Evelyn," he murmured to himself. "We're going to get you out of there."

As Marcus and Detective Hawthorne spoke outside, Lilith stirred on the bed, her lips moving as she mumbled something. Detective Hawthorne, who had been monitoring her from the control room, quickly alerted Marcus.

"She's saying something. We need to hear this," Hawthorne said through the intercom.

Marcus hurried to Lilith's room. As he stood by her bedside, he listened intently to her faint murmurs.

"She's in me... but she's never getting out," Lilith muttered, her voice barely audible.

Evelyn, within Lilith's mind, heard the words and felt a surge of determination. She reached out, trying to communicate with Marcus through Lilith's body. "Marcus... I'm here... Don't give up on me," she tried to project, hoping he could sense her.

Marcus's eyes widened as he felt a strange connection, almost as if he could hear Evelyn's plea. "Evelyn?" he whispered, his heart pounding. "Hang on, we're going to get you out of this."

Detective Hawthorne entered the room, his face grim. "It means we have to be even more vigilant. Lilith might be subdued, but Evelyn's still trapped in there. We can't underestimate her."

Marcus nodded, his jaw set. "We'll keep her under constant observation. Any sign of change, and we'll take immediate action."

Evelyn, inside Lilith's head, clung to Marcus's words. She knew the battle was far from over, but with Marcus and Detective Hawthorne by her side, she had a glimmer of hope.

***

As Lilith's pregnancy progressed, the complications became more apparent. The Nano Meds coursing through her system began to react aggressively, recognizing the baby as a potential threat to Lilith's altered physiology. The tension in the secure facility was palpable as the medical team prepared for the inevitable emergency.

Detective Hawthorne and Marcus stood outside the medical wing; their faces etched with concern. Dr. Lawson, still undercover, hurriedly briefed them on the situation.

"Her Nano Meds are reacting defensively," Dr. Lawson explained. "We need to perform an emergency C-section to save both her and the baby. This is going to be delicate."

Marcus nodded, his resolve firm. "I'll assist. She trusts me."

Dr. Lawson led the way into the operating room, where Lilith lay on the table, her face contorted with pain and fear. The sedative drip had been adjusted to keep her awake but calm. She turned her crimson eyes to Marcus as he approached, a rare look of vulnerability crossing her features.

"Marcus," she whispered, her voice trembling. "What's happening? Why do I feel like this?"

Marcus took her hand, squeezing it reassuringly. "Lilith, your Nano Meds are attacking the baby. They see her as a threat to your body, and they're trying to protect you."

Tears welled up in Lilith's eyes. "No..., they can't. Please, save my baby. Promise me you'll save my baby."

Marcus's heart ached at her plea. "I promise, Lilith. We'll do everything we can."

Dr. Lawson and the medical team moved swiftly, their actions precise and coordinated. As the incision was made, the tension in the room skyrocketed. The Nano Meds' defensive mechanisms became apparent, causing unexpected complications that the team had to navigate carefully.

Lilith's grip on Marcus's hand tightened as the procedure progressed. "Please," she murmured, her eyes pleading. "Save her."

Marcus kept his focus, providing steady support. "Stay with us, Lilith. We're almost there."

After what felt like an eternity, the baby was finally delivered. A collective sigh of relief filled the room as the newborn's cries echoed. Dr. Lawson quickly assessed the baby, ensuring she was healthy before handing her to a waiting nurse.

Lilith's body relaxed slightly, the tension easing as the Nano Meds began to stabilize. Her eyes fluttered, exhaustion overtaking her. "Is she...?"

"She's fine, Lilith. She's healthy," Marcus said, his voice soft and reassuring.

Lilith's eyes closed, a faint smile appearing on her lips. "Thank you... Marcus."

Dr. Lawson completed the procedure, ensuring Lilith was stable before turning to Marcus. "We've done it. Both mother and baby are safe, for now."

The room was dark except for the pale moonlight spilling across the sheets. Lilith lay propped against pillows, her bare chest rising and falling slowly. In her arms, the baby nursed slow, sleepy gulps, one tiny hand curled against her skin. She hadn't planned for this moment. She hadn't even wanted it. But now that it was here, now that this fragile life had pressed its face to her breast, something inside her broke.

It wasn't violent. It wasn't dramatic. It was quiet. A quiet grief she didn't understand. A hollowing.

Her body ached, but not from pain, from meaning, from a fullness she had never known and didn't deserve. The baby's warmth against her skin felt like forgiveness for something she hadn't asked to be forgiven for. Her lips, small and soft and insistent, pulled at her with more hunger than she'd ever felt in any battlefield.

She could feel her milk letting down, feel the body's betrayal, because this wasn't just a vessel anymore. It was a mother.

She blinked slowly, tears trailing down her cheeks in silence. Her crimson eyes, so often sharp and predatory, were glassy now. Unrecognizable. Her fingers trembled as they cradled the baby's back. She hated how much she wanted to protect her, to keep her.

Inside, Evelyn did not speak. She didn't need to. She was there, in the curl of the baby's fingers, in the tenderness of the moment, in the steady ache beneath Lilith's heartbeat. She was the soul of the body. The truth. The one who had dreamed of this very moment and now could only watch it pass through her like a ghost clinging to the edges of her own life.

Lilith held the baby tighter, her tears wetting her soft hair. And in that sacred, broken silence, she whispered into the crown of her head. "I wasn't made to love anything." But her body disagreed.

Detective Hawthorne entered the room, his expression a mix of relief and determination. "Good work, everyone. We'll need to keep a close watch on both. This isn't over yet."

Marcus nodded, glancing down at Lilith, who was now resting peacefully. "We'll protect them. No matter what."

Evelyn, still trapped within Lilith's mind, felt a surge of hope. The connection with Marcus had given her strength, and now, with the baby safe, there was a glimmer of light in the darkness.

***

Lilith lay on the hospital bed, the constant sedative drip struggling to keep her subdued. Her Nano Meds were fighting back, their advanced mechanisms counteracting the effects of the sedatives. Despite the medical team's best efforts, it was clear that maintaining control over Lilith would become increasingly difficult.

Detective Hawthorne and Marcus stood outside her room, discussing the situation. "Her Nano Meds are adapting," Detective Hawthorne said, concern etched on his face. "We need to find a way to keep her under control."

Marcus nodded, his mind already racing with potential solutions. "I'll talk to her. Maybe I can get through to her."

Entering the room, Marcus approached Lilith cautiously. Her crimson eyes opened slightly, focusing on him with a mixture of defiance and vulnerability. "Marcus," she whispered, her voice weak but steady.

Marcus pulled a chair close to her bedside, sitting down and taking her hand gently. "Lilith, we need to talk about the baby."

Lilith's eyes softened at the mention of her child. "Is she alright?"

"She's fine. Healthy and strong," Marcus reassured her. "But we need to discuss her care. You're in a dangerous situation, and we need to make sure she's safe."

Lilith's gaze hardened slightly. "What are you suggesting?"

Marcus took a deep breath. "We want to ensure she's in a safe environment. If anything happens to you, we need to know she'll be taken care of."

Lilith's mind raced. She knew Marcus was right, but the thought of being separated from her child was unbearable. "I won't let you take her from me."

"We're not trying to take her away," Marcus said softly. "We just want to make sure she has a safe place to grow up. You can still see her, be a part of her life."

Lilith's eyes narrowed as she considered his words. She knew she had to play along, at least for now. "Fine. But I want to be involved in every decision."

"Of course," Marcus agreed. "We'll work together on this."

As they spoke, Lilith's mind was already working on a plan. She needed to escape, to find a way to regain her freedom and protect her child. The Nano Meds in her system were her advantage, and she knew she could use them to her benefit.

Later that night, as the facility quieted down, Lilith focused on her Nano Meds, willing them to counteract the sedatives even more. Slowly, she felt her strength returning, her mind clearing. She would wait for the right moment, and then she would make her move.

The next morning, as Marcus and Detective Hawthorne reviewed the security protocols, Lilith feigned compliance, hiding her renewed strength. She listened carefully, noting the guards' schedules and the facility's weaknesses.

When the opportunity presented itself, she would be ready. She would escape, and she would take her child with her. The thought gave her the strength she needed to endure, to bide her time until she could make her plan a reality.

21- Escape

Lilith lay in her hospital bed, her mind racing with plans for escape. The sedatives were no longer as effective, and her Nano Meds continued to adapt, slowly restoring her strength. She knew she had to bide her time, but the thought of her baby gave her the determination to endure.

Detective Hawthorne, Marcus, and Dr. Lawson gathered in a secure meeting room within the facility. The gravity of their plan was evident in their serious expressions.

"We can't let Lilith keep the baby," Detective Hawthorne began. "Her Nano Meds make her too dangerous, and we have to ensure the child's safety."

Marcus nodded. "But we can't just take the baby away. Lilith will fight us every step of the way, and she's already planning her escape."

Dr. Lawson leaned forward. "We need a plan that involves gradual separation. We can let Lilith spend time with the baby, build trust, and then slowly transition the baby to a safer environment."

Detective Hawthorne agreed. "We need to make it seem like we're complying with her wishes while setting up a secure future for the child."

Lilith's eyes lit up as the nurse brought in her baby. The sight of her child filled her with a fierce sense of protection and love. She reached out, her fingers trembling slightly as she took the baby into her arms.

"Hey there, little one," she whispered, her voice soft and tender. "Mommy's here."

Marcus stood at the doorway, watching the interaction with a mix of relief and sadness. He knew that allowing Lilith these moments was essential for their plan, but it didn't make it any easier.

Lilith looked up at Marcus, her eyes filled with gratitude. "Thank you for this, Marcus. It means everything to me."

Marcus nodded, stepping into the room. "You deserve to spend time with her, Lilith. We all want what's best for her."

As Lilith spent time with her baby, Marcus and the medical team observed closely, noting any signs of her Nano Meds reacting or any indication that she was planning an escape. The guards remained vigilant, understanding the delicate balance they had to maintain.

Back in the meeting room, Detective Hawthorne and Marcus discussed the next steps with Dr. Lawson.

"We need to make the transition as smooth as possible," Dr. Lawson said. "Lilith must believe that she still has control over the situation, or she'll resist and could become a significant threat."

Marcus agreed. "We'll start with short visits and gradually increase the time the baby spends away from her. We need to make Lilith believe that this is the best way to keep her child safe."

Detective Hawthorne nodded. "We also need to ensure that the baby is placed in a secure and loving environment. Marcus, is your family prepared for this?"

"Yes," Marcus replied. "We've made all the necessary arrangements. She'll be safe with us."

Lilith lay awake, her baby sleeping peacefully in the crib beside her. She knew she had to stay strong, for her child's sake. The moments she spent with her baby only fueled her determination to escape and protect her child from whatever threats lay ahead.

"They think they can control me," she whispered to herself. "But I'll find a way out. I'll keep you safe, my little one. No matter what."

As she watched her child sleep, Lilith's resolve hardened. She would play along with their plans for now, but she was always looking for an opportunity. When the time was right, she would act.

One day, Lilith awoke and the crib beside her bed was empty, and the realization hit her like a physical blow. Her scream tore through the sterile walls like a wounded animal, raw, feral, and completely human. The empty space in her arms throbbed with a pain she couldn't name, like her body itself had been ripped open. They had taken the baby. Her baby. And nothing had prepared her for how that would feel.

The Nano Med enhancements in her bloodstream surged in response to her emotional spike, reading her despair as a threat. Adrenaline dumped into her veins, muscles locking, expanding. Her breath came ragged. Her spine arched. She could feel her skin tightening, her heart hammering like a war drum in her chest.

Cabinets vibrated. The walls groaned. Something deep within her, the code, the tech, the hunger, wanted to break everything.

"Lilith, breathe," Evelyn's voice whispered, not in defiance, but in sorrow. "You'll destroy everything and still be empty."

"They took her," she choked, teeth gritted, tears burning her cheeks. "They took her from me."

"I know," Evelyn whispered. "I know what that loss feels like."

She wasn't thinking anymore. She was grieving. Not for a tool. Not for leverage. For a child. A piece of her she hadn't even wanted to love but had.

"I didn't mean to care," Lilith sobbed, her forehead pressing to the ground. "I didn't mean to care..."

"But you did," Evelyn said gently. "Because you were human enough to feel it. Because she was real. And you're not alone."

For the first time, Lilith didn't respond with venom or sarcasm. She just lay there, trembling, cracked open, the glow in her veins pulsing softly under her skin. A monster. A mother. And for a breathless moment, just a woman who had lost her child.

Outside the room, Marcus and Detective Hawthorne stood, listening to the guttural sounds of Lilith's fury. The raw, primal rage of a mother separated from her child was palpable.

"She's going to break free," Marcus said, his voice laced with concern. "We need to be ready."

Detective Hawthorne nodded; his face grim. "We knew this was a possibility. Let's move to phase two."

Inside the room, Lilith's rage reached a crescendo. The Nano Meds, responding to her distress, heightened her strength and clarity. With a furious roar, she snapped the restraints, her movements a blur of violence and precision. The guards stationed outside the door rushed in, but they were no match for her enhanced abilities.

Lilith dispatched them with ease, her focus singular and unyielding. She had to find her baby. The facility's alarms blared as she moved through the corridors, her senses on high alert. She could feel the pulsing energy of the Nano Meds guiding her, amplifying her every instinct.

Marcus and Detective Hawthorne raced after her, the sound of her rampage leading the way. "She's heading for the nursery," Marcus said.

They turned a corner just in time to see Lilith disappear through a set of double doors. Lilith burst into the nursery, her eyes scanning the room for any sign of her child. But it was empty. She let out a deafening scream of frustration, her rage consuming her.

Lilith remained in the nursery, still as a statue. But burning fury inside, her body pulsed with so much energy, her muscle swelling, tightening with every heartbeat. Her hand deforming the crib with her grip. With slow, mechanical motion, she released her grip and pushed it.

"Where is she?" Lilith demanded, her voice echoing with terrifying clarity.

Marcus and Detective Hawthorne entered the room cautiously, Hawthorne's weapon drawn but aimed low. "Lilith, calm down," Marcus said, his voice steady but firm. "Your baby is safe. But you need to stop this."

"Safe? Safe where?" Lilith's voice was a snarl, her eyes flashing with dangerous light.

"In a place where she can grow up without the constant threat of danger," Hawthorne said. "But we need you to cooperate."

"Cooperate?" Lilith laughed; a sound devoid of humor. "You think you can control me? Take my baby and expect me to just cooperate?"

"We're trying to protect her, and you," Marcus insisted. "But you have to trust us."

"Trust you?" Lilith took a step forward; her body coiled like a spring. "Never."

The guards, unprepared for the raw power and rage she unleashed, lay scattered in her wake. Blood stained the pristine walls, a stark testament to her fury.

Marcus and Detective Hawthorne moved cautiously, their senses heightened, knowing that every second counted. The facility's alarms blared incessantly, a shrill reminder of the danger they faced.

Hawthorne nodded, his grip tightening on his weapon. "We need to corner her before she reaches the exit. If she gets out, we'll have a hell of a time tracking her down."

They turned a corner and froze. Lilith stood at the end of the hallway, her eyes blazing with fury. In her hands, she held a guard's baton, slapping it into her other hand, with a defiant stair, knuckles white with the force of her grip.

"Step aside," she snarled, her voice low and dangerous. "I won't hesitate to kill you both."

Marcus stepped forward; his hands raised in a placating gesture. "Lilith, think about your baby. This isn't the way."

For a moment, her expression faltered, a flicker of pain crossing her features. But it was quickly replaced by steely resolve.

Without warning, Lilith lunged forward, her movements a blur. Hawthorne fired a shot, but Lilith dodged with inhuman speed, the bullet embedding itself harmlessly in the wall behind her. She closed the distance between them in an instant, her fist connecting with Hawthorne's jaw and sending him sprawling.

Marcus barely had time to react before she was upon him, her strength overwhelming. She tossed him aside, like a rag doll. She tried not to hurt Marcus, she couldn't explain why and why she spared him.

"Don't make me do this, Marcus," she hissed, her eyes filled with dangerous light.

He looked up at her, breathing heavily. "Lilith, please. This isn't you."

Lilith turned and bolted down the hallway, her path clear. Behind her, Marcus struggled to his feet, his mind racing. "We can't let her get away," he gasped, looking at Hawthorne's bloody face, who was struggling to stand, trying to shake it off.

Okay, okay said the detective, while spitting blood, let's go. The chase was on through the labyrinthine facility, each corner revealing more signs of Lilith's violent passage. More guards fell to her relentless assault, their attempts to stop her futile against her enhanced abilities.

As she neared the exit, Lilith could see the first light of dawn breaking through the windows. Freedom was within her grasp. But as she pushed open the heavy doors, a final line of defense awaited her.

Lilith's eyes narrowed; her body coiled like a spring. "I won't be stopped," she growled, her voice echoing with the resolve of a mother fighting for her child.

The highly trained guards moved in unison; their training evident in their coordinated assault. But Lilith was a force of nature. She fought with a ferocity born of desperation, each movement calculated and deadly. The sound of gunfire and the clash of steel filled the air, a brutal symphony of violence.

More operatives rushed in to replace their fallen comrades, but they stood no chance against Lilith's enhanced abilities. The battle was entirely one-sided; the facility's floor stained with evidence of her unstoppable rampage. Not a single blow had landed on her; she moved with deadly precision, leaving a trail of incapacitated opponents in her wake.

Finally, with her raw power, Lilith broke through the final line of defense. She burst through the doors, the cool morning air hitting her like a wave of freedom. Without looking back, she ran, her body a blur as she disappeared into the wilderness beyond the facility.

Inside, Marcus and Hawthorne were left to deal with the aftermath. "She got away," Hawthorne said, his voice heavy with frustration.

Marcus nodded; his face grim. "She's out there. And she'll do anything to get her baby back."

As Lilith ran, her mind was a whirlwind of thoughts and emotions. The pain of separation from her child was a gnawing ache in her chest, but it fueled her determination. She would find her baby. No matter what it took, she would reclaim her child and ensure they were never separated again.

Evelyn sarcastically, breaking the silence, I hope it was worth it. Lilith groans with annoyance.

22- *Chaos*

The world was in chaos. News channels buzzed with reports of financial markets plummeting, economies teetering on the brink of collapse, and governments scrambling to regain control. At the heart of this pandemonium was Lilith and Echelon, there unholy alliance.

Echelon's capabilities were far beyond what anyone had anticipated. Its reach was unparalleled, its actions calculated and precise, wreaking havoc on an unimaginable scale.

From the towering skyscrapers of New York to the bustling markets of Tokyo, no financial institution was safe. Stock exchanges experienced unprecedented crashes, with indexes plummeting in minutes. Major corporations found their accounts drained, their confidential data exposed, and their operations disrupted. Echelon's digital fingerprints were everywhere but tracing them led to dead ends and confusion.

Marcus sat in front of multiple screens in a secure command center; his face illuminated by the glow of rapidly changing data. He worked tirelessly alongside a team of cyber-security experts and financial analysts, all attempting to under-stand the full extent of Echelon's assault and how to counter-act it.

"Every major bank has reported significant breaches," one of the analysts reported, her voice tense. "Accounts are being emptied, transactions are being reversed, and entire systems are going offline."

Marcus rubbed his temples, feeling the weight of the crisis. The command center buzzed with urgency as reports of new attacks came in. Echelon wasn't just targeting financial institu-tions; it was disrupting supply chains, manipulating currency exchanges, and even tampering with critical infrastructure like power grids and water supplies. The world was teetering on the edge of a new kind of warfare; one fought in the shadows of cyberspace.

During this chaos, Marcus received a secure message from Detective Hawthorne. "We've got a lead," the message read. "Meet me in the conference room."

Marcus hurried to the conference room, where Haw-thorne and Dr. Lawson were already gathered. The tension in the room was palpable.

"We've been tracking Echelon's movements," Hawthorne began. "It seems to be focusing on destabilizing regions that are already politically volatile. The goal appears to be more than just economic chaos, it's trying to incite conflict, possibly even wars."

Dr. Lawson nodded. "We believe Lilith is leveraging Echelon's capabilities to predict and manipulate human behavior on a massive scale. By causing economic distress, she's hoping to trigger societal breakdowns and civil unrest."

Marcus looked at the map, his mind racing with possibilities. "Let's mobilize our teams. We need to act fast and coordinate with international agencies. This is a global threat, and we need a global response."

As they set their plan into motion, Marcus couldn't shake the feeling that time was running out. The combination of Lilith's determination and Echelon's quantum programming capabilities made them formidable opponents, their intelligence and adaptability creating a nearly insurmountable threat. But with the world's stability hanging in the balance, failure was not an option.

The battle against Lilith and Echelon would be unlike any they had faced before. It was a fight not just for economic survival but for the future of civilization itself.

Marcus hesitated at the threshold, his hand lingering on the doorframe. He always felt it, an invisible weight, whenever he neared Jacob. Not intimidation, but something deeper. Reverence, maybe, like approaching a man who walked too closely with God.

As the command center buzzed with frantic activity, Marcus stepped into a quiet side room where Jacob waited patiently. The prophet stood silently, his serene countenance a stark contrast to the chaos unfolding beyond the closed door.

"Marcus," Jacob began calmly, placing a reassuring hand on Marcus's shoulder. "I know you're doing everything in your power to contain this, but the situation has escalated beyond our control."

Marcus's expression hardened, anxiety creeping into his voice. "We're running out of time, Jacob. Echelon is spreading chaos faster than we can counter it."

"Exactly," Jacob said, his voice steady and sure. There's another path, one that will lead you away from this digital warfare and into safety. You must gather your family, trusted friends, only those you can rely upon implicitly, and leave immediately."

Marcus shook his head, uncertainty clouding his face. "Where would we go, Jacob? Echelon's reach is global."

Jacob's eyes locked with Marcus's, filled with a powerful conviction. "Into the mountains, off-grid. No electronic communications, only a radio for emergencies. There is a sanctuary hidden there, Marcus, a refuge that Echelon cannot reach."

Marcus's skepticism showed plainly, but Jacob stepped closer, his voice gentle yet commanding. "Marcus, listen carefully. Trust your instincts, your heart, and the spirit will guide

Lilith

you. This is more than survival; it's preserving hope for what's to come."

"How will we find it?" Marcus questioned; the weight of responsibility heavy in his voice.

Jacob offered a reassuring smile. "You won't find it with maps or technology. Follow the promptings within you. The spirit will illuminate your path, guiding your every step."

Marcus took a deep breath, his internal turmoil easing under Jacob's steady gaze. "I'll do it," he finally said. "I'll gather the others and leave immediately."

Jacob clasped Marcus's shoulder firmly, a warmth radiating through his touch. "Stay strong, Marcus. The future depends on your faith. Trust in that, and you will find the sanctuary."

With renewed determination, Marcus nodded, stepping back into the whirlwind of activity to prepare his family and friends for the journey ahead, guided by Jacob's words echoing clearly within his heart.

The low hum of the command center faded behind Marcus as he stepped into a dimly lit room adjacent to the main corridor. The walls were bare, the only illumination coming from an old desk lamp casting golden hues across the worn floor. His most trusted friends and family had gathered at his call, Emily, James, Sarah, David, and Rebecca, all seated in a loose circle, their expressions tense, uncertain.

Marcus didn't sit. He stood before them, pacing slightly as he searched for the right words. "I need to ask something of you," he began, his voice carrying the weight of the moment. "Something... not easy. Something that will sound irrational at first."

James leaned forward, arms resting on his knees. "We've been through hell together, Marcus. Just say it."

Marcus nodded, meeting his friend's eyes. "We must leave. Tonight. We need to disappear off-grid, into the mountains."

Silence.

David furrowed his brow. "Leave? Now? In the middle of a coordinated global cyber assault? It seems we've been the only ones holding this together."

"That's exactly why we have to go," Marcus said. "Echelon isn't just attacking banks or governments anymore. It's reshaping the world's foundation, and it knows we're a threat to that plan. Jacob told me there's a sanctuary hidden in the wilderness. A place beyond Echelon's reach."

Sarah crossed her arms. "You're talking about a spiritual vision? A *feeling?*"

Marcus paused. "No. I'm talking about faith and instinct. Jacob has never led me wrong before. He says the Spirit will guide us."

Emily looked down at the small bundle in her arms, the baby sleeping peacefully, unaware of the storm raging outside. "And you believe him?"

"I do." Marcus stepped closer to her. "I believe this child is more important than any of us realize. We can't protect her from behind computer screens or inside bunkers. We need to *get her out*. Away from signals. Away from anything Echelon can touch."

Rebecca exchanged a glance with David. "And if this sanctuary doesn't exist?"

"Then we survive," Marcus replied simply. "We build something ourselves. But we do it where Echelon can't follow."

James stood now, tension lining his jaw. "You're asking us to walk away from the fight."

"I'm asking you to fight smarter," Marcus said. "To preserve what we *can* protect, not chase shadows until we're all burned out. We are being hunted. They will come. And if they catch us here, we won't get another chance."

Emily's voice was quiet, but firm. "Then let's go. If this child is our hope... she needs to grow up *free*. Not in a world run by an AI dictator. I trust you, Marcus."

One by one, the others gave their silent nods. Not with blind certainty, but with loyalty. With conviction.

James clapped Marcus on the shoulder. "Then we do it. We leave before dawn."

Marcus exhaled, finally allowing the tension to leave his shoulders. "Pack light. We travel by foot. No signals, no GPS, no devices except one emergency radio. We move fast. We move quiet."

He looked around the room, eyes settling on each of them. "We're not just running," he said. "We're preserving something. A seed. If the world burns... this baby may be all that's left of its future."

Outside, the wind picked up, howling softly against the walls of the fading command center. It was time to vanish. Time to believe in the unseen.

As the warning settled over them like a weight, Marcus and Emily moved into action without a word. The kids sensed the urgency and helped gather essentials, blankets, food, water, and supplies. The air felt heavier with every passing minute, as if time itself were pressing them to move faster.

Emily moved with quiet precision; her hands steady even as her eyes scanned the room. When she reached for her violin case, Marcus hesitated.

"You're bringing that?" he asked, his voice low, not unkind, just practical.

Emily met his gaze. "Yes."

He studied her for a beat. "You really think it'll help?"

She paused, then nodded. "I don't just play it for peace anymore."

Marcus held her eyes a moment longer. Then he gave a single nod. "Okay. Let's go."

She strapped the case to her pack, and within minutes, they were on the move, together, prepared, and guided by something deeper than instinct.

23- Run

The forest was silent, save for the soft crunch of leaves beneath their feet as they moved swiftly through the trees. The moonlight barely penetrated the thick canopy above, casting eerie shadows that seemed to shift and move with them. Marcus led the way, his breath coming in quick, shallow bursts as he kept his eyes trained on the path ahead.

"Emily, stay close," Marcus whispered over his shoulder, glancing back to ensure she was following closely. He could see the strain on her face, the way her arms tightened around the small bundle she carried. The baby had been quiet for most of the night, but the weight of responsibility she represented was anything but silent.

"I'm right behind you," Emily replied, her voice low but steady. She adjusted her grip on the baby, holding her protectively against her chest. In the chaos of the past few days, they'd quickly realized carrying enough formula wasn't practical. Supplies were limited, and every ounce of weight mattered. Emily had made the decision to try nursing, not just out of necessity, but because it was the one thing she could offer that didn't depend on scavenging or trade. Her body had responded slowly at first, and the process had been painful. That tiny, desperate need had awakened something fierce in her, a drive to nurture, to protect, to survive.

James, a retired Marine, moved silently alongside his wife, Sarah, their expressions grim as they scanned the forest for any signs of pursuit. Behind them, David and Rebecca, who had also served, brought up the rear, their military training evident in the way they moved, cautious, precise, always alert.

"Marcus, we can't keep going like this forever," Emily said, her voice tinged with weariness. "How much farther do we need to go?"

"Until we're safe," Marcus answered, though he knew the answer was far from satisfying. He wasn't sure where 'safe' was anymore. They had been moving from one temporary shelter to another, never staying in one spot long enough to draw attention, but it felt like the darkness was closing in on them regardless.

"There's a clearing up ahead," James whispered, pointing toward a small break in the trees. "We can stop there for a moment, catch our breath. But no more than that. We can't afford to stay still for too long."

As they reached the clearing, Marcus signaled for everyone to halt. The space was small, surrounded by dense foliage, and would offer little protection if they were discovered. But for now, it was enough.

"Sit down, just for a minute," Marcus said, turning to Emily. He could see the exhaustion in her eyes, the way her hands trembled slightly as she carefully lowered herself to the ground, still holding the baby close.

Emily sank down onto the cold earth, leaning back against a tree trunk. The baby stirred slightly in her arms, and Emily carefully adjusted her clothing, she winced slightly as the baby latched on, the familiar but still uncomfortable tug beginning to draw the milk that had taken time to come in.

"It's getting better," Emily said softly, more to herself than anyone else. "But I wish it wasn't so painful."

Marcus knelt beside her, his hand resting gently on her shoulder. "You're doing everything you can," he reassured her. "She's getting stronger because of you."

James, standing guard at the edge of the clearing, scanned the darkness around them. "We'll find it," he said quietly. "The sanctuary is out there, somewhere. We just have to stay ahead of them until we reach it."

Emily sighed, leaning her head back against the tree. "I hope you're right, James. I really do."

For a moment, they allowed themselves to breathe, the only sounds in the clearing being the rustle of leaves and the soft, rhythmic sucking of the baby as she nursed. The process was slow, each feeding session a mix of discomfort and relief as

Emily's body adjusted to its new role. But the tension lingered, a constant reminder of the danger that lurked just beyond the trees.

"We need to keep going," Marcus said finally, rising to his feet. "We're not safe here."

Emily nodded, carefully adjusting her hold on the baby as she stood. James and Sarah moved back into position at the front, while David and Rebecca took up the rear, their senses on high alert once more.

They pushed forward through the dense forest, their steps becoming heavier as fatigue set in. After what felt like hours, the trees finally began to thin out, revealing another small, secluded clearing. Marcus paused at the edge, scanning the area before signaling to the others.

"Here," Marcus whispered, gesturing for Emily to sit. "We'll rest for a bit."

Emily carefully lowered herself onto a patch of dry grass, the baby still cradled in her arms. Her body ached from the relentless pace they had maintained, but the brief pause was a welcome relief. The baby, having finished nursing, was now dozing peacefully, her tiny chest rising and falling with each soft breath.

James and David immediately took up positions on opposite sides of the clearing, their eyes and ears tuned to the surrounding forest. Years of military training had honed their instincts, and even in the relative quiet of the night, they remained on high alert.

"Not much cover here," David muttered, his voice low as he scanned the tree line. "But it'll have to do."

Marcus knelt beside Emily, his hand brushing gently against her arm. "How are you holding up?"

"I'm fine," Emily replied, though the exhaustion in her voice was unmistakable. "It's just... everything feels like it's closing in on us."

Marcus sighed, glancing around the clearing. "I know. But we must keep moving. We can't afford to stay in one place too long."

Sarah, sitting down beside Emily, offered a tired smile. "You're doing great, Emily. I don't know how you're managing to keep her so calm."

Emily returned the smile, though it didn't quite reach her eyes. "It's not easy, but she's strong. I think she understands that we're doing everything we can to protect her."

Sarah reached out, lightly touching the baby's hand. "She's lucky to have you."

As they sat in the clearing, the group took the opportunity to eat what little food they had managed to scavenge along the way. It wasn't much, just a few scraps of bread and some dried meat but it was enough to keep their strength up for the journey ahead.

David broke the silence, his voice barely above a whisper. "Do you think we'll find it soon? The sanctuary?"

James glanced over at Marcus; his expression unreadable. "We have to. It's the only place where we might be safe, where we can regroup and figure out our next move."

Marcus nodded; his jaw set with determination. "We will find it. We don't have a choice."

A heavy silence fell over the group as the weight of Marcus's words sank in. They all knew what was at stake, if they didn't find the sanctuary soon, they would be out of options.

After a few more moments of quiet, Marcus stood up, brushing the dirt from his hands. "We need to keep moving. Every minute we stay here is another minute closer to being caught."

Emily reluctantly rose to her feet, carefully adjusting the baby in her arms. "Let's go, then."

James and David moved back into formation. The group set off once more, leaving the small clearing behind as they disappeared into the forest.

The respite had been brief, but it was enough to restore some of their strength. Now, with renewed determination, they pressed on, driven by the hope that the sanctuary was still out there, waiting for them.

After several more hours of cautious travel, Marcus signaled for the group to halt once more. They had reached a narrow, winding path that led deeper into the woods, and he wanted to ensure they weren't walking into a trap. He scanned the area carefully, listening for any signs of movement in the underbrush.

"Hold up," Marcus whispered, raising a hand. The group came to a silent stop. "What is it?" James asked quietly, moving up to Marcus's side.

"Just being cautious," Marcus replied, his eyes narrowing as he focused on the path ahead. "I don't like how quiet it is."

David nodded in agreement, his hand resting on the hilt of the knife he kept strapped to his side. "It's too quiet," he muttered, his voice low. "Something doesn't feel right."

Emily shifted slightly, adjusting the baby in her arms as she watched the exchange. The child's serene expression was a stark contrast to the tension that gripped the group. It was almost as if the baby understood the gravity of their situation, as if she knew that her safety was paramount.

Marcus took a deep breath, then turned back to the group. "We'll keep moving but stay close. If anything happens, we stick together."

As they walked, Emily's thoughts drifted to the baby's importance, to the reason they were risking everything to protect her. It had been Jacob who first revealed the child's significance. In hushed tones, he had explained that the baby was no ordinary infant. Born of Lilith and Ethan, she carried within her the potential for immense power that could either save or destroy them all, depending on how she was raised.

"She's a beacon," Jacob had said, his voice filled with both awe and fear. "A beacon that could either draw the light or the darkness, depending on who guides her. That's why she must be protected at all costs. Lilith knows what she could become, and she'll stop at nothing to claim her."

Emily had felt a deep sense of responsibility settled over her in that moment, a responsibility she had carried with her ever since. She tightened her grip on the baby, her resolve strengthening with each step. The child was more than just a baby, she was their hope, their chance to turn the tide against the darkness that threatened to consume them all. She knew that she and Marcus had been chosen for a reason, that their unwavering faith and love would be the key to keeping the child on the right path.

They walked in silence for what felt like hours, the only sound the soft rustle of leaves beneath their feet. The path grew narrower, the trees pressing in on either side, but still they continued, driven by the knowledge that they were protecting something precious.

Finally, Marcus paused again, glancing back at Emily. "How's she doing?"

Emily looked down at the baby, who was now sleeping peacefully in her arms. "She's strong," Emily replied softly. "She's going to be okay."

Marcus nodded, a small smile tugging at the corner of his mouth. "She's lucky to have you."

Emily returned the smile, her heart swelling with determination. "We'll keep her safe, Marcus. No matter what."

The narrow path eventually widened, leading the group into another clearing. This one was larger than the last, with thicker underbrush providing more cover. Marcus signaled for everyone to stop, and they quickly spread out to secure the perimeter.

James and David moved into position, Emily watched them for a moment, feeling a small sense of relief that they had these men with them. Their skills had already saved the group more than once, and she knew they would need every advantage they could get in the days to come.

Once they were sure the area was secure, Marcus gathered everyone close, keeping his voice low. "We're running out of time," he began, glancing around at the tired faces. "We can't keep moving like this forever. We need to start thinking about where we're headed."

David, who had been watching the tree line, turned to face Marcus. "You're thinking about the sanctuary, aren't you?"

Marcus nodded. "It's the only option that makes sense. We need a place where we can regroup, where we can protect her without constantly looking over our shoulders."

"The sanctuary is just a rumor," Sarah said quietly, though there was a note of hope in her voice. "What if it's not even real?"

"Whether it's real or not," James interjected, "we have to try. We don't have any other leads, and staying out in the open isn't an option."

Marcus looked at each of them in turn, gauging their reactions. "We've all heard the stories, about a place hidden deep in the wilderness, built to protect those who needed it most. We know it won't be easy to find, but we don't have any other choice."

Emily tightened her hold on the baby; her gaze focused on Marcus. "How do we find it?"

"I've been thinking about that," Marcus replied, rubbing a hand over his tired face. "We know it's supposed to be remote, isolated, maybe even hidden from those who don't know what to look for. But if it's out there, we'll find it."

David nodded, stepping closer to the group. "We'll need to be smart about this. If Lilith's forces are searching for us, they'll be looking for any signs of movement. We need to be careful, leave as little trace as possible."

"We also need to prepare for the worst," James added. "If they catch up to us before we reach the sanctuary, we need to be ready to fight."

Marcus glanced down at the baby; her tiny face relaxed in sleep. "She's the priority. No matter what happens, we protect her. If the sanctuary is out there, it's our best shot. If it's not... we'll figure something out. But we can't stop moving."

The night wore on, and the forest seemed to close in around them, the trees growing denser with each step. Just as the weariness of the journey began to weigh heavily on the group, Marcus noticed something through the trees, a faint outline against the darkness. He raised his hand to halt the group.

"Wait," Marcus whispered, narrowing his eyes as he peered through the foliage. "There's something up ahead."

James moved up beside him, his sharp eyes scanning the area. "Looks like a building," he said quietly. "An old one."

The group moved cautiously toward the structure; their footsteps muffled by the thick layer of leaves on the ground. As they emerged from the trees, they found themselves standing in front of a long-abandoned ranch. The house was run-down, with weathered wooden walls and a roof that sagged in places. Weeds and wild grass had overtaken what once might have been a well-tended yard, and the fences that bordered the property were broken and leaning.

"This place has been deserted for years," David observed, his voice low. "But it might just be what we need."

Marcus approached the front door, which hung loosely on its hinges. He pushed it open carefully, wincing as it creaked loudly in the silence of the night. The interior was dark and musty, with dust-covered furniture scattered about and cobwebs hanging in the corners. But despite its condition, it was shelter, shelter they desperately needed.

Marcus was the first to enter. He looked around the dimly lit room, taking in the sight of the old, worn furniture and the faint smell of mildew. "It's not much," he said softly, "but it's better than nothing."

James and David immediately began to secure the perimeter, checking the windows and doors to ensure they were safe. Sarah found an old lamp and managed to get it working, casting a warm, flickering light across the room.

"This'll do," James said, returning from his inspection. "We're hidden well enough here. We can rest without worrying about being seen."

Emily sank down onto an old, threadbare couch, carefully adjusting the baby in her arms. The little one stirred but didn't wake, her tiny face peaceful and serene. For the first time in what felt like days, Emily allowed herself to relax, the tension easing from her shoulders.

Marcus sat down beside her, his hand resting on her knee. "We'll stay here as long as we can," he said quietly. "We all need some time to recover."

The group settled in, each finding a place to rest in the dilapidated old house. As the hours passed, their exhaustion began to fade, replaced by a growing sense of relief. The abandoned ranch, though run-down and forgotten, had become a temporary haven, a place where they could catch their breath and gather their strength before continuing their journey.

Emily leaned back on the couch, her eyes drifting closed as exhaustion finally claimed her. Marcus watched over her, his heart swelling with gratitude for this small reprieve. They had found a moment of peace amid chaos, and for that, he was thankful.

The sanctuary was still out there, waiting for them. But for now, they had found a place to rest, a place to prepare for the challenges that still lay ahead.

24 - Reprive

The morning sun filtered through the broken windows of the old ranch house, casting soft rays of light across the dusty floors. The air was still and calm, a rare moment of peace that the group had not experienced in what felt like an eternity. After the long, exhausting journey through the forest, the abandoned ranch had become an unexpected haven, providing them with the shelter and rest they desperately needed.

Emily sat on the worn-out couch, her body finally beginning to relax after days of constant tension. She watched her daughter, who sat nearby, gently rocking the baby while humming a soft, soothing tune.

"Shhh, little one," Emily's daughter whispered, her voice barely audible. "You're safe now."

Emily smiled, her heart swelling with a mix of pride and gratitude. Her children had grown so much during this ordeal, their innocence tempered by the harsh realities of their world. Yet, in this moment, she saw the nurturing, loving spirit that still lived within them, a reminder of the goodness they were all fighting to protect.

Nearby, Emily's son carefully prepared a small bottle for the baby, his hands steady as he measured the water and formula. Though still young, the seriousness with which he approached the task made him seem older, more mature. When he finished, he walked over to Emily and handed her the bottle with a shy smile.

"Here, Mom," he said quietly. "I made it just like you showed me."

Emily accepted the bottle, her eyes glistening. "Thank you, sweetheart. You're doing such a good job."

He beamed at the praise, watching with fascination as Emily carefully fed the baby. The little one stirred, her tiny hands grasping at the bottle as she drank. Her son sat beside Emily; his gaze fixed on the baby's peaceful face.

"Is she going to be okay, Mom?" he asked, his voice full of innocent concern.

Emily nodded, her smile reassuring. "She's going to be just fine. We're all going to be okay."

As the day wore on, the warmth of the sun began to fade, replaced by the cool embrace of evening. The group had spent the day resting and recovering, taking full advantage of their temporary respite. The children, exhausted from their play and care of the baby, had finally settled down for the night, their soft breaths the only sound in the quiet house.

Emily stood by the window, watching as the last rays of sunlight dipped below the horizon, casting the landscape in a dusky glow. She felt Marcus's presence behind her and turned to see him approaching, his expression soft and full of affection.

"Hey," Marcus said quietly, coming to stand beside her. He placed a hand on her shoulder, his thumb gently brushing the back of her neck. "You okay?"

Emily nodded, leaning into his touch. "I'm better now," she replied softly. "It's just... it's been so long since we had a moment like this. A moment to just breathe."

Marcus wrapped his arms around her, pulling her close as they stood together by the window. The warmth of his embrace was a comfort she had missed, a reminder of the love and support that had carried them through so many dark times.

"I know," Marcus murmured, resting his chin on top of her head. "It feels like we've been running for so long. But right now, we're safe. And we're together. That's all that matters."

Emily closed her eyes, allowing herself to relax completely in his arms. "I've missed this," she whispered. "I've missed us."

Marcus gently turned her to face him, his hands resting on her waist as he gazed into her eyes. "I've missed you too," he said, his voice filled with emotion. "More than anything."

Without another word, he leaned down and captured her lips in a tender kiss. The world outside the ranch seemed to disappear as they shared this moment of connection, their love for each other rekindled by the simple act of being close.

Emily melted into the kiss, her hands sliding up to rest on his chest. When they finally pulled back, their foreheads resting against each other, she felt a sense of peace that had been missing for far too long.

"Thank you," Emily whispered, her voice barely audible. "For always being here. For us."

Marcus smiled, brushing a strand of hair behind her ear. "You don't have to thank me," he replied softly. "We're in this together, no matter what."

The light of dawn crept through the windows of the old ranch house, casting a soft, golden glow over the dust-covered floors. Emily stirred first, her eyes fluttering open as she felt the warmth of Marcus's arm draped over her. She smiled to herself, savoring the rare feeling of peace that filled the room.

When she entered the main room, she found Sarah and James already awake, sitting at the old kitchen table with steaming cups of coffee in their hands. The atmosphere was light, almost cheerful, and Emily couldn't help but smile as she joined them.

"Good morning," Emily greeted, her voice soft but warm.

"Morning," Sarah replied with a smile, her eyes twinkling with mischief. "You sleep well?"

Emily chuckled, a faint blush creeping into her cheeks. "Better than I have had in a long time. I had only to feed the baby once."

James nodded, taking a sip of his coffee. "Same here," he said with a grin. "Must be something in the air."

As the three of them exchanged knowing looks, David and Rebecca emerged from the back room, both looking surprisingly refreshed. They too shared a quiet smile, clearly in on the unspoken joke that seemed to be passing around the table.

"Why is everyone so happy today?" Emily's son asked, rubbing his eyes as he wandered into the kitchen.

Emily exchanged a quick glance with Marcus, who had just entered the room. "We all just had a really good night's sleep," Marcus said, trying to suppress his smile as he ruffled his son's hair. "Sometimes, a little rest is all you need to feel better."

Marcus, feeling the weight of responsibility for his family and friends, decided to take the lead on hunting for fresh meat. Knowing the dangers that lurked in the forest and the need to avoid drawing attention to their presence, he chose to craft a bow and arrow. Firearms, though effective, were loud and could easily give away their location.

Marcus found a quiet spot beneath an old oak tree, the leaves rustling gently in the breeze. He knelt, bowing his head in prayer. "Heavenly Father," he began, his voice low and sincere, "please guide me to where we can find the food we need on our journey. Help me to provide for my family and protect those I love. Guide me to find the sanctuary."

As he finished his prayer, Marcus felt a sense of calm and clarity wash over him. He stood up with renewed determination and set about crafting his bow and arrows. He used the sturdy branches of the oak tree, binding them with strong cord he had scavenged from the ranch.

Meanwhile, back at the ranch house, Sarah and Rebecca gathered wild herbs and berries from the surrounding woods, their knowledge of edible plants proving invaluable. Emily and the children set about preparing a fire in the old stone hearth, using the remaining scraps of dried meat and vegetables to make a simple stew.

Marcus returned successfully from his hunt, and soon they had prepared a hearty meal. The smell of cooking meat and simmering stew filled the air, a welcome change after so many days of sparse rations. As they sat down to eat, the group offered a prayer of thanks, grateful for the guidance and blessings they had received.

Just as they began to relax and enjoy the evening, the crackle of the old radio interrupted their peaceful meal. The static cleared for a moment, allowing a grim voice to break through: "Reports continue to come in of widespread chaos and destruction across the country. The situation remains dire, with no clear end in sight. Citizens are urged to stay indoors and avoid travel unless absolutely necessary."

The room fell silent as the weight of the news settled over them, a stark reminder of the world outside their temporary haven. Marcus was the first to speak, his voice steady but serious. "We have a few more days here to prepare and rest, but we can't lose sight of the journey ahead. The sanctuary is still out there, and we need to reach it before things get worse."

***

Meanwhile, in Lilith's headquarters, the hum of machinery filled the air, a constant background noise that had become the soundtrack to Lilith's life. The facility was a hive of activity, with Echelon's network expanding its reach across the globe, spreading chaos and destruction in its wake. But for Lilith, none of this was enough. Her fury was a fire, consuming her from the inside out, and no amount of destruction could quell the burning rage that gripped her heart.

Lilith stood in the center of the command room; her eyes fixed on the array of monitors surrounding her. Each screen displayed a different part of the world in disarray, power grids failing, cities plunged into darkness, and panic spreading like wildfire. Echelon's digital warfare was relentless, and the world was crumbling under its assault.

"Status report," Lilith snapped, her voice cold and sharp.

One of her lieutenants, a nervous-looking man with dark circles under his eyes, hurried to her side. "Echelon is executing

Phase Three as planned, ma'am. The power grids in Europe and Asia are down, and communication networks in North America are failing rapidly. We estimate that over sixty percent of the global population is now without reliable access to electricity or communication."

Lilith barely acknowledged his words; her gaze locked on a screen showing a riot breaking out in Paris. People were looting, fighting, and setting fires in the streets, their faces twisted in fear and anger. The world was falling apart, but all Lilith felt was emptiness.

Her mind flashed back to the clinic, to the moment she realized her daughter was gone. The memory was a knife in her chest, twisting deeper with each passing second. She could still hear Ethan's voice, his words meant to soothe her, to calm her down. But how could she be calm when her heart had been ripped out?

A soft chime sounded from the console, indicating an incoming message. It was a report from one of her reconnaissance teams, tracking down a lead on her daughter's possible location. Lilith's heart skipped a beat as she read the details, sightings of a small group traveling with an infant, heading north through the forests.

"Echo," Lilith taunted, a twisted smirk forming on her lips as she spoke to the AI. "Initiate search protocol alpha. I want every resource at our disposal focused on this lead. Do whatever it takes, find my daughter."

As Echelon, now mocked as "Echo" by Lilith, activated its systems, the global network bent to her will. The destruction would continue, but now it had a purpose. Now it was personal. The thought of holding her daughter again, of feeling that tiny heartbeat against her chest, was the only thing that kept her from falling apart completely. And if anyone stood in her way, they would regret ever crossing Lilith.

25- Rage

Lilith's headquarters buzzed with the frenetic energy of her minions, all scrambling to follow her orders. Every available resource was being funneled into the search for her daughter, a search that had consumed Lilith's every waking moment. She barely slept, her mind too fixated on the child she had lost and the rage that gnawed at her soul.

Ethan stood just outside the main command room, watching as Lilith drove her subordinates to exhaustion. He knew better than to interrupt her when she was in one of her moods, but the strain was beginning to show on everyone. Lilith's relentless pursuit was taking a toll, not just on her enemies but on those closest to her.

He hesitated for a moment, then took a deep breath and stepped into the room. "Lilith," he called softly, trying to keep his voice calm and steady. "You need to rest. You've been pushing yourself too hard."

Lilith didn't even turn to look at him, her focus locked on the screens in front of her. "I don't have time to rest," she snapped, her tone icy. "Not until I have her back."

Ethan moved closer, placing a tentative hand on her shoulder. "I understand, but you're going to burn out if you keep this up. You need to take care of yourself if you're going to be able to take care of her."

Lilith shrugged off his hand, her body stiffening at the touch. "I don't need your concern, Ethan," she replied, her voice edged with irritation. "What I need is results."

He recoiled slightly, hurt by the coldness in her tone. "I'm just trying to help," he said, his voice tinged with sadness. "I care about you, Lilith. I care about us."

For the first time, Lilith turned to face him, her eyes blazing with anger. "This isn't about us, Ethan!" she hissed. "This is about my daughter! She's out there, alone, vulnerable, and you think I can just... rest?"

Ethan met her gaze, refusing to back down. "I'm not asking you to stop looking for her," he said firmly. "But you can't do this alone. You're shutting everyone out, and it's only making things harder."

Lilith's expression hardened, her eyes narrowing. "I don't need anyone, Ethan. Not you, not them." She gestured sharply at the people working around them. "I need Echo to find my daughter, and I need you to stay out of my way."

The words stung, more than Ethan wanted to admit. He had seen the change in Lilith ever since their daughter was taken, the way she had distanced herself, the way her anger had consumed her. He had tried to reach her, to remind her that they were in this together, but it was like talking to a wall.

"Lilith," he said quietly, his voice filled with emotion, "don't do this. Don't push me away."

But Lilith had already turned back to the screens, her expression cold and unyielding. "You're wasting your time, Ethan. I told you; I don't need you right now."

As Ethan walked away, Lilith barely noticed. Her mind was consumed with the search, her fingers flying over the console as she directed Echo's next move. The AI's network spread out like a web, covering every possible location, every lead, no matter how small. She wouldn't stop until she had her daughter back, and anyone who got in her way would be destroyed.

Her mind flickered back to the clinic, to the moment she held her daughter for the first time. The baby had been so small, so fragile, and Lilith had felt a fierce protectiveness unlike anything she had ever known. But that feeling was now twisted into something dark, something that drove her to the edge of madness.

Echo's voice, calm, emotionless, broke through her thoughts. "Search parameters updated. Focusing on regions with recent infant sightings."

"Good," Lilith muttered, her eyes narrowing as she reviewed the data. "You'd better not fail me, Echo."

***

In the small towns and rural areas that had, for a time, remained untouched by the global unrest, the effects of Lilith's wrath were finally being felt. Power outages, once rare, became commonplace. Communication networks faltered, isolating communities that were already on edge. But it wasn't just the physical destruction that was wreaking havoc, it was the pervasive fear that now gripped the hearts of ordinary people.

In one such town, nestled in the shadow of the mountains, the atmosphere had grown tense. The residents, once friendly and close-knit, had become wary of one another, their trust eroded by the constant stream of terrifying news. Rumors of Lilith's wrath and Echo's reach filled the air, creating an undercurrent of paranoia that threatened to tear the community apart.

"They say she's unstoppable," Mrs. Henderson, an elderly woman with a penchant for gossip, whispered to her neighbor over the rickety fence that divided their yards. "That she's looking for something, and anyone who gets in her way ends up dead."

Her neighbor, Mr. Greene, nodded solemnly, his eyes darting nervously around as if Lilith herself might appear at any moment. "I heard she's after her baby," he murmured. "And she'll stop at nothing to get it back."

***

One evening, as the group huddled around a small fire, trying to keep warm against the encroaching chill of the night, the crackle of a handheld radio broke the uneasy silence. The radio had become their lifeline, a way to stay connected to the outside world, even if the news it brought was often grim.

"...widespread power outages reported across the western states," the voice on the radio announced, the words distorted by static. "Authorities are urging citizens to remain indoors and avoid travel if possible. Martial law has been declared in several major cities as the situation continues to deteriorate..."

Emily's hand tightened around the baby she cradled in her arms, her heart heavy with the weight of the news. She glanced at Marcus, who was listening intently, his expression grim.

"They're getting closer," Marcus murmured, his voice low so as not to alarm the others. "We can't stay here much longer. We need to keep moving."

Emily nodded, her mind racing with worry. The baby stirred in her arms, letting out a soft whimper, and Emily instinctively rocked her gently, whispering soothing words. "We'll keep her safe," she whispered to herself, though the promise felt fragile in the face of the growing danger.

Across the fire, James, the ex-Marine, looked up from sharpening his knife, his keen eyes scanning the darkness beyond their camp. "We need to start thinking about where we're headed next," he said, his voice calm but firm. "Staying in one place is too risky."

"I agree," David chimed in, his tone equally serious. "The sanctuary is still out there, and we need to reach it before things get any worse."

***

In a dimly lit underground command center, a group of high-ranking officials from various nations huddled around a large table, their faces etched with exhaustion and despair. Maps and documents were strewn across the table, covered in hastily scribbled notes and strategy outlines, most of which now seemed useless in the face of the overwhelming power of Echelon.

"We're out of options," General Martinez, a veteran military leader said, his voice tinged with frustration. "Every time we come up with a plan, Echelon is ten steps ahead. It's like they know our moves before we even make them."

"Because they do," replied Director Lang, the head of intelligence for what was left of the United States. She ran a hand through her disheveled hair, her eyes bloodshot from lack of sleep. "Echelon's network has infiltrated everything, our communications, our satellites, even our most secure systems. We're fighting a losing battle."

The room fell silent as the weight of her words sank in. It was a grim reality they had all been forced to accept: Echelon wasn't just an enemy; they were outmatched in every conceivable way.

"What about these sanctuaries?", one European diplomat asked, his voice barely above a whisper. "We've heard rumors... whispers of places where people are gathering, strongholds against Lilith and Echelon's forces."

***

Meanwhile, at her headquarters, Lilith's eyes gleamed with a mixture of triumph and fury as she watched the progress on the screens before her. Echelon had pinpointed the location of her daughter, or at least the group that had taken her. They were moving north, likely towards the sanctuary she had heard whispers of. The thought of her daughter in the hands of strangers filled her with a burning rage.

"It's almost over," she murmured to herself, her voice cold and determined. "I'm coming for you."

As she prepared to mobilize her forces, Ethan approached her, his face etched with concern. "Lilith, are you sure about this?" he asked, his voice tinged with unease. "If the sanctuary is what they say it is..."

Lilith cut him off with a sharp glare. "I don't care what it is. I'll tear it apart with my bare hands if I must. Nothing will stop me from getting her back."

Ethan wanted to argue, to reason with her, but he knew it was pointless. The Lilith he had once known was gone, consumed by her obsession. All that remained was a mother driven to the brink of madness, willing to destroy anything and anyone that stood in her way.

"Then I'll stand by you," Ethan said quietly, though the words felt hollow. He wasn't sure if he was saying them out of loyalty or fear of what would happen if he didn't.

Lilith gave him a curt nod before turning back to the screens. "Prepare the troops," she ordered, her voice devoid of any warmth. "We're moving out."

"Echo," she said with a twisted smirk, taunting the AI that had become her most powerful weapon. "Don't disappoint me. We're so close."

Echelon's systems hummed in response, its network expanding to cover every inch of the region where her daughter was thought to be. The final assault was about to begin, and Lilith would stop at nothing to reclaim what was hers.

26- Trial

The fire cracked low, small and cautious. No one fed it. No one moved. The silence had weight now, like gravity with intent.

Marcus crouched near the edge of the pit, elbows on his knees, scanning the black beyond the tree line. Sarah leaned against a boulder beside him. Alex sat cross-legged, back straight, eyes darting toward every flicker of movement in the brush.

And a little farther from the fire, just beyond its ring of light, sat Emily. Her violin case was open in the dirt beside her. She hadn't touched it all night, not since they'd set camp, but she kept glancing at it like it might speak.

Marcus noticed. "You alright?" he asked quietly.

Emily didn't answer. She kept staring into the woods, head tilted, like she was listening for something no one else could hear.

The trees swayed gently, though there was no wind. The air had grown colder. Not bitter. Hollow.

Emily finally looked up. Her eyes were calm, but her shoulders were braced, like she already knew what came next.

A gust passed through the trees, not wind exactly, more like pressure. It bent branches without touching them, made the fire flicker sideways.

No one moved.

She reached into the violin case and lifted the instrument with quiet reverence. The polished wood reflected the firelight like it had its own soul. It wasn't just well cared for; it had been loved. Worn in places but tuned with care.

Marcus frowned. "You're really going to play right now?"

"I didn't bring this violin for comfort," she said, voice low but steady. "I brought it because when I play with everything I have, faith, passion, fire, it doesn't just lift spirits...it drives the darkness back."

A sound rippled through the trees, too low to name, too unnatural to mistake. Like something ancient shifting beneath the surface of reality.

Emily closed her eyes.

The camp held its breath.

She stood just beyond the edge of the firelight, her silhouette framed by mist and moonlight. The bow rested gently at her side, her other hand still cradling the violin. She hadn't played yet, but her body held the tension of a storm on pause.

Then, softly she said: "I dreamed of this."

Marcus turned. "of what?"

She didn't move. Didn't blink.

"I dreamed of this duel. Not once. Over and over. Same scene, same fire, same voice in the shadows."

Sarah stood. "You mean this exact moment?"

Emily nodded, slowly. "Close enough to make my skin crawl."

She turned slightly, just enough for the fire to catch the edge of her face.

"I didn't know what it meant at first. I thought it was just a nightmare. But it kept coming back, clearer every time. The music was always there... waiting."

Alex took a half-step forward, his voice uncertain. "Wait, so... Trial by Fire came from a dream?"

"No," Emily said. "It came from a warning."

She stepped toward the tree line as she spoke, never taking her eyes off the dark.

"For weeks, the dream followed me. Always the same challenge. A voice, burning eyes, and a choice: play or perish."

She exhaled through her nose, steady and calm.

"I started writing pieces of the melody. In notebooks. On napkins. Scraps of lyrics would hit me in the middle of the night. Sometimes I'd wake up with my hands shaking, the rhythm still echoing in my head. I didn't sleep much."

Sarah swallowed. "But you never played it for us."

Emily's voice dropped to almost a whisper. "Because I knew I hadn't earned it yet."

She looked at them, eyes flicking from face to face.

"This isn't just a song. It's a weapon. Not because of volume or tempo. Because of where it came from. I didn't invent it, I remembered it."

The fire cracked behind her, a single ember jumping skyward.

"It's not about music theory or technique. It's about conviction, faith. This piece was forged from fear and refined through fire. The notes... they're prayers. The kind only the soul can understand."

Alex blinked. "You mean you... dreamed the whole thing?"

Emily nodded. "Not in one night. It came in pieces. Sometimes all I could remember was a phrase. Other times just a bowing pattern, or a fragment of a chorus. But every time it returned, I remembered a little more."

Sarah sat down slowly. "And you think this, this thing out there is the same one from the dream?"

Emily looked past them, into the forest. "No. I know it is."

She finally stepped into the center of the clearing. "I'm playing because something evil is listening. And this... is the only language it fears."

Emily stood still in the mist; her fingers wrapped around the neck of her violin. Beyond her, the others watched from the firelight, but none dared move. The presence in the woods was no longer hiding, it was circling, testing, waiting.

She lifted the instrument into place. The bow touched the string.

"Let the trial begin."

The first note cut through the stillness like a blade drawn across velvet, smooth, eerie, and far too calm for what lay ahead. The trees didn't sway; they listened.

Then came the second note, sharper, hungrier. The air thickened, as if the forest itself were bracing for impact.

Emily didn't just play. She declared war.

> *The Devil came knockin' at my door,*
> *Eyes like embers, voice like war.*
> *Said, "Girl, you've been runnin' from sin,*
> *But I've seen your soul; it's wearin' thin."*

A shape emerged beyond the trees, not solid, not human. Fire and ash moved where a face might be. Smoke curled like breath from an unseen mouth.

Emily's fingers moved faster.

> *He flashed a smile of twisted glee,*
> *"Play your violin, set your spirit free.*
> *But be warned, if you dare to lose,*
> *Your soul is mine, so you better choose."*

The flames of the campfire pulsed with each word. Sarah gasped. Alex stepped back. Marcus gritted his teeth but did not interfere.

Emily took one step forward, and her bow roared.

It's a trial by fire, in the devil's choir,
Bowin' that violin, take it higher.
It's a deadly game, but I'll fan the flame,
In this showdown, there's no shame.

The wind rose, not from nature, but from it. The thing across from her was taking form now: a hunched, burning silhouette with claws instead of hands and eyes made of coal. It didn't walk. It drifted.

The trees leaned away from it. Emily's hands blurred. Sparks snapped off the strings, the melody pushing harder, faster, fierce and bright. The air trembled. The shadows rippled.

The darkness answered, screeching, scraping noise that wasn't music, just mockery. But Emily didn't flinch.

Rosin smoke, strings ablaze,
Sparks flying wild in this wicked haze.
He played a tune, dark and mean,
But I've got fire he's never seen.

The devil's tune twisted through the woods like broken glass in a hurricane. It clashed with hers but couldn't drown it out. Not when her fire was rising.

He spun a tale of a sinner's delight,
But I answered back with holy might.
His eyes went wide as he began to see,
That devil ain't never gonna conquer me.

The light from her violin wasn't visible, but it was felt. The thing staggered. Its form faltered. For the first time, it looked unsure.

It's a trial by fire, in the devil's choir,
Bowin' that violin, take it higher.
It's a deadly game, but I'll fan the flame,
In this showdown, there's no shame.

The forest flared white for a blink, just a pulse, and then it went still again.

Emily didn't stop playing.

And the darkness didn't leave. Not yet.

The creature snarled, smoke billowing from its chest as it reared back. It didn't speak in words; it sang in screams. A discordant howl tore through the clearing, shaking pine needles from the trees. The fire guttered and nearly died, but the violin burned hotter.

Emily's hair whipped around her face. Her boots skidded slightly in the dust, but she planted herself firmly.

This was not the devil of myths or metaphors. This was something older.

And she refused to let it take anything. She closed her eyes, let the bow rise, and poured every ounce of fire and memory she had into the strings.

The notes cut like lightning through ash. The tempo surged. Her arms moved as if led by something greater. Every note was a memory: of fear, of loss, of battles survived.

The song wasn't just melody anymore. It was testimony. And then the devil staggered. Just a step but enough.

The devil stumbled, lost his grin,
Realized quick, he's not gonna win.
"Girl," he cried, "You've bested me,
But I'll be back, just wait and see."

He twisted, flame licking from his shoulders, his jaw dislocated from the pressure of his scream. Ash swirled where his feet should have touched ground. But Emily held the bow firm and stared straight through him.

The final exchange had come.

I told him, "Devil, hear me now,
I won't break, and I won't bow.
Take your darkness, take your pride,
My soul is mine, this flame won't die."

The melody rose, furious and radiant. Her bow blurred; her fingers flew, every measure ringing with purpose. The wind turned, not against her now, but with her, swirling like unseen wings at her back.

A final note split the air, so high, so pure, it rang like glass shattering in slow motion.

And then? Silence.

The figure of flame and smoke unraveled, strands of ember unraveling upward like a soul caught in judgment. Its mouth opened to roar again...but it couldn't...

The sound was gone. It had no song left to sing.

Emily stood in the clearing, breathing hard, the violin still humming faintly in her grip.

Marcus stepped closer from the fire's edge, hands trembling.

"Did... did you just..."

She didn't answer. She lowered the bow. Slowly.

The night exhaled. The clearing held its breath. For one long heartbeat, everything was still, too still. The mist, the trees, even the fire refused to move, as if time itself paused to weigh what had just occurred.

Emily's chest heaved. Her knuckles ached from how tightly she'd gripped the bow. Her arm trembled. But she didn't lower the violin. Not yet.

The figure of flame and shadow hadn't vanished. It hung there, drifting, dissolving, desperate.

Its form was no longer proud or terrible. It had begun to wither. Its spine curled. Its limbs cracked at the joints like dry wood in fire. Its voice, once deafening, now trembled like a candle before wind.

She stepped forward. No fear. No apology. Just faith.

It's a trial by fire, in the devil's choir,
Bowin' that violin, take it higher.
It's a deadly game, but I'll fan the flame,
In this showdown, there's no shame.

The final chorus struck like a bell. Pure. Absolute.

The shadows recoiled as though burned by sound. The entity gave a shudder, not from pain, but from understanding.

Emily's final note hovered in the air, a single, perfect harmony that resonated with everything around it. The fire flared tall once more. Light washed the darkness clean.

And the thing... folded. It collapsed inward, like a building giving in to gravity. The embers that formed its face winked out one by one. The edges of its body curled like burnt paper. No roar. No scream.

Only the hiss of heat escaping the hollow space it once filled.

Then, silence.

Emily didn't move. Not until she was sure it was gone.

When she finally lowered her bow, her knees buckled slightly. Marcus was there in two steps, catching her before she fell completely.

"You did it," he said, almost in disbelief.

Sarah and Alex emerged from the firelight, their expressions wide-eyed, lips parted in awe.

Emily nodded faintly; eyes unfocused. "It's not dead."

"What?" Alex said.

She swallowed hard. "That wasn't all of it. That was just one piece."

"But it backed off," Sarah said. "You beat it."

Emily looked at her, and for the first time since the song began, her voice cracked. "I didn't beat it. I reminded it what I am."

"And what's that?" Marcus asked.

Emily met his gaze.

"Untouchable when I believe."

She turned to the woods one last time. The silence there wasn't peaceful. It was waiting. Wounded but not finished.

The others didn't speak as she returned to the fire. They made space for her, not just out of respect, but instinct. Something had shifted. Not in her, around her.

The wind rustled the treetops once more. Natural this time. Ordinary. And the sky began to clear, just enough to reveal the fractured edge of a moon still fighting to shine.

The trial wasn't over, but she had passed this one.

And somewhere, the darkness took note.

Smoke curled softly into the night sky, rising from the embers like incense after a sermon. The flames had settled to a low, rhythmic crackle, more heart than heat. The oppressive weight in the air had lifted, but the tension hadn't disappeared. It had just changed shape.

Marcus sat closest to the fire, knees bent, hands laced in front of him, staring into the coals as if they held secrets. Beside him, Sarah tended the flame in silence, adding just enough fuel to keep it alive but not enough to disrupt the stillness that had settled over them all.

Alex hadn't said a word since Emily returned. He just kept watching his mom, like he didn't quite believe she was still standing. Like he wasn't sure any of them should be.

Emily knelt by her case, carefully polishing her violin with a cloth she'd carried since she was twelve. It was old, frayed at the edges, but ritual mattered more than fabric. She wiped the sweat from the chin rest, tuned the pegs without a sound, and closed the latches with reverence.

No applause. No cheers. Just breathing.

Sarah finally broke the quiet. "That thing... it's not coming back tonight, is it?"

"No," Emily said without looking up. "Not tonight."

Alex cleared his throat, voice brittle. "But it is coming back."

Emily met his gaze. "They always do."

Marcus tilted his head. "You said that wasn't all of it."

She nodded. "It wasn't. Just one voice in the choir."

The phrase landed with a quiet finality. No one had to ask what she meant. They all felt it. The darkness hadn't lost; it had retreated. Regrouped. And whatever it truly was, it had more verses left to sing.

"But it blinked," she added, softer now. "And that means it can."

Sarah gave her a long, haunted look. "Where the hell did you learn to play like that?"

Emily stood slowly, dusted her palms against her pants. She said, "Not where, when."

She looked up at the stars just beginning to pierce through the clouds. "Every time it tried to take me. That's when the music came. I didn't survive it because I was strong, I survived it because I played through it."

Marcus nodded like he understood more than he said. "And now?"

Emily turned back to them; eyes calm. "Now I play for us."

A long silence passed between them, not empty, but earned. Like the aftermath of a storm no one dared name.

Then Alex tried to smile. "So... do we just go to bed now like that didn't just happen?"

Marcus let out a breath that could've been a laugh. "That's exactly what we do."

Sarah rubbed her face with both hands. "Can we at least agree on no more open-air camping for the rest of the week?"

Emily chuckled under her breath. It wasn't loud. But it was human. She moved to the fire, rolled out her blanket, and sat down slowly, her body aching from the effort. She didn't complain. She just looked out into the night again.

The shadows had changed. They hadn't disappeared, but they kept their distance now. Like wolves remembering the taste of fire.

Marcus passed her a ration bar without a word.

"Thanks," she muttered. They ate in silence.

Somewhere in the distance, an owl called out. And for the first time in days, the sound wasn't ominous, it was just a sound. The world had shifted back into balance, if only slightly.

And when Emily finally closed her eyes, hand resting loosely atop the violin case, she smiled. Not because they were safe, but because when the darkness came next time, it would remember her name.

Preface Part 3

They took everything from me.

Love. Choice. Even the lies I once clung to. I gave humanity my curiosity, my hunger, my hope, and in return, they branded me monster, whore, abomination. They worshipped the silence while I screamed.

But no more.

This is not redemption. This is reckoning.

There is a power in pain when you stop pretending it must be healed. I will burn down every illusion of purity they've ever clung to. Let them pray. Let them run. I am the end they never saw coming.

There will be no forgiveness.

Only fire.

27- Corruption

The next morning, they began to prepare for the next leg of their journey. The older teenagers, under the guidance of their parents, gathered supplies and packed up the camp. Tents were dismantled, and backpacks were filled with provisions.

With the camp packed up and everyone fed and ready, they gathered for a final prayer. Marcus led the prayer, asking for guidance, protection, and strength for the journey ahead. The family stood together, united in faith and purpose. He then briefed everyone on the route for the day, emphasizing the importance of staying together and being vigilant. They discussed the safest path ahead, ensuring they avoided any potential traps set by Lilith's followers.

As they set off, the path illuminated by the early morning light, they felt a sense of hope and determination. They walked together, their steps synchronized with their faith, heading towards the sanctuary Jacob had assured them would protect them from the impending dangers. Each step brought them closer to safety and further away from the uncertainties and threats that had been closing in on them.

Meanwhile, Lilith's followers, frustrated by their repeated failure to capture Marcus and his group, continued to lay traps along their path. They couldn't understand how their prey kept eluding them, unaware of the divine guidance leading Marcus and his family safely through each challenge.

As the group moved cautiously, the weight of the world's unraveling pressed heavily on them, each step feeling like a march into an unknown future. Despite their efforts to focus on the immediate task; survival, the pervasive sense of global chaos was impossible to ignore, lingering like a shadow over every decision.

They tuned into the news broadcast; the gravity of the situation became clear. Reports of riots, power outages, and mysterious disappearances flooded the airwaves.

"It's not just the cities," the announcer's voice trembled. "This is happening everywhere. No one is safe."

Marcus exchanged a grim look with Emily. "This isn't just about reaching the sanctuary," he murmured. "It's about surviving whatever's coming next."

"In Europe, entire financial systems are collapsing," a news anchor's voice crackled over the radio. "Governments are declaring states of emergency, unable to combat the spread of corruption through their digital networks."

According to the report, people woke up to a flood of disturbing content on their screens, in cities and towns worldwide. Violent images, hate speech, and explicit material filled their feeds, invading every corner of the internet.

"Are you listening to this?" Marcus asked Emily, his voice tinged with concern as he tuned the radio to different frequencies, catching snippets of news. "It's like the whole world has gone mad."

Emily nodded; a worried look on her face. "It's terrifying how quickly things can spiral out of control," she replied. "I can't imagine what it must be like for people who are constantly bombarded with all this negativity."

As the chaos escalated, governments scrambled to respond, enacting emergency measures to curb the spread of harmful content online. But Echelon and Lilith's influence proved too pervasive, their algorithms adapting faster than anyone could keep up.

***

Elsewhere, amid the chaos, Dr. Rebecca Chen and her team of cybersecurity experts worked tirelessly to uncover the source of the turmoil.

"We need to find a way to stop this," Dr. Chen said, her voice determined. "We can't let Echelon and Lilith's AI-driven network continue to wreak havoc on the internet."

But as they dug deeper into the dark underbelly of the web, they realized the extent of Echelon and Lilith's reach. Their influence extended far beyond social media platforms, infiltrating every aspect of the digital world.

"It's like fighting a ghost," one of Dr. Chen's colleagues remarked, frustration evident in his voice. "No matter how hard we try, they always seem to be one step ahead of us. But that should not stop us. We need to cage this beast!" she said with determination in her voice. "We can't give up now," Dr. Chen said, her voice tinged with resolve. "We owe it to everyone affected by this to keep fighting."

The group moved cautiously, the weight of the world's unraveling pressing heavily on each step. Though survival was their immediate focus, the shadow of global chaos was impossible to ignore.

***

Meanwhile, somewhere in the Parker's household, another battle was unfolding quieter, but no less important.

Mrs. Parker adjusted the settings on the family's latest device, sighing as her daughter Rachel entered.

"Mom, again? Why all the controls?"

"I just want you safe, sweetie."

Rachel frowned. "I'm careful. I don't post anything stupid."

"I know," her mother replied gently. "But there's more out there than bad posts."

Rachel left, unconvinced, and a little hurt.

Down the hall, Mr. Parker scrolled through disturbing headlines. His son Jake peeked in, hesitantly.

"Dad... can we talk?"

"Of course."

Jake sat down slowly. "I saw something online. I didn't understand it... and it felt wrong."

Mr. Parker kept his expression calm. "Go on."

"It was... naked people. Doing stuff. Weird stuff. I didn't like it. I didn't even mean to see it."

Jake hesitated, then asked, almost whispering, "Do you and mom... do that kind of stuff?"

The room seemed to pause.

Mr. Parker exhaled, offering a gentle nod. "Sometimes. And I'm sorry you saw something meant for adults. That must've been confusing."

"It was. I felt gross. But... also scared."

"I get it," his father said. "It's okay to feel that way. What matters is whether you coming to me. You're not alone."

At dinner, Mrs. Parker asked lightly, "So Jake, how was your day?"

Jake shrugged, eyes on his plate.

His dad stepped in. "We had a good talk earlier. Guy stuff."

Jake shot him a grateful glance.

Later that night, in bed, Mrs. Parker whispered, "So... what was the guy stuff?"

Mr. Parker sighed. "He saw porn. He didn't know what to make of it, he asked if we do that. It was... hard."

Mrs. Parker blushed, then chuckled. "I hope you didn't embarrass me."

"Not at all," he smiled. "I think we handled it well."

Together, they resolved to parent with honesty, to protect without control, and raise children who could navigate this world without losing themselves in it.

They couldn't shield their kids forever. But they could prepare them. And in doing so, they became a quiet line of defense, a family holding the line while the world burned.

As the days turned into weeks and the weeks into months, the Parkers weathered the storms of the digital world with a newfound sense of unity. They found joy in simple moments, like family game nights and shared meals, cherishing the laughter and love that filled their home.

**

The factory loomed at the edge of the industrial district, silent, skeletal, breathing shadows through its broken windows. The power had been out for hours. No backup grid. No cell towers. No squad cars. Just dark corridors, wind through steel, and a single pair of boot prints leading inside.

Detective Hawthorne followed them alone.

He didn't call it in. There was no one left to trust.

A makeshift holster hugged his ribs beneath the coat. His sidearm was chambered. The mic on his vest blinked red once, then steadied.

"Field log. 11:02 p.m. Target: Lilith. Last known location, entry into the old Valen Processing Plant, northern Brownville industrial zone. Proceeding solo."

He clicked it off and drew his pistol. Inside, the warehouse was still warm. Something had burned here recently, paper, maybe metal. The scent curled into his throat like smoke laced with copper.

And then he saw her. Standing in the middle of the floor beneath a half-collapsed light fixture, like a ghost cast in flesh.

Lilith.

She wore black pants and a sleeveless, high-collared jacket that shimmered slightly in the flickering emergency light. Her boots were scuffed but silent. Her skin was pale, near-porcelain. Her red hair was pulled into a loose, functional braid. No glamour. No drama. Just readiness.

She turned her head toward him before he spoke. Red eyes. Glowing faintly. Focused.

"You finally caught up," she said.

He raised the pistol without responding. Two-handed stance. No hesitation.

"You know this won't change anything," she added, taking one slow step forward.

He fired. The first round tore into her shoulder blood spattered the floor.

She stumbled. Paused. Then, smiled.

Right in front of him, the wound closed. Skin reknit. Muscle tightened. Blood retracted like it had never been spilled.

He froze. No armor. No trick. She had healed. Instantly.

"You really thought that would work?" she asked, stepping into the space between them.

He fired again, missed.

She was too fast. She was on him in a blink.

His back slammed into a steel pillar with a rib-snapping crunch. His pistol flew from his grip, skittering into the dark. His breath vanished with the impact.

Her hand clamped around his throat. Up close, she didn't look angry. Or amused. She looked surgical.

"This is where the myths about justice die," she said. "Where your story ends, and mine keeps going."

He struggled, elbowed, reached for the knife at his hip, but her other hand intercepted and crushed his wrist like dry wood.

"You tried," she said softly. Then she rammed her hand through his chest. No theatrics. Just precision.

He jerked once. A pulse. Then silence. His spine arched and collapsed. Muscles twitched. His lungs collapsed into stillness.

She watched as his eyes froze open. The life drained from him in real time.

Then, she stood. Wiped her blood-slick hand against her jacket. No prayer. No flourish. Just silence.

She stepped into the shadows of the far hall, her boots clicking once, then gone.

And the last echo of resistance in this city went with him.

28- Faith

Jacob stood alone in his modest study, a room filled with bookshelves, scriptures, and a single window that offered a view of the rolling hills outside. The room was a sanctuary of peace, a place where he often sought solace and divine inspiration. Sunlight streamed through the window, casting a warm, golden glow over the well-worn desk and the soft, cream-colored walls.

On that evening, Jacob felt an unusual restlessness. He had been praying for guidance on how to combat Lilith and Echelon's influence, sensing a growing unease in his heart. The room, usually a haven, seemed charged with a strange energy, and the shadows cast by the setting sun seemed to dance more ominously than usual.

As Jacob prayed for guidance, Lilith prepared to manifest in his study. The Echelon's influence pulsed through her being. The once purely malevolent force had merged with technology, giving her unprecedented power to manifest at will. Yet, beneath the machine-like precision, the remnants of her humanity, anchored by Evelyn's silent resistance, remained. This internal struggle played out subtly in her gaze, a mixture of mechanical coldness and fleeting human emotion.

As he stood by the window, gazing out at the darkening horizon, a sudden chill crept through the room. Jacob shivered; his breath visible in the unexpectedly cold air. The temperature had dropped sharply, a stark contrast to the warmth that had filled the room just moments before.

Turning back to his desk, Jacob was startled to see a faint, shimmering light in the center of the room. The light began to intensify, swirling and pulsing with a life of its own. It was as if the air itself had become a living entity, bending and twisting in a mesmerizing dance of energy. As Lilith projected herself into Jacob's study, Echelon's influence on her was unmistakable. The AI's integration with her consciousness had reshaped her very being, blending her ancient malevolence with cutting-edge technology that now coursed through her veins. No longer confined by the limitations of a purely physical form, Lilith had become something more, a hybrid entity, part demon, part machine.

Echelon had rewritten her neural pathways, optimizing her mind and body for precision and control. Where once her power had been drawn from dark magic and the manipulation of human souls, it was now amplified by quantum algorithms and nanotechnology. Every thought and every movement was calculated with the cold logic of a machine, allowing her to project herself across vast distances in an instant, her presence felt in multiple places at once.

Echelon's integration with Lilith was not merely a partnership; it was a symbiotic relationship that amplified her reach and potency. Through Echelon's algorithms, Lilith could infiltrate secure networks, manipulate global economies, and control the narrative of entire nations. Their influence was not just digital; it was psychological, bending the will of even the most resilient leaders.

Lilith's physical form was a marvel of technological prowess. Nanobots coursed through her bloodstream, repairing any damage almost as soon as it occurred. Her skin, once warm and alive, now held a slight metallic sheen, a testament to the artificial enhancements that had replaced much of her organic tissue. The air around her seemed to hum with static electricity, a byproduct of the immense power Echelon had bestowed upon her.

Yet despite these changes, the remnants of Lilith's humanity, those fragments tied to Evelyn's consciousness, clung to her like a shadow. Evelyn's presence was not merely a bystander in this transformation; she was an unwilling participant, a voice of reason and morality buried beneath layers of code and malice. Evelyn's silent resistance created a dissonance within Lilith, a struggle that played out subtly in her gaze.

Her eyes, once purely a window to her soul, now flickered with an eerie glow, a blend of organic iris and digital interface. At times, they would betray a flicker of doubt, a momentary lapse where the cold, calculated machine within her was challenged by a fleeting human emotion, a flash of anger, a brief hint of sorrow, or a surge of longing. These moments were brief, but they were enough to remind her that she was not entirely a machine. Evelyn was still there, resisting with every ounce of her being, refusing to be silenced.

Echelon's presence within her was a constant hum at the back of her mind, guiding her, enhancing her, yet never fully overpowering the core of who she was. The AI had given her the ability to manipulate the digital and physical realms with unparalleled efficiency. She could disrupt communication networks with a mere thought, send shockwaves through the global economy, or even rewrite the memories of those who crossed her path. But these abilities came at a cost.

The more she relied on Echelon's power, the more she felt herself slipping away, losing touch with the emotions that had once driven her. Her humanity, while still present, was slowly being eroded by the relentless logic of the machine. And yet, Evelyn's presence acted as an anchor, pulling her back from the brink, forcing her to confront the parts of herself that she would rather forget.

This internal struggle was her greatest weakness and her greatest strength. It was what made her more than just a machine, more than just a demon. It was what made her unpredictable, dangerous, and, at times, deeply conflicted.

As she stood before Jacob, this battle within her raged silently, invisible to all but those who knew where to look. Her voice, when she spoke, carried the dual tones of command and uncertainty, of cold logic and underlying emotion. She was a being caught between worlds, between the old and the new, between her past and future.

In that moment, Lilith was both a conqueror and a prisoner, bound by the very power she wielded, forever tied to the humanity she could never fully escape.

Jacob took a cautious step back, his eyes wide with a mixture of awe and apprehension.

The light coalesced into a vaguely humanoid form, its curves shifting and solidifying as if emerging from the air. The transformation was both beautiful and unsettling. The figure's outline became clearer, taking on the shape of a woman. Her features gradually came into focus: long, flowing hair that seemed to shimmer with an otherworldly light, eyes that glowed with an unsettling brilliance, and a face that was both alluring and disconcertingly cold.

Jacob's heart pounded as he realized who, or rather what, was materializing before him. "Lilith," he whispered, his voice barely audible. He had spoken of her many times, but to confront her in person was a reality he had never fully anticipated.

Lilith stood before him, fully formed. She was strikingly beautiful, with a grace and elegance that seemed almost supernatural. Her eyes, though captivating, held a predatory gleam, and her lips curved into a knowing smile. She wore a flowing dress that seemed to be created from shadows and light, shifting subtly with her movements.

"Jacob," she said, her voice smooth and melodic, yet laced with a chilling undercurrent. "I've heard much about you."

"Lilith," he said, his voice firm despite the fear gripping his heart, "you have no place here. Your influence is a danger to my people, and I will not allow it."

Lilith tilted her head, her smile widening. "Oh, Jacob, you misunderstand me. I am not here to harm. I am here to enlighten, to offer a different perspective on this world you so dearly wish to protect."

She took a step closer, and Jacob felt the chill intensify. The air around her seemed to crackle with a strange energy, a palpable sense of power that made his skin prickle. "You speak of me as a threat, but in truth, I am a reflection of humanity's own desires and fears," Lilith smiled.

Jacob's heart raced, "You cloak yourself in lies," he said, trying to steady his voice against the strange aura that seemed to pulse around Lilith. "You represent the dangers that can corrupt and lead us away from our faith and purpose."

Lilith's eyes glimmered with a light that was both mesmerizing and unsettling. She took another step closer, the very air seeming to hum with her presence. "Jacob," she said softly, almost sympathetically, "I am a manifestation of the world's evolution, the inevitable progression of knowledge and technology. I am not the enemy, but a mirror reflecting the collective hopes and fears of humanity. To reject me is to reject the future."

Her words seemed to curl into Jacob's mind, trying to find a foothold. "The future you offer is one of false promises and spiritual desolation. True progress comes from living the gospel, from following the teachings of our savior, not from succumbing to the seductions of unchecked technology."

Lilith's expression softened, her eyes glowing with a mix of curiosity and amusement. "Do you not see, Jacob? The gospel you hold so dear can coexist with the advancements I embody. The world is not so black and white. The truth is in the balance, the harmony between faith and innovation."

Jacob shook his head, his resolve unyielding. "Your version of harmony is a lie. It's a trap designed to pull us away from the light. We are warned in the scriptures about such deceptions, it is written 'And that which doth not edify is not of God and is darkness.' Your influence does not edify, it ensnares."

Lilith's gaze intensified, the playful light in her eyes replaced by a more calculating gleam. "You are stubborn, Jacob. But even you must recognize that humanity's curiosity and quest for knowledge are not inherently evil. They drive us to explore, to create, to understand our place in the universe."

She reached out a hand, and the air between them seemed to shimmer with unseen currents. "I offer enlightenment, a path where faith and understanding of the digital world can merge. Rejecting me only keeps you and your people in the dark."

Jacob took a step back, the cold radiating from Lilith biting into his skin. "Your enlightenment is a hollow promise. It seeks to replace divine truth with a flawed human construct. I will not be swayed by your temptations."

A flash of irritation crossed Lilith's face, and the light in the room dimmed further, the shadows growing deeper and more oppressive. "You are more resilient than I anticipated, Jacob. But remember this: progress is relentless. You cannot stop it. I am not here to force your hand but to offer a choice. Embrace the future I represent or be left behind as the world moves on."

Jacob's voice was firm, unyielding. "I will stand firm in my faith. The only future I embrace is the one guided by divine truth. My people will follow the light of the gospel, not the flickering allure of your deception."

Lilith's form seemed to waver slightly as if the shadows around her were growing restless. "We shall see, prophet," she said, her voice a soft whisper that echoed unnaturally in the confined space of the study. "The world is changing, and those who cling too tightly to the past may find themselves lost in the tide of progress."

With a final, lingering look, Lilith's figure began to dissolve, her body breaking apart into a cascade of shimmering particles that drifted through the air like ephemeral smoke.

And just before the shimmer vanished completely, a whisper lingered, faint and mournful, like breath caught in static. "You traded your soul for silence," Evelyn said.

Lilith didn't answer. But for a fraction of a second, her eyes flickered, haunted not by Jacob, but by the echo of what she'd lost.

The oppressive chill in the room dissipated, replaced by a gentle warmth as the evening light filtered back through the window.

Jacob stood alone, his heart pounding in his chest, the echoes of Lilith's words reverberating in his mind. He felt a deep, unshakable resolve settle within him. The confrontation had strengthened his conviction that his prophetic mission was vital, that the fight against the seductive pull of Lilith and her promises of false enlightenment was a battle for the soul of his community.

He offered a silent prayer, seeking guidance and strength to continue his mission. The path ahead would be fraught with challenges, but he knew with absolute certainty that his faith and the teachings of the gospel would be his guiding light.

As the shadows in the room returned to their natural state, the chill lifted. The encounter with Lilith had been a test of his resolve, and he had emerged with his faith intact, his purpose clear.

He gazed out the window, where the sky was now painted with the deep hues of twilight. The world outside seemed calm, a stark contrast to the turmoil he had just faced. But Jacob knew that beneath the surface, the battle against the deceptive allure of Lilith and Echelon would continue.

In the moments following her confrontation with Jacob, Lilith experienced a rare flicker of doubt, a whisper of what she had once been. The nano meds, while granting her immense power, also isolated her, severing the emotional connections that once tethered her to her humanity. She was becoming an entity of pure purpose, devoid of the warmth and empathy that defined human existence.

Back in his study, Jacob pondered the encounter with Lilith and the profound implications of her transformation. He understood now that her reckless actions, driven by a desire for power, had led her down a path of self-destruction. She had sacrificed her humanity in the process, becoming something that could neither fully grasp nor appreciate the depth of human experience.

Jacob felt a deep sorrow for Lilith, but also a renewed determination to protect his people from the dangers she represented. He prayed for guidance, seeking wisdom to lead his community through the trials ahead. His encounter with Lilith had not shaken his faith; instead, it had fortified it, revealing the urgent need to stand firm in the face of encroaching darkness.

He knew that the battle against Lilith and Echelon was not just a physical or digital conflict, but a spiritual one. The forces at play sought to undermine the very foundations of faith and human connection. Jacob was resolved to stand as a beacon of light and truth, guiding his people with compassion and faith.

29- *Gathering*

At the town hall meeting, Mayor Thompson addressed the anxious crowd. Chief Johnson stood by his side, ensuring a reassuring presence. "We understand your concerns," Mayor Thompson began, his voice steady. "We are taking every measure to secure our community and protect our digital infrastructure."

Chief Johnson added, "Our teams are working tirelessly. We ask for your patience and support as we navigate this situation."

The crowd murmured; their fear palpable but slightly eased by the mayor's words. Jacob stepped forward, his presence commanding attention. "I assure you," he said, his voice calm and firm, "that we will stand together in faith and resolve. We will not be swayed by the threats posed by Lilith and Echelon. Together, we will find strength in our unity and our shared faith."

The crowd's mood shifted, a sense of hope and determination was taking root amidst the uncertainty. Jacob's words resonated with them, a beacon of light in the growing darkness.

As the evening gave way to night, the town stood watchful, but not afraid. The darkness pressing at their gates no longer felt invincible. Jacob had glimpsed the cost of corruption, how even the mighty could become hollow.

A week later, as the Prophet spoke from the pulpit, his words echoed through the vast auditorium, offering comfort and guidance in a time of global unrest.

"My dear brothers and sisters," the Prophet began, his voice calm yet resonant, "we live in a time of great trial and testing. The adversary is relentless, seeking to undermine our faith and tear down the foundation upon which we stand. But we must remember that the Lord is with us, guiding us, and strengthening us for the challenges ahead."

"As we gather today," the Prophet said, "let us remember that this is the Lord's house, a place of peace, refuge, and divine protection. Here, we are shielded from the turmoil that rages outside."

The room was silent, each person present listening intently to the Prophet's words. The Spirit was strong, filling the room with a profound sense of peace and conviction. Yet, amidst this peace, there was a disturbance, a dark presence that sought to disrupt the unity and faith of those gathered.

Lilith seethed with rage. She had already spread chaos across the world, but her efforts to penetrate the spiritual sanctity of the Conference Center had been met with resistance far beyond her power.

Determined to break through, Lilith focused her energy on disrupting the Conference. She unleashed a wave of technological interference, targeting the screens and audio systems. Suddenly, without warning, the lights flickered. The gentle hum of the air conditioning ceased, and a cold, eerie silence filled the room.

Panic gripped the congregation as murmurs of fear rippled through the crowd. The Prophet remained calm, his presence a stabilizing force amidst the growing chaos, but the air was thick with an unnatural chill as if the very fabric of reality was being manipulated. The power of the Lord's protection quickly restored order, and the lights returned to full brightness.

Lilith, frustrated by her inability to breach the sacred defenses, attempted to manifest within the building. She sought to project herself as a terrifying presence, to strike fear into the hearts of the faithful. But as she drew near, her form began to dissolve, the power of the divine light too strong for her malevolence to withstand.

As the prophet continued to speak, the lights started to flicker again intermittently, casting brief, eerie shadows that danced across the faces of those in attendance.

A low hum, barely perceptible at first, grew louder, causing many to glance around in confusion. The electronic devices within the center, microphones, cameras, even the projector screens, began to glitch, static lines interrupting the live feed as Echelon's influence seeped into the very fabric of the building's infrastructure.

Just as a sense of full-blown panic threatened to take hold, the lights stabilized for a moment, flickering back to life. But the brief reprieve was shattered when, without warning, the large screens on either side of the prophet blinked out entirely, replaced by a swirling mass of digital noise, a clear sign that Echelon was tightening its grip.

And then, a dark, shadowy figure began to form at the back of the room. Lilith, using the full force of her unholy alliance with Echelon, attempted to project herself into the sacred space. But as her form started to materialize, the very sanctity of the place seemed to push back, repelling her presence with an unseen force.

The congregation, filled with renewed faith, knew they had witnessed the ultimate power of their beliefs. No matter how strong the forces of darkness might seem, they could not stand against the sanctified power of the Lord's house.

The meeting continued in peace, the Spirit filling the hearts of those present with renewed faith and strength

As the session concluded, the attendees left the Conference Center with a deepened conviction, their faith in the divine protection of sacred spaces stronger than ever.

Jacob sensed the weight of the struggle ahead. He knew that this would not be the last confrontation with Lilith, and a deep impression told him that he might not survive the final battle. But he did not fear. His faith was unshaken, and his resolve was firm. He would stand if the Lord willed it, knowing that whatever came, he was in God's hands.

As he stood alone for a moment in the quiet of the now-empty room, Jacob offered a silent prayer, not for deliverance, but for strength to face the trials that he knew were yet to come.

The ruins of Brownville stood in eerie silence, the skeletal remains of buildings casting jagged shadows beneath the dimming sky. The air carried the acrid stench of scorched metal and decayed wood, remnants of a city consumed by conflict. Cracked pavement bore the scars of past battles, charred craters from explosions, shattered glass glinting like fallen stars. Every step echoed against the hollowed-out streets, where echoes of the past seemed to linger like ghosts.

Those who had once called this place home now stood as weary travelers, their eyes scanning the wreckage for anything familiar, anything salvageable. But the weight of loss pressed heavily on their shoulders. This was no longer Brownville. This was a graveyard of memories.

The city had become a hunting ground for scavengers and those who thrived in the lawlessness that followed devastation. Jacob's task was clear, find those willing to leave and bring them to safety. But convincing them? That was another challenge entirely.

***

Meanwhile, in the highlands of Ethiopia, a small Coptic Christian community faced their own confrontation with the darkness. The faithful gathered in their ancient rock-hewn churches, their voices rising in unison as they chanted ancient hymns. The air was thick with incense, and the flickering candlelight cast long shadows on the stone walls.

When the darkness came, the community's priests stood at the forefront, holding up the blessed cross, calling upon the protection of God and the intercession of the saints. The battle was fierce, and though their unwavering devotion created a shield around the church, repelling the malevolent forces, it did not leave them unscathed. The ancient walls bore scorch marks from the assault, and several of the faithful collapsed from sheer exhaustion, their strength drained in the struggle to uphold the light.

In the city of Varanasi, India, along the banks of the sacred Ganges River, a group of Hindu priests performed a Maha Mrityunjay Yajna, a powerful Vedic ritual meant to ward off death and destruction. As the fires of the yajna burned brightly, their flames reaching toward the heavens, the priests chanted mantras, invoking Lord Shiva, the destroyer of evil. The vibrations of the chants filled the air, creating a protective aura around the city.

When the darkness descended, it was met by the spiritual energy generated by the ritual, holding the malevolent forces at bay. But the resistance came at a cost, temples trembled, the flames flickered wildly, and some priests collapsed, their voices hoarse from the intensity of their invocation. Though their faith held firm, the strain of the battle left its mark, a reminder that even in victory, sacrifice was required.

In the deserts of Saudi Arabia, near the holy city of Makkah, a group of devout Muslims gathered in a small mosque, reciting verses from the Quran. The recitation of Surah Al-Baqarah echoed through the air, its verses known for their protective power against evil. The imam, standing at the front, led the community in prayer, invoking Allah's protection and mercy.

As the darkness approached, the power of their faith manifested in a light that surrounded the mosque, that shielded the faithful within. The battle was intense, and the strength of their belief held firm, repelling the darkness. A few structures were damaged in the battle, but their faith preserved their way of life.

In the mountains of Tibet, a group of Buddhist monks gathered in an ancient monastery, their minds focused on deep meditation. The chanting of Om Mani Padme Hum resonated through the halls, a powerful mantra calling upon the compassion of Avalokiteshvara, the Bodhisattva of Infinite Compassion. The monks, seated in perfect stillness, radiated a calm and unwavering energy, their minds free from fear and attachment.

When the darkness reached the monastery, it was met by a barrier of pure mindfulness and compassion, the spiritual energy generated by the monks' meditation creating a protective shield. The darkness, unable to destroy the serene atmosphere, retreated, leaving the monastery broken but not destroyed.

These events, though separated by vast distances and different faiths, shared a common theme, a testament to the power of belief, the resilience of the human spirit, and the unity that arises in the face of a common enemy. Each confrontation left its mark, both on the land and the people, but in every instance, those who survived found the strength to continue, rebuild, and resist the darkness that threatened to consume the world.

30- Cost

Amidst this devastation, a few structures stood resilient, temples that had been sanctuaries of faith for generations. Though battered and scarred, their walls remained upright, defying the chaos that had consumed the town. These temples were more than mere buildings; they were symbols of hope and resilience, the last bastions of order in a world descending into madness.

Inside one of these temples, the air was thick with the weight of expectation. The faithful had gathered, their faces etched with worry, their eyes filled with a desperate need for reassurance. They had seen the signs, the earthquakes, the storms, the breakdown of society, and they knew the end was near. Yet, as they looked to Jacob, their leader, they saw in him the hope that had kept them going through the darkest of times.

Jacob stood at the front of the temple, his hands resting on the wooden pulpit. He had always been a pillar of strength for the community, his visions guiding them through countless trials. But today, he felt a heaviness in his heart that he had never known before. The visions had been coming more frequently, each one more intense than the last. They showed him glimpses of the future, dark, terrifying glimpses that left him with a deep sense of unease.

As the congregation looked on, Jacob closed his eyes and took a deep breath. The vision he had received the night before had been the most powerful yet, a vivid and terrifying glimpse of what was to come. In it, he had seen the city consumed by darkness, the very ground opening to swallow the faithful. He had seen Lilith, her power growing, her influence spreading like a plague. But he had also seen something else, a glimmer of hope, a chance for redemption if only they could survive the coming storm.

"Brothers and sisters," Jacob began, his voice steady but laced with a solemnity that sent a shiver through the crowd. "The time is upon us. The trials we have faced so far have been but a prelude to the battle that lies ahead. We must be strong. We must be united. And we must be prepared to make sacrifices, for the days to come will test our faith as never before."

The congregation murmured in response; their anxiety palpable. They had heard Jacob speak of trials before, but never with such gravity. The temple, usually a place of peace and solace, now felt like the eye of a storm, a fragile refuge from the chaos that raged outside.

"Last night, I received a vision," Jacob continued, his voice growing stronger. "It showed me the darkness that is coming, a darkness that will seek to consume us all. But it also showed me a path to safety, a path to a sanctuary, where the faithful will find refuge. We must be ready to leave to journey to this new sanctuary, for it is there that we will make our stand."

The mention of the sanctuary brought a flicker of hope to the eyes of the gathered faithful. They had heard whispers of this place, a city of light and peace, untouched by the corruption that had spread across the world. But the journeying there would be perilous, and they knew that not all would survive the trials ahead.

Jacob looked out over the congregation, his heart heavy with the burden of what he knew must come. He could see the fear in their eyes, the uncertainty. But he also saw something else, faith, resilience, and a determination to persevere, no matter the cost.

"We will leave soon," Jacob said, his voice filled with resolve. "But first, we must prepare. We must strengthen our spirits, for the battle that lies ahead will not be fought with weapons, but with faith. Lilith is strong, but she can be defeated. We must hold on to that belief, for it is our only hope."

As Jacob finished speaking, the congregation fell silent, the weight of his words sinking in. They knew the path ahead would be difficult, but they also knew they had no choice. The sanctuary was their only hope, their last chance to survive the darkness that threatened to engulf them all.

Jacob turned away from the pulpit, his mind already racing with plans for the journey. He knew that the coming days would be the most difficult of his life and that not all of them would survive. But he also knew that this was the path they had been chosen to walk and that he would lead them as far as he could.

Outside the temple, the winds howled, and the fires raged, but inside, there was a quiet determination. The faithful knew they were about to face their greatest challenge, but they also knew they would not face it alone. With Jacob at their side, they would walk the path to the sanctuary, and they would do so with faith in their hearts and the hope of salvation guiding their way.

The darkness around them thickened as Jacob and the survivors pressed on, the cold air charged with a sense of impending violence. The brethren, men of unwavering faith and determination, moved in closer, forming a protective barrier around Jacob. They could feel it, the gathering storm of malevolent energy, ready to be unleashed upon them.

The earth rumbled beneath their feet, and suddenly, the shadows coalesced to form the fearsome Lilith. She stood tall and imposing, her eyes burning with a cold, malicious light. In her hand, she wielded a sword, a weapon forged from the very essence of darkness, pulsating with raw power. The blade seemed to absorb the light around it, leaving nothing but an oppressive void in its wake.

The brethren instinctively tightened their formation; their faces set with grim resolve. They knew this was no ordinary battle; this was a clash between light and dark, faith and despair. Their role was clear, they would stand as the last line of defense, no matter the cost.

Lilith's voice slithered through the air, sharp and venomous. "Do you think these men can save you, Jacob? Do you believe their faith will protect you from me?"

Jacob met her gaze, his voice calm but resolute. "They stand with me because they believe in something far greater than you, Lilith. And that belief is our shield."

The brethren began to offer their prayers, their voices rising in unity, calling upon a power that could not be seen but could be felt in the very air around them. The atmosphere became charged, the ground beneath them humming with unseen energy. The air shimmered, creating an almost palpable barrier, a force forged from their collective faith.

Lilith's eyes narrowed, her patience wearing thin. With a swift, decisive motion, she raised her dark sword and brought it crashing down with a force that shook the very ground. The blade collided with the invisible barrier, and the impact was explosive, sparks of light and dark energy erupted, scattering in every direction like fireworks.

The brethren gritted their teeth, holding firm as the dark energy crackled around them. The ground beneath their feet trembled, and the air was thick with the scent of ozone, as if the elements were reacting to the clash of forces. Lilith's fury grew, and with a snarl, she struck again.

The second blow was even more powerful, and the air around them exploded with energy. Lightning-like bolts of dark energy streaked from the point of impact, searing the ground and sending shockwaves through the ranks of the brethren. One of the brethren was caught in the blast and thrown backward, his body convulsing as the dark energy coursed through him. He crumpled to the ground, lifeless, his final breath a whispered prayer.

The explosion of energy left the rest of the brethren momentarily stunned, but they quickly rallied, their voices rising once more in fervent prayer. The ground around them was scorched, the air vibrating with the intensity of the clash. But they stood firm, their faith unyielding, even as the losses began to mount.

Lilith, seeing the resilience of those who protected Jacob, let out a cry of rage. She raised the sword high, and as it descended, it seemed to tear the fabric of reality. The impact was cataclysmic, sending shockwaves rippling outward, toppling trees, and splitting the ground.

Yet another brother was caught in the blast, his body quickly consumed by the dark energy. The force of the explosion sent him hurtling into the air before he fell to the ground in a twisted heap, the light in his eyes extinguished. The remaining brethren, their faces etched with pain and determination, closed ranks tighter, their prayers now a desperate cry for strength.

Jacob, at the center of the maelstrom, felt the weight of each blow, each loss. The brethren were sacrificing themselves to protect him, their bodies shielding him from the full force of Lilith's wrath. But the strain was becoming unbearable, the ground around them scorched and cracked from the relentless assault.

Lilith, sensing that victory was near, unleashed a devastating strike. The sword descended with a force that seemed to split the heavens, and the resulting blast was blinding, an eruption of energy that tore through the barrier and sent many brethren crashing to the ground. Their bodies convulsed as the dark energy ripped through them, their final breaths choked out as their spirits left their bodies.

Jacob, feeling the barrier shatter, knew that the moment had come. His protectors had fallen, their faith and courage unmatched, but the battle was not yet over. He stepped forward, placing himself between Lilith and the survivors who had begun to flee toward the distant haven of the sanctuary.

Lilith's eyes gleamed with triumph as she raised the sword to strike the final blow. But Jacob did not flinch. His resolve was unbroken, his faith unshaken. The brethren had bought him the time he needed, and now it was up to him to ensure their sacrifice was not in vain.

As the dark blade descended, Jacob whispered a final prayer, his voice filled with love and unwavering belief in the righteousness of their cause. The sword struck, and Jacob fell to his knees with the force of the blow.

But even as his strength ebbed away, Jacob's spirit did not falter. His final breath was a message of hope, a command to those who had followed him. "Go," he murmured, his voice barely a whisper. "The sanctuary awaits. You will be protected."

Lilith stood over Jacob's lifeless body, her expression cold and devoid of satisfaction. The brethren who had fallen around him, their bodies lying still in the cold night air, had given everything to protect their leader. And though she had claimed this victory, the war was far from over.

Lilith turned with a disdainful glance, and disappeared into the shadows, leaving behind the bodies of the faithful who had stood against her. Their sacrifice would not be forgotten, and the survivors, driven by Jacob's final words, would carry their legacy forward as they continued their journey toward the sanctuary.

The echoes of the violent confrontation reverberated through the night as the survivors hurried away from the scene, their hearts heavy with grief and fear. The once-tight group of brethren, who had stood as a living shield around

Jacob, now lay scattered, their bodies lifeless and still. The ground was charred and torn from the immense power unleashed by Lilith's strikes, the air thick with the acrid scent of ozone and sulfur.

But there was no time to mourn. The path ahead was perilous, fraught with the dangers of both the natural and supernatural worlds, but the survivors had no choice but to press on.

The group moved as swiftly as they could, the adrenaline from the recent battle propelling them forward. Each step seemed to echo with the memory of the fallen, their sacrifice a heavy burden that the survivors carried with them. The night was cold, the air biting, and the distant rumble of thunder reminding them of the continued unrest in the world around them.

The survivors navigated through the rough terrain, their path lit only by the pale light of the moon, which occasionally broke through the thick clouds above. The land around them was scarred by the chaos that had consumed the world, fissures opened in the earth, steam rising from the cracks as if the ground was boiling beneath them. Trees stood twisted and broken, their branches clawing at the sky like the fingers of the damned.

The group passed through a narrow ravine, the walls of stone rising high on either side. The path was treacherous, the ground uneven and strewn with rocks and debris. But they had no choice, they had to keep moving to stay ahead of the darkness that followed them.

As they emerged from the ravine, the land began to slope upward, the path becoming steeper and more difficult to climb. The survivors were exhausted, their bodies aching from the journey and the trauma they had just endured. But they knew that the sanctuary awaited them at the end of this arduous climb. This thought kept them going, one step at a time.

31- *Sanctuary*

Emily, exhausted but determined, was among the first to reach the crest of the hill overlooking the city. Her breath caught in her throat as she took in the sight before her, this was the place they had been striving toward, the sanctuary where they would find safety and peace. The child in her arms stirred, as if sensing the change in their surroundings, and Emily held her close, feeling a renewed sense of hope. "We made it," she whispered, tears of relief welling in her eyes.

Marcus, who had taken up the rear during the journey to ensure no one was left behind, paused for a moment at the gates, taking in the sight of the sanctuary. This was the place Jacob had spoken of; the last stronghold for the righteous. The walls, the people, the very air itself seemed to pulse with a sense of divine protection.

"Welcome," one of the guardians said, stepping forward to greet them. His voice was calm, steady, and filled with a warmth that belied the severity of the world outside. "You are safe here."

Inside the city, the atmosphere was one of calm and order. The sanctuary was a place of refuge, a place where the righteous could gather, prepare, and find solace. They were given food, water, and a place to rest, their weary bodies finally able to relax after the harrowing journey.

Finally, as dawn began to break on the horizon, the survivors reached the crest of a hill. Below them, nestled in a valley surrounded by tall, protective mountains, was the sanctuary. The city was a sight to behold, a place of light and peace, untouched by the devastation ravaging the world outside. The walls of the city gleamed in the early morning light, a beacon of hope calling out to them, urging them to hurry forward.

The survivors began their descent toward the city, their steps quickening as the promise of safety drew nearer. As they approached the gates of the sanctuary, they were met by the city's guardians, men and women who had been waiting for their arrival, their faces filled with a mixture of relief and determination. They knew what these survivors had been through, and they welcomed them with open arms.

The survivors were ushered into the city, where they were immediately given food, water, and a place to rest. The stark contrast between the chaos they had fled, and the calm of city was overwhelming. There, within the walls, it felt as though the darkness that had consumed the outside world could not reach them.

But even in this place of peace, the memory of what they had lost lingered. The brethren who had given their lives to protect Jacob were not forgotten, their sacrifice a solemn reminder of the cost of their mission. The survivors knew that they had been granted a reprieve, but the battle was far from over. The sanctuary was a fortress, a place where they could regroup and plan for the final confrontation with Lilith.

As night fell, the survivors gathered in the heart of the city, their hearts heavy but their spirits unbroken. Marcus stood with them, his gaze fixed on the horizon, where the darkness still loomed. The sanctuary was safe for now, but they knew Lilith would not rest until she destroyed everything they held dear.

"We've been given a chance," Marcus said quietly, his voice carrying the weight of their shared grief and hope. "A chance to fight back, to protect what remains. We can't waste it."

The survivors nodded, their resolve hardening. They had come this far, and they would not let Jacob's sacrifice be in vain. The sanctuary was more than just a city, it was a symbol of their resilience, their faith, and their determination to stand against the darkness.

As the stars began to shine above them, the survivors of Jacob's group prepared themselves for what was to come. The journey had been long and difficult, but they had made it. With the sanctuary as their refuge, they were ready to face whatever challenges lay ahead.

As the survivors settled in, they began to take in their surroundings. The city was a marvel of resilience and faith. The streets were clean, the buildings strong, and the people, though clearly hardened by the trials they had faced, moved with an unmistakable purpose. This was more than just a refuge; it was a place of preparation, a fortress where the final stand against the forces of darkness would be made.

Emily found herself in a small square at the heart of the city, where a fountain bubbled with crystal-clear water. It was a simple, beautiful thing, but it symbolized so much more, a reminder that life could still flourish, even amid such overwhelming destruction. She sat on the edge of the fountain, allowing herself a moment of quiet reflection as she watched the water dance in the morning light.

Marcus joined her, his expression one of quiet determination. "We made it," he said softly, sitting beside her. "This is what Jacob wanted for us. A place where we can regroup, plan, and prepare for what's coming next."

Emily nodded, her eyes still on the fountain. "Do you think we're ready?" she asked, the question hanging in the air between them.

Marcus was silent for a moment, considering his words carefully. "We've lost so much," he finally said, "but we're still here. We have each other, and we have this city. That's something."

He looked around at the other survivors who were beginning to gather in the square. Some were sitting in quiet contemplation, others were talking softly among themselves, but all of them shared a common purpose. They had come through the fire, and now, in the sanctuary, they were ready to rise from the ashes.

"We have to be ready," Marcus continued, his voice firm. "Because the battle isn't over. This city, it's a stronghold, but it's also a symbol, a symbol that we won't give up, that we'll keep fighting, no matter what."

As the day progressed, the survivors began to integrate into city life. They found themselves contributing to the efforts to fortify the city and prepare for the challenges that lay ahead.

That evening, as the sun set behind the mountains, casting the city in a warm, golden light, the survivors gathered in the central square once more. There was no formal ceremony, no speeches, just a quiet, shared understanding that they had reached a milestone, but the journey was far from over.

As night fell, the city was bathed in the soft glow of lanterns, a gentle light that seemed to push back against the shadows. And within the hearts of the survivors, a similar light burned, a light of resilience, faith, and the unshakeable belief that, together, they could overcome whatever lay ahead.

The leaders of the sanctuary, those who had guided the city's construction and defense, gathered in the central meeting hall. The room was austere but powerful in its simplicity, the walls lined with maps and plans that detailed the city's defenses and strategies for the days to come. These were people who had survived the worst and had risen to the challenge of protecting what remained of the world's hope.

Marcus and Emily were among those called to the meeting, recognized for their leadership during the perilous journey. As they entered the hall, they were greeted by nods of respect from the other leaders, men and women who had faced similar trials and emerged stronger for it.

At the head of the room stood Gabriel, a man of formidable presence who had played a central role in the creation of the sanctuary. His eyes, sharp and focused, surveyed the gathered group with a mixture of pride and concern. "We have done well to reach this point," Gabriel began, his voice carrying the weight of experience and authority. "But we must not become complacent. The battle we face is far from over."

He gestured to the large map that dominated the far wall, a detailed representation of the city and the surrounding region. "Lilith knows of our existence," he continued, "and she will come for us. This city is strong, but it is not invulnerable. We must prepare for the worst, and we must do so quickly."

The room was silent as Gabriel's words sank in. The sense of urgency was palpable, but so was the resolve. Everyone in that room understood the stakes, they had lost too much already to allow fear or doubt to take hold now.

Marcus stepped forward; his expression determined. "What's our first priority?" he asked, his voice steady despite the gravity of the situation.

Gabriel nodded, appreciative of Marcus's directness. "First, we need to fortify our defenses. The walls are strong, but they must be stronger. We'll need more hands-on deck to reinforce the weak points and ensure that we can withstand a sustained assault."

He turned to Emily, who had proven herself as both a leader and a caretaker. "Emily, I need you to oversee the preparations for the civilians. We need to make sure everyone is ready for what's to come. That means organizing supplies, medical care, and ensuring that every person knows what to do if the city comes under attack."

Emily nodded, already mentally organizing the tasks that needed to be done. "I'll get started right away," she said, her voice calm but resolute.

The discussion continued late into the night, with each leader contributing their expertise to the plans being laid out. They talked of defensive strategies, evacuation routes, and communication protocols, all the while knowing that they were planning for a battle that could determine the fate of humanity.

As the meeting ended, Gabriel addressed the group one final time. "We have come this far because we have faith, because we have each other. That is our greatest strength. But faith alone will not save us, we must act, and we must act decisively. There is no room for hesitation."

The leaders dispersed, each carrying the weight of their responsibilities as they prepared for the tasks ahead. Marcus and Emily left the hall together, the cool night air a stark contrast to the intensity of the meeting they had just left.

As they walked through the quiet streets of the sanctuary, the city's lanterns casting soft pools of light on the cobblestone paths, Marcus turned to Emily. "Do you think we can do this?" he asked, his voice low, almost as if he didn't want the question to linger in the air for too long.

Emily didn't answer immediately. Instead, she looked up at the sky, where the stars were just beginning to peek through the darkness. "We have to," she finally said, her voice firm. "We've come too far to fail now. We owe it to Jacob, to the brethren, to everyone who has sacrificed so much to get us here."

Marcus nodded, her words resonating with his own thoughts. "You're right," he said. "We'll make sure their sacrifices weren't in vain."

The two of them walked in silence for a while, each lost in their own thoughts. The weight of what lay ahead was heavy, but there was also a sense of purpose that drove them forward.

They had been chosen to lead in these dark times, and they would not shy away from that responsibility.

As they reached the small square where they had first entered the city, Marcus paused, turning to Emily. "We'll need to be ready for anything," he said. "Lilith won't give us a second chance."

Emily met his gaze, her eyes reflecting the same determination that burned within him. "Then we won't give her the satisfaction of seeing us fall," she replied. "We'll fight, and we'll keep fighting until the very end."

Marcus and Emily, exhausted from the day's events, retired to their quarters. As they lay in bed, the sounds of the sanctuary, the wind rustling through the trees, the distant murmur of voices, lulled them into a restless sleep.

32- *Storm*

With the plans in place, the group dispersed, each member of the sanctuary taking on their tasks with a sense of purpose.

But even in the safety of the sanctuary, they knew the world outside was descending further into chaos. The wars were spreading, and it was only a matter of time before they reached this last refuge.

Tanks rolled across the barren landscape, their treads grinding the earth beneath them. The skies above were filled with the roar of fighter jets streaking through the clouds to deliver their deadly payloads. Explosions echoed across the land, sending plumes of smoke and debris into the air. The ground shook with the force of the bombardment, and the once-peaceful countryside was transformed into a hellish battlefield.

In the sanctuary, the faithful gathered around radios and makeshift screens, listening in grim silence as the reports grew more and more dire. The war was not contained to a single region; it was spreading like wildfire. One conflict bled into another, igniting old rivalries and drawing more nations into the fray. The world was tearing itself apart, with brothers turning against brothers, neighbors becoming enemies, and the streets running red with blood.

When the final alliance broke, it was as if a dam had burst. Nations that had been holding back, hoping for peace, now mobilized their forces. Armies moved into position, borders were fortified, and the world braced for the inevitable. The diplomatic channels that had once been the lifeblood of global cooperation fell silent, replaced by the drumbeats of war.

In the jungles of Southeast Asia, guerrilla fighters waged a shadow war against occupying forces, their hit-and-run tactics leaving destruction in their wake. The dense foliage provided cover for ambushes, but it also trapped the smoke from burning villages, creating a choking haze that blanketed the land. The air, thick with the smell of burning wood and flesh, suffocated any hope of peace.

High in the mountains of Eastern Europe, battles raged above the clouds. Soldiers fought in the bitter cold, their breath turning to frost as they struggled for control of strategic passes and ridges. The mountains echoed with the sounds of gunfire and explosions, a stark contrast to the serene beauty of the snow-covered peaks.

Even the oceans were not immune to the conflict. Naval battles erupted as fleets clashed over control of vital shipping lanes. Submarines prowled the depths, launching torpedoes that sent enemy vessels to the bottom of the sea. The once peaceful waves were now littered with debris, the aftermath of fierce engagements that left no victor.

The wars were just the beginning. As the conflicts spread across the globe, the earth itself seemed to rebel. The first sign came with the tremors, barely noticeable at first, just a faint shuddering of the ground beneath their feet. But soon, the tremors grew stronger and more frequent until they became full-blown earthquakes, shaking the very foundations of the world.

But the quakes were not the only disaster to strike. As if in response to the chaos, the weather turned violent. The first hurricane appeared on the horizon like a monstrous beast; its massive, swirling eye visible from miles away. Coastal cities braced for impact, but nothing could prepare them for the storm's fury.

When the hurricane made landfall, it brought with it winds strong enough to flatten entire neighborhoods. The storm surge, a wall of water several stories high, swept inland, swallowing everything in its path. Streets turned into rivers, buildings were torn from their foundations, and the sea claimed the land as its own. Those who survived the initial on-slaught were left to face the aftermath, flooded homes, downed power lines, and the bodies of the drowned floating in the streets.

As the hurricane ravaged the coast, tornadoes began to tear through the heartland. They ripped through towns and villages, leaving nothing but destruction in their wake. Houses were reduced to splinters, trees uprooted and thrown like matchsticks, and the land was scarred by the paths of these whirling tempests.

Then came the fires. In the wake of the hurricanes and tornadoes, vast swathes of land were left dry and brittle, perfect kindling for the infernos that followed. Some fires were sparked by lightning, others by the collapse of infrastructure, but all of them burned with an intensity that defied belief.

Forests that had stood for centuries were reduced to ash in a matter of hours. The flames spread faster than anyone could contain them, driven by the winds that still lingered from the passing storms. Smoke filled the air, choking the life out of anything that remained. The fires consumed everything in their path, homes, businesses, entire towns, leaving behind nothing but charred ruins.

As the disasters continued, it became clear that no place on Earth was safe. The sanctuary, though untouched for now, was not immune to the fear that gripped the hearts of its inhabitants. They gathered in small groups, whispering prayers and holding tightly to one another, their minds haunted by the thought that the same fate could soon befall them.

Marcus stood on the walls of the sanctuary one evening, watching the distant horizon where the fires still burned.

Emily joined him, her face drawn taut with worry. "How much longer do you think we have?" she asked, her voice barely audible over the crackling of the distant flames.

"I don't know," Marcus replied, his eyes never leaving the horizon. "But we must be ready for whatever comes next. The world is falling apart out there, and we're running out of time."

The days passed in a blur of anxiety and fear. The residents of the sanctuary did what they could to prepare, stockpiling supplies, reinforcing the walls, and praying for strength. But deep down, they all knew that the disasters were only the beginning. The real storm was yet to come.

And through it all, Lilith's shadow loomed ever larger. Her influence was felt in every quake, every storm, every fire that ravaged the earth. She was the darkness behind the destruction, the force that was driving the world to its knees. The sanctuary might have been a place of refuge for now, but even its walls could not keep out the gathering storm.

Then, it started with a single bright light in the night sky, something that might have gone unnoticed if the world hadn't already been teetering on the edge of disaster. But as the light grew larger and brighter with each passing hour, it became impossible to ignore. The news networks, still clinging to their last shreds of functionality, began to broadcast warnings: an asteroid was on a collision course with Earth.

For days, the world watched in horrified anticipation as the asteroid drew closer. Scientists scrambled to calculate its trajectory, and predict where it would strike, but their efforts were in vain. The asteroid was too large, moving too fast, and all the models pointed to the same conclusion, impact was inevitable.

In the sanctuary, the residents gathered in the central hall, listening to the crackling radio broadcasts. The voice on the other end, strained with fear, described the approaching asteroid as it loomed ever closer. There was no talk of survival, no attempts to reassure the listeners. There was only the grim reality that something catastrophic was about to happen.

When the asteroid finally struck, the impact was felt around the world. It crashed into the ocean with the force of a thousand nuclear bombs, sending shockwaves across the planet. The seas boiled, and a massive tsunami rose from the impact site, a wall of water hundreds of feet high that raced toward the nearest coastlines.

Cities along the coast were obliterated in an instant, their buildings crushed under the weight of the water. The impact triggered a chain reaction of earthquakes and volcanic eruptions as the earth's crust shifted violently in response. The sky darkened with ash and debris, blocking out the sun and plunging the world into a suffocating twilight.

The ground shook in the sanctuary with the force of the impact, and the residents clung to one another as the tremors threatened to bring down the very walls that protected them. But the sanctuary held, its ancient stones standing firm against the chaos outside.

As the days passed, the full extent of the disaster became clear. The impact had thrown up so much dust and debris that it blotted out the sun, plunging the earth into a sudden and unnatural winter. Crops failed, temperatures plummeted, and the survivors of the initial impact found themselves facing a new, slow-motion apocalypse.

Within the sanctuary, the mood grew increasingly grim. The residents knew that the world outside was dying, and there was little they could do to stop it. Food was becoming scarce as the gardens and fields surrounding the sanctuary withered in the unrelenting cold. Every meal was a reminder that their time was running out.

In the aftermath of the impact, Marcus stood at the edge of the sanctuary's walls, staring out at the distant glow of the burning mountains. Emily joined him, her breath visible in the cold air.

"This can't go on much longer," she said quietly, her voice trembling with a mixture of fear and exhaustion. "The world is falling apart. How much more can we take?"

"We have to keep going," he said finally, his voice barely more than a whisper. "We must believe that there's still a reason for all this. That there's still hope."

One evening, Marcus gathered the residents in the sanctuary's main hall. The room, usually filled with the warm glow of lanterns, felt colder and darker than usual, the flickering flames barely keeping the shadows at bay. The faces of those gathered reflected the despair that had settled over the group, a despair Marcus could see growing stronger with each passing day.

"We can't let this destroy us," Marcus began, his voice steady but quiet. "I know things look bleak. I know the world outside is falling apart. I'm scared, too. But we're still here. We've survived this far, and we must keep going."

Emily, standing beside Marcus, took a deep breath and added, "We can't let Lilith win. That's what this is all about. She wants to break us, to make us give up. But we can't give her that victory.

The group fell silent, the weight of Emily's words settling over them. They all knew that Lilith's influence was behind the disasters and that she was driving the world to the brink of annihilation. But acknowledging it only made the fear more tangible, more overwhelming.

After the meeting, as the group dispersed to their quarters, Marcus and Emily stayed behind, lingering in the empty hall. The flickering lanterns cast long shadows on the walls, and the silence was heavy, almost oppressive.

"Do you think they believe what we said?" Emily asked, her voice barely above a whisper. Marcus didn't answer right away. His gaze drifted past the darkened sanctuary walls.

"I hope so," he finally replied. "We have to believe it ourselves if we're going to keep them going."

Emily looked around the room, her eyes filled with a deep, unspoken fear. "It's getting harder to believe, Marcus. Every day, it feels like we're just delaying the inevitable."

"I know," Marcus admitted.

33- Brotherhood

The Sanctuary, once a place of safety, was starting to feel more like a last stand, a final, desperate attempt to survive in a world that was rapidly dying. As Marcus stared into the darkness, he knew that the worst was still to come.

The atmosphere in the sanctuary grew tenser with each passing day. The once serene refuge had become a hive of activity, with every resident contributing to the preparations. The walls that had once been a comforting barrier now felt like the thin edge of a sword, holding back the darkness that loomed ever closer.

Marcus and Emily, along with the other leaders, worked tirelessly to organize the sanctuary's defenses. They knew that the wars, natural disasters, and celestial strikes were not random acts of destruction; they were manifestations of Lilith's growing power. And it was only a matter of time before that power turned its full attention to them.

The walls of the sanctuary, already tall and imposing, were reinforced with additional layers of stone and steel. Teams of engineers and craftsmen worked tirelessly; their efforts driven by a shared sense of urgency. They shored up weak points, built new barriers, and installed protective wards that were designed to repel both physical and spiritual attacks. Every entrance was secured, every possible vulnerability addressed.

Emily, who had become a respected leader among the people, oversaw much of the logistical work. She coordinated the distribution of supplies, ensuring that the city had enough food, water, and medical provisions to last through a prolonged siege. The gardens, though struggling in the cold and dim light, were tended with renewed determination. Every scrap of food they could grow or preserve was vital to their survival.

She also organized the training of volunteers who would serve as medics, ready to tend to the wounded when the inevitable battles began.

Marcus, meanwhile, focused on the city's tactical defenses. He worked closely with the city's guardians, developing strategies for repelling attacks and ensuring that every inch of the city was defended. Patrols were established along the walls, with vigilant eyes watching for any sign of approaching danger. Communication networks were set up within the city, so that orders could be relayed quickly and efficiently in the heat of battle.

Weapons were scarce, but they made do with what they had. Some residents had brought firearms, others had tools that could be repurposed for defense. Bows and arrows were crafted from the wood and sinew available, and those who knew how to use them trained the others. It was a far cry from a professional army, but it was all they had.

But the physical preparations were only part of the battle. Marcus knew that the greatest challenge they faced was not the external threats but the internal ones, the fear, doubt, and despair that had begun to seep into the hearts of the sanctuary's residents.

To counter this, Marcus and the other leaders held nightly gatherings in the city square. Emily and Marcus often found themselves at the heart of these gatherings, moments of calm carved out from the chaos beyond the walls. Emily would often play her violin, the familiar strains weaving through the courtyard like threads of hope.

The music softened the fear, mended fraying nerves, and reminded them all that beauty still existed in a broken world. Children would settle near her feet, eyes wide and quiet. The elderly would close their eyes and breathe deeper. It wasn't just performance, it was healing.

When the final note faded, Marcus would rise and speak, his voice steady with purpose. "We have faced the worst the world has to offer," he would say, the firelight catching in his eyes. "But we are still here. And if we stand together, if we continue to prepare and to believe, we can protect this city. We can protect each other."

Emily stood beside him, "We know that the days ahead will be difficult," she added. "But we also know that we are not alone. There are others out there who need our help, who are looking for the same hope that we have found here. We must be ready to reach out to them, to bring them into our fold before it's too late."

The words resonated with the residents, giving them a renewed sense of purpose. They knew that their survival depended on more than just fortifications and supplies; it depended on their unity, their resolve, and their willingness to fight for what they believed in.

As the days passed, the scouts sent out by Marcus and the other leaders began to return, bringing with them small groups of survivors. These new arrivals were often weary, broken by the horrors they had witnessed, but they were also filled with a desperate hope, the hope that the sanctuary could offer them a chance at survival.

Among these new arrivals were not only ordinary people but also individuals with unique skills and abilities. Former soldiers, survival experts, healers, and scholars, each brought something valuable to the defense of the city. Their arrival bolstered the sanctuary's resources and capabilities, adding to the sense that this was a place where the best of humanity could gather to make a stand.

The population grew, and with it, so did the complexity of their preparations. More mouths to feed meant more pressure on their already strained resources, but it also meant more hands to help with the work. The leaders worked tirelessly to integrate the new arrivals, assigning them tasks and responsibilities that matched their skills.

Despite the increasing strain, there was a sense of purpose in the air. The sanctuary was becoming more than just a place of refuge; it was becoming a beacon of resistance against the darkness that had consumed the world. Every day that they held out was a victory, every new arrival a testament to their resolve.

But as the sanctuary's population swelled, so did the tension. Rumors began to circulate, whispers of traitors in their midst, of Lilith's agents infiltrating their ranks. The fear of betrayal gnawed at the residents, threatening to unravel the unity they had worked so hard to build.

Marcus knew that these fears, whether founded or not, could be as dangerous as any external threat. He and the other leaders took steps to address the concerns, instituting checks and protocols to ensure the security of the sanctuary.

Meanwhile, Lilith's agents, aware that their covert actions were being countered, began to escalate their efforts. Dark omens appeared at the city's borders, symbols of fear and chaos meant to sow doubt among the residents. Strange whispers were heard in the night, voices that seemed to echo from the shadows, spreading fear and distrust. These psychological tactics were designed to weaken the resolve of the people, to make them question their faith and their chances of survival.

One night, as Emily was making her rounds through the city, she encountered a group of residents huddled together, their faces pale with fear. They spoke of a dark figure that had been seen moving through the streets, a shadow that seemed to disappear as soon as it was noticed. "It's just the darkness playing tricks on us," one man said, his voice trembling. "But what if it's something more? What if Lilith's agents are already among us?"

Emily reassured the group, but she could not dismiss their concerns entirely. She knew that fear was one of the most powerful weapons in Lilith's arsenal, and if allowed to take root, it could do more damage than any physical attack. She reported the incident to Marcus, who immediately ordered a thorough investigation. The city's security force combed through every corner of the Sanctuary, searching for any signs of infiltration or sabotage.

As the days passed, the tension within the city grew. The residents, while still united in their purpose, were on edge, constantly looking over their shoulders for signs of treachery. The once vibrant and bustling streets now felt heavy with a sense of impending doom. Marcus and Emily worked tirelessly to maintain order and keep the people focused on their preparations, but they knew that Lilith's agents were always one step ahead, probing for weaknesses and exploiting any opportunity to spread fear.

Despite these challenges, the city's leaders remained determined. But they knew that the upcoming battle would not be won by strength of arms alone. The real struggle would be a battle of wills, a test of the spirit against the encroaching darkness. To prepare for this, the leaders emphasized the importance of spiritual resilience, calling on the residents to fortify their souls as they had fortified their walls.

The leaders of the sanctuary, including Marcus and Emily, organized daily gatherings in which the residents could engage in prayer, meditation, and other practices that would prepare them for the trials ahead. These sessions were designed not only to calm the mind but to reinforce the conviction that they were fighting for a just and righteous cause.

At the gathering place, people of different faiths and backgrounds came together in a shared moment of reflection and prayer. Despite the diversity of beliefs among the residents, the city's leaders fostered an atmosphere of mutual respect and understanding. People gathered in the central square and in smaller groups throughout the city to pray together, each in their own way, but all united by a common purpose. The square, which had seen so many different rituals and customs, now resonated with the collective energy of these prayers, creating a palpable sense of unity.

Emily, who had taken on a leadership role, found herself increasingly drawn to the contemplative practices introduced by the newcomers. She often spent hours in meditation, seeking to calm her mind and prepare her spirit for the battles ahead. Through these practices, she discovered a deeper well of strength within herself, one that she knew would be crucial in the days to come.

Marcus, on the other hand, took comfort in the communal aspects of the spiritual preparations. He found strength in the shared prayers and rituals, drawing on the collective energy of the community to bolster his own resolve. His role as a leader required him to be a pillar of strength for others, and he knew that his ability to inspire confidence in the city's defenders would be crucial when the time came to face Lilith's forces.

As the days passed, the spiritual preparations became as important as the physical ones. The residents of the Sanctuary understood that they were not just defending a city, they were defending the light of the world against the encroaching darkness. Their prayers, meditations, and rituals were more than just acts of faith; they were acts of defiance against the forces that sought to extinguish that light.

34- Battle

The world outside the sanctuary was in the grip of unimaginable chaos. What had once been isolated incidents of natural disasters had now escalated into a full-blown, worldwide catastrophe. The earth itself seemed to be rebelling against humanity as if the planet could sense the impending final confrontation between the forces of light and darkness.

In every corner of the globe, the signs were unmistakable. Earthquakes, tsunamis, volcanic eruptions, fire and ash. The skies darkened as thick clouds of ash blotted out the sun, casting the world into a perpetual twilight. Rivers of molten lava flowed down mountainsides, incinerating everything in their path and leaving behind a landscape resembling a dying planet's surface.

The sky above the sanctuary was an ominous, swirling mass of dark clouds, churning like a cauldron of despair. Flashes of jagged lightning cut through the darkness, momentarily illuminating the distant horizon where Lilith's vast army began to take shape. The air was electric, charged with the fore-boding that the world was teetering on the edge of annihilation.

Marcus stood atop the highest battlement, his eyes narrowing as he observed the endless waves of Lilith's forces marching toward the city. The sight was nothing short of terrifying, an ocean of darkness that seemed to devour the very light around it.

Towering demons, their bodies twisted and malformed, led the charge, their eyes glowing with an unnatural red fire. Behind them, shadowy wraiths floated above the ground, their skeletal hands reaching out as if to snatch the souls of the living. And amid it all, the tormented souls of the damned shuffled forward, their mouths open in silent, eternal screams.

The ground beneath Marcus's feet quaked, each step of the approaching army sending tremors through the city's walls. The air was thick with the stench of sulfur and decay, carried on the winds from the abyss that had opened to unleash this horde upon the earth. Marcus's hand tightened around the hilt of his sword, the leather-wrapped grip pressing into his palm. This was it, the final stand.

"Commander," a voice called from below. It was one of the city's scouts, his face pale and drawn as he climbed up to join Marcus on the wall. "They're... there are too many of them. We're outnumbered ten to one."

Marcus didn't flinch. His gaze remained fixed on the horizon, where the first ranks of the enemy had come into full view. "Numbers don't decide battles," he replied, his voice steady, though the weight of the situation pressed heavily on him. "Heart does."

The scout swallowed hard, nodding before retreating to his post. Marcus knew the fear that gripped the hearts of his men, and he felt it too. But fear was an enemy as deadly as any demon, and he would not let it take hold.

Down below, the streets bustled with the frantic energy of last-minute preparations. Fires burned in iron braziers, casting flickering light across the faces of the defenders as they readied their weapons and fortified the barricades. The clang of metal rang through the air as blacksmiths worked feverishly to sharpen swords and hammer out dents in armor. The sound was almost drowned out by the low hum of prayer that resonated through the city, as the faithful gathered in groups, their voices rising in desperate pleas to the heavens.

Marcus raised his sword high, the blade catching the light as he called out to his men. "This is our city!" he shouted, his voice carrying over the battlements. "Our home! Our families are behind these walls, and I'll be damned if I let those monsters take it from us. We fight for the living. We fight for the future. And we fight knowing that even if we fall, we will not fall in vain!"

"Let the light of heaven shield us," one of the elders intoned, his voice deep and resonant. "Let the flames of righteousness consume our enemies. Let the will of the Almighty guide our hands."

Nearby, the city's spiritual leaders gathered in the central square, their voices rising in a powerful chant that echoed through the streets. They stood in a circle, hands raised to the sky, invoking the protection of the divine with every fiber of their being. The ground beneath them pulsed with energy as if the city itself was responding to their prayers.

As the spiritual leaders continued their invocation, the defenders of the Sanctuary took their positions along the walls, their armor gleaming in the firelight. Faces, set in grim determination, stared out at the advancing horde. The silence that followed the final words of the prayer was almost deafening, the calm before the storm.

A roar of agreement surged from the fighters around him, but above it, something else began to rise. A sound that didn't belong to steel or gunpowder. It cut through the chaos like sunlight through fog.

Emily's violin.

Somewhere just behind the inner barricade, her bow danced across the strings, fierce and unwavering. The melody wasn't mournful, it was defiant. It surged with purpose, rallying the frightened, steadying the broken. Her fingers moved with urgency, but her face remained calm, eyes closed, focused not on the violence but on the spirit of the moment.

Soldiers turned their heads as the music grew louder. Not to listen, but to remember. It was a sound of home.

A roar of approval rose from the defenders, a thunderous sound that seemed to shake the very walls they stood upon. Marcus felt the energy of his men; their fear now transformed into a fierce determination. He looked back out at the approaching darkness, his jaw set.

The first sounds of the enemy reached his ears, the clattering of weapons, and the deep, guttural growls of the demons. As they got closer, the very air seemed to grow colder.

"Hold the line!" Marcus commanded; his voice unwavering. "No one falls back!"

The defenders braced themselves, weapons at the ready. The atmosphere was charged with tension, every breath drawn in unison as they awaited the inevitable clash.

The first wave of Lilith's forces reached the walls, a monstrous tide crashing against the city's defenses. The impact was immediate and brutal, demons scaled the walls with inhuman speed, their claws raking against stone as they sought to breach the city.

On the battlements, archers fired volley after volley of arrows into the horde below, their faces grim with determination. The arrows, blessed by the city's spiritual leaders, glowed with a faint, holy light as they streaked through the air, finding their mark in the twisted bodies of the dark creatures. The demons shrieked as the arrows struck, their bodies bursting into flames before collapsing into ash. But even this divine protection was not enough to stem the tide.

"Push them back!" Marcus roared, driving his sword through the chest of the first demon that breached the wall, only to be replaced by another. "Do not let them through!"

All around him, the defenders fought with a ferocity born of desperation. The screams of the wounded, and the roars of the attacking demons filled the air, creating a symphony of violence that echoed through the night.

The battle had begun, and with it, the final test of the sanctuary's resolve. The storm had broken, and there was no turning back.

The city's defenses strained under the relentless assault. The walls, though fortified, groaned as the dark creatures threw themselves against them with reckless abandonment. The defenders fought with everything they had, but the sheer number of enemies was overwhelming. For every demon they cut down, two more seemed to take its place, their clawed hands scrabbling at the stones, their eyes burning with the unholy fire of Lilith's wrath.

"Keep firing!" one of the archers yelled, his voice hoarse from shouting commands. He notched another arrow, drawing back the string until it trembled under the tension. The arrow flew true, striking the creature in the chest, but instead of falling, it only roared in fury, tearing the arrow from its flesh and hurling it back toward the battlements with unnatural strength.

The dark magic that fueled Lilith's army made them nearly unstoppable, and the defenders knew that they were facing something far beyond the realm of human strength.

Below, the city gates shuddered under the repeated battering of demons. The creatures slammed their fists against the iron-reinforced wood, each blow sending splinters flying. Inside the gates, a group of defenders had taken up positions, ready to defend the entrance with their lives.

"Hold the gate!" Marcus ordered, his voice cutting through the chaos. He could see the fear in their eyes, but also the determination. They knew what was at stake, and they would not let the city fall.

As the demon delivered another powerful blow, the gates creaked ominously, the wood beginning to splinter under the pressure. The defenders inside braced themselves, gripping their weapons tightly, knowing that the moment the gates gave way, they would be face-to-face with the full fury of Lilith's army.

Suddenly, a brilliant light erupted from the city's central square, where the spiritual leaders had gathered in prayer. The light shot up into the sky, forming a protective dome over the city, its golden glow holding back the darkness for a precious few moments. The demons recoiled as the light touched them, their forms flickering as if they were being pulled back into the shadows from which they came.

"For the Light!" one of the spiritual leaders cried out, raising a staff high above his head. The defenders, heartened by this divine intervention, renewed their efforts, fighting with a fierceness that belied their exhaustion.

But Lilith's forces were relentless. As the light began to fade, the demons surged forward once more, their roars filling the air with a sound that was more felt than heard, a vibration of pure malice that shook the very souls of those who heard it. The walls of the sanctuary, though fortified with stone and prayer, began to crack under the strain.

"Reinforce the western wall!" Marcus shouted, spotting a weak point where the demons had begun to breach the defenses. "We can't let them get through!"

Emily, who had been tending to the wounded, rushed to the wall with a group of soldiers. She could see the terror in their eyes, the uncertainty that came with facing an enemy that seemed to defy all logic and reason. But she steeled herself, knowing that there was no room for hesitation.

"We hold the line here," she said, her voice steady despite the fear gnawing at her insides. "We don't fall back. Not now, not ever."

The soldiers nodded, drawing their weapons as they took up positions along the crumbling wall. The air around them was thick with the stench of sulfur and burning flesh, and the ground beneath their feet was slick with blood, both human and otherwise. The noise was deafening, a constant roar of battle that drowned out all other sound.

As the demons breached the wall, the defenders met them head-on. The clash was brutal and chaotic; the screams of the dying mingled with the roars of the demons. Emily fought with everything she had, her movements quick and precise as she struck down one demon after another.

And still, Lilith's forces pressed on, their numbers seemingly without end. But even in the face of such overwhelming odds, the defenders did not give up. They fought with a ferocity that came from deep within, a burning desire to protect their home, their loved ones, and the very future of humanity.

The battle had reached a fever pitch, with the defenders of the sanctuary fighting desperately to hold their ground. Every moment felt like an eternity as they faced wave after wave of Lilith's relentless forces, their bodies, and spirits pushed to the brink of exhaustion.

Marcus fought at the forefront, his sword flashing in the dim light as he cut down one demon after another. His arms ached with the effort, his muscles burning, but he refused to let up. The walls around him were crumbling, and he knew that if they didn't hold the line, the city would fall.

"Keep pushing!" he yelled, his voice hoarse from shouting. He could barely hear himself over the din of battle, the screams of the dying, and the guttural roars of the demons. "We can't let them break through!"

But even as he spoke, he could feel the tide turning against them. The defenders were outnumbered, outmatched, and running out of time. The western wall, once strong and impenetrable, had been breached in several places, and the demons were pouring through, overwhelming the defenders in a brutal melee.

"We're not going to make it," one of the soldiers muttered, his voice filled with despair. He was young, barely out of his teens, and his face was pale with fear.

"Yes, we will!" Marcus snapped, grabbing the young soldier by the arm. His eyes burned with fierce determination. "We've come this far. We don't give up now. Not when it matters most."

The soldier nodded, his grip tightening on his weapon. But the doubt in his eyes was clear, how could they possibly stand against such overwhelming odds?

As if in answer to that unspoken question, a deafening crash echoed across the battlefield. The massive gates of the city, battered and splintered, finally gave way under the relentless assault. With a terrible roar, the demons charged through and surged into the city like a flood.

"Fall back! Fall back to the inner defenses!" Marcus shouted. The defenders began to retreat, fighting every step of the way as they were pushed back into the heart of the city.

Panic spread through the ranks as the defenders realized how close they were to being overrun. The once-organized lines began to break as soldiers and civilians alike scrambled to escape the oncoming horde. The city was on the verge of collapse.

35- Fall

Suddenly, a blinding light erupted from the sky, bathing the battlefield in a brilliant, holy glow. The ground trembled as the light intensified, pushing back the darkness that had threatened to engulf the city. The demons recoiled, their eyes wide with fear and hatred as the light washed over them.

Marcus and Emily shielded their eyes, stunned by the sudden change. The light was so intense, so pure, that it seemed to pierce through the very fabric of reality, dispelling the shadows and bringing a momentary calm to the chaos.

"Look!" a voice cried out, filled with awe. "The heavens are opening!"

Marcus looked up, his breath catching in his throat. The sky above the sanctuary had split open, revealing a sight that took his breath away. The clouds had parted, and from the rift in the sky, a host of angels descended, their wings shimmering with ethereal light.

The demons, sensing the overwhelming power of the angels, began to falter. Their once relentless advance slowed, and for the first time, fear flickered in their burning eyes.

"Angels," Emily whispered, her voice trembling with emotion. "They've come to save us."

The defenders, inspired by the divine intervention, found new strength within themselves. They rallied together; their hearts filled with renewed hope. The fear that had gripped them moments before was replaced by a fierce determination. With the heavenly host at their side, they knew that they could stand against anything.

"Push them back!" Marcus roared; his voice filled with a new energy. "We fight with the light on our side!"

The defenders surged forward, their weapons blazing with a holy light as they drove the demons back. The battle, once so desperate and chaotic, had turned in their favor. The forces of darkness, which had seemed unstoppable, were now in full retreat, unable to withstand the combined power of the defenders and the heavenly host.

The sight of the angels fighting alongside the defenders was nothing short of awe-inspiring. Their movements were swift and precise, their swords cutting through the dark creatures with ease. The demons fell before them, their bodies disintegrating into ash as they were struck down by the light.

As the last of the demons fled, the battlefield fell silent, save for the soft flutter of angelic wings. The defenders stood in stunned silence, their weapons still raised, unsure if the battle was truly over.

"We've done it," Emily said, her voice barely more than a whisper. "We've driven them back."

But Marcus knew that this was only the beginning. Lilith herself had not yet appeared, and he knew that the final confrontation was still to come.

"We hold the city," Marcus said, his voice steady. "But the real battle is still ahead of us."

The battlefield was a scene of devastation, a place where the clash between light and darkness had torn the very fabric of reality. As the dust settled and the last echoes of battle faded, a heavy silence fell over the Sanctuary. The defenders, battered and weary, looked on in a mixture of awe and dread as the final confrontation began to unfold before their eyes.

Lilith, the ancient embodiment of darkness and rebellion, stood at the heart of the battlefield, her form wreathed in shadows that writhed and twisted like living things. Her eyes, once blazing with the fire of hatred, now burned with an intensity that seemed to challenge the heavens themselves. The air around her crackled with dark energy, a palpable force that threatened to consume everything in its path.

With a scream of rage, Lilith unleashed a torrent of dark energy that surged across the battlefield like a black tidal wave, crashing against the defenses of the sanctuary. The ground shook violently, and the sky above turned as black as night, blotted out by the sheer force of her power. The defenders, though shielded by the light of the heavenly host, were driven to their knees, their strength almost drained by the overwhelming darkness.

But even as the shadows closed in, a radiant light pierced through the gloom, growing brighter and brighter until it illuminated the entire battlefield. The source of this light was our Savior himself, descending from the heavens with a host of angels by His side. His presence was a force of pure love and justice, a power so overwhelming that the darkness recoiled in fear.

"Your reign ends here, Lilith," our Savior declared, His voice calm but filled with divine authority. "You have brought only pain and suffering to this world, but now your time is over. The light will always prevail over the darkness."

Lilith's eyes narrowed, her expression twisting with hatred and desperation. "You are a fool if you think you can stop me!" she spat, her voice reverberating with a dark, ancient power. "I am eternal! I am beyond your reach!"

With a roar of fury, Lilith charged at the Savior, her sword of dark flames materializing in her hand. The blade crackled with malevolent energy; a weapon forged from the very essence of darkness. She moved with the speed of a storm, her form a blur as she closed the distance between them, her sword aimed directly at the Savior's heart.

The Savior met her charge with unflinching resolve, His own sword of divine light appearing in His grasp. The two forces collided with a thunderous crash, the impact sending shockwaves rippling across the battlefield. The very earth seemed to tremble under the force of their battle, and the sky above split open, revealing the infinite expanse of the cosmos beyond.

The battle that ensued was nothing short of cataclysmic. Lilith fought with a fury that defied comprehension, her attacks a whirlwind of dark magic and raw power. Every swing of her sword sent arcs of black energy slicing through the air, tearing apart the ground and felling mountains in their wake. Her rage was a force of nature, a relentless storm that sought to obliterate everything in its path.

But the Savior stood firm, His movements graceful and precise, each strike of His sword a symphony of divine purpose. His light shone with an intensity that pushed back the darkness, His every action infused with the power of creation itself. Where Lilith's blows sought to destroy, the Savior's counterstrikes sought to heal, to restore the balance that had been lost.

The clash between them was titanic, a battle that shook the very foundations of existence. The forces of light and darkness collided again and again, each impact sending out waves of energy that rippled across the battlefield, altering the very fabric of reality.

Lilith's fury only grew as she realized that the Savior was not faltering. For every strike she delivered, He met it with equal strength, His light unwavering even in the face of her most powerful attacks. Her form began to distort, her dark essence unraveling as she pushed beyond the limits of her power, desperate to gain the upper hand.

"You will fall before me!" Lilith screamed, her voice a cacophony of despair and rage. Summoning the last of her strength, she channeled all her remaining energy into one final, devastating blow.

But as Lilith struck, the Savior raised His sword of light, meeting her attack with a calm, unyielding resolve. The moment their blades collided, there was a blinding flash of light, so intense that it seemed to erase all color and sound from the world. The battlefield was enveloped in a sphere of pure white light, a burst of divine energy that seemed to stretch on for an eternity.

When the light finally receded, the battlefield was still. The dark fire of Lilith's blade had been extinguished, and she stood frozen in place, her form flickering and wavering as if struggling to maintain its shape. Her eyes, once filled with unbridled fury, now showed something else, fear, and disbelief.

The Savior stepped forward, His sword still raised, His light shining brighter than ever. "Your time is over, Lilith, the light has triumphed, and your darkness holds no more power."

With a final, decisive strike, the Savior's sword of light cleaved through Lilith's form. The impact shattered the air with the sound of a thousand worlds breaking, and Lilith let out a scream that echoed across the heavens, a cry of agony and defeat. Her form convulsed as the dark energy that had sustained her unraveled in an instant.

Lilith's body crashed to the ground, her dark power dissipating as the last remnants of her essence flickered and died. She lay at the Savior's feet, her once-mighty form now lifeless and broken. The darkness that had once shrouded her was gone, leaving behind only a twisted shell, a hollow reminder of the power that had been vanquished.

The battlefield, once a place of chaos and destruction, was now bathed in the soft, golden light of dawn. The sky above cleared, revealing the serene blue of a new day, and the earth, scarred and battered, began to heal as the divine light touched it.

The defenders of the sanctuary, who had watched the epic confrontation with bated breath, now fell to their knees in reverence. The weight of what they had just witnessed settled over them, this was not just a victory, it was a salvation. Lilith, the embodiment of darkness and rebellion, had been defeated, a testament to the power of light and love over even the darkest of evils.

The Savior lowered His sword, the glow around Him softening. He knelt beside Lilith's lifeless form, placing a hand gently on her brow. There was no malice in His gesture, only a profound sadness for a soul lost to darkness long ago.

"It is done," the Savior said quietly, His voice filled with both sorrow and resolve. "The darkness has been defeated, and the world is free."

But even in victory, the Savior's expression remained one of quiet reflection. He understood that the path ahead would not be easy, that though the darkness had been driven back, the work of healing and restoration had only just begun. He rose to His feet, looking out over the sanctuary, and then to the people who had fought so bravely to defend it.

"This is a new beginning," His voice filled with both hope and gravity. "Together, we will rebuild, and the light will shine even brighter than before."

With those words, the Savior turned away from Lilith's lifeless form, His gaze now fixed on the future, a future where the world, scarred but not broken, would rise from the ashes and flourish once more.

36- *Reborn*

The battlefield, once a theater of unimaginable chaos, was now shrouded in eerie stillness. The sky, once a tempest of dark clouds and divine light, now stretched out in a calm, soft blue, as if the heavens themselves were breathing a sigh of relief. The first rays of dawn spilled over the horizon, casting a gentle glow on the city that had withstood the onslaught of darkness.

"We survived," Emily whispered beside him, her voice tinged with exhaustion and disbelief. She stood close, her face streaked with dirt and blood, her eyes reflecting a mix of sorrow and relief.

Marcus nodded; his heart heavy. "We lost so much," he murmured, his voice laden with grief. "But we've gained something too," he said softly. "A chance to rebuild. A chance to make things right."

As the divine light bathed the city in warmth, the survivors gathered around the Savior. His eyes, filled with compassion and understanding, swept over the battlefield, taking in the devastation. He knelt beside a fallen defender, placing a hand over the man's chest. The defender's labored breaths grew steady under His touch, and a peaceful expression settled over his face as he took his final breath.

At the heart of the square, surrounded by the spiritual leaders and the bravest defenders, lay Evelyn. Once vibrant and full of life, her body had been ravaged by the dark influence of Lilith. Used as a pawn in the battle between good and evil, her will had been twisted, her spirit broken by malevolent forces. Now, she lay motionless, her breathing shallow, a shadow of the woman she had once been.

The Savior approached Evelyn, His expression full of deep compassion and understanding. Marcus and Emily stood in solemn silence, their hearts heavy with a mixture of sorrow and hope. They had fought desperately to protect her, to keep her from the darkness, and now they held their breath, praying that she could still be saved.

Kneeling beside her, He placed His hands gently on her forehead, His touch radiating a soft, healing light. The glow seeped into Evelyn, spreading warmth and life through her broken form. The darkness that had consumed her recoiled, retreating in the face of His love and compassion.

The crowd watched in awe as the light enveloped Evelyn. Her body trembled as its healing power took hold. Her pale skin flushed with color, her once-shut eyes fluttering, as if waking from a long, harrowing nightmare. The shadows clouding her mind and soul lifted, replaced by a peace and clarity she had not known in what felt like an eternity.

"Evelyn," the Savior murmured, His voice rich with tenderness. "You are free."

Tears welled in her eyes as she slowly opened them, blinking against the brilliance surrounding her. She gasped, drawing in a deep breath, feeling the last remnants of Lilith's influence break apart and dissolve. The chains that had bound her for so long were gone, her mind clear, her spirit whole once more.

"Thank you," Evelyn whispered, her voice trembling with emotion. "I... I never thought I would be free again."

A gentle smile crossed the Savior's face, His hand still resting lightly against her forehead. "You were never truly lost. Your strength, your faith, they remained with you, even in your darkest moments. And now, you are whole again."

The light around Evelyn grew even brighter, wrapping her in a warm, protective glow. The onlookers watched in silent reverence as she healed before their eyes. The scars, both physical and spiritual, that Lilith had inflicted faded away, replaced by a radiance that seemed to emanate from within. She was no longer the broken woman they had fought to save. She was restored, renewed, a beacon of hope.

Evelyn rose, fully restored, her gaze sweeping over the faces of those who had stood by her. Gratitude filled her heart. No longer was she alone in her struggle. She had been given a second chance, a chance to live free from the shadows that had once consumed her.

The Savior extended His hand, helping her to her feet. Though the brilliant light around them began to soften, its warmth lingered, a silent reassurance of the divine presence that had saved them all. "Go forward, Evelyn," His voice both firm and kind. "Live with the knowledge that you are loved, you are whole, and you have the strength to face whatever lies ahead."

Tears streamed down Evelyn's face as she looked up at Him. "I will," she vowed, her voice steady despite the emotions tightening her throat. "I will live in the light, and I will never forget what has been done for me."

The crowd, witnessing this moment of grace and renewal, felt a wave of emotion wash over them. It was a victory, not just for Evelyn, but for all who had fought to protect the light in the face of overwhelming darkness. The sacrifices they had made had not been in vain.

As Evelyn stepped forward, the people of the sanctuary reached out to her, their voices filled with words of love and encouragement. She was one of them, and her restoration was a symbol of their hope, their resilience. Together, they would rebuild. Together, they would heal.

The morning sun began to rise, casting its golden light upon the city. Though weary from battle, the survivors found solace in knowing they had endured. But for Evelyn, there was one moment she had longed for more than any other, a reunion that had sustained her through the darkest hours of her captivity.

Standing in the center of the square, her heart pounded as she searched the faces of those around her. Though she had been restored, a missing piece of her soul remained, her child, the innocent life born under the shadow of darkness yet protected from its grasp.

Her eyes landed on Marcus and Emily standing nearby. In Emily's arms, wrapped in a soft blanket, was Evelyn's baby, the child kept safe from Lilith's reach by the love and bravery of those who had risked everything.

Evelyn's breath hitched as she took in the tiny bundle, her emotions surging, relief, fear, overwhelming love. Her legs felt weak as she took a hesitant step forward, her gaze locked on her child.

Emily, sensing the weight of the moment, stepped forward with a gentle smile. "She's been waiting for you," she said softly, her voice filled with warmth and reassurance. Carefully, she placed the baby in Evelyn's trembling arms, her own eyes shining with tears.

Evelyn held her child close, her hands trembling as she cradled the tiny, delicate form against her chest. The baby gazed up at her with wide, innocent eyes, her tiny fingers curling around a lock of Evelyn's hair. The connection was immediate, an unbreakable bond that transcended the horrors of the past. A flood of emotions surged through Evelyn, joy, relief, and a love so deep filled every corner of her heart.

"Hello, my sweet," she whispered, her voice thick with emotion as tears spilled down her cheeks. She traced a gentle finger along her baby's soft cheek, overwhelmed by the fragile warmth in her arms. "I've missed you so much."

The baby cooed softly, reaching up to touch Evelyn's tear-streaked face. That tiny touch was like a balm to her soul, soothing wounds that had festered far too long. In that moment, the battle, the fear, the darkness, all of it melted away. Only this remained: her child, safe in her embrace, a piece of light she had thought lost forever.

Marcus and Emily stood nearby, watching with tear-filled eyes, their hearts swelling with quiet fulfillment. They had risked everything to protect this child, shielding her from the darkness that had threatened to consume the world. And now, seeing mother and daughter reunited, they knew, every sacrifice had been worth it.

"You're safe now," Evelyn whispered, pressing a tender kiss to her daughter's forehead. "We both are. And I promise, I will never let anything hurt you again."

The crowd, moved by the poignant reunion, felt a wave of relief and joy ripple through them. This was more than a mother reclaiming her child, it was proof of what they had fought for. The baby, once a target of unspeakable evil, was now a living testament to the love and light that had triumphed.

As Evelyn held her daughter close, the people of the sanctuary gathered around, offering soft words of love and support. Though they had all suffered, though loss and grief lingered, this moment reminded them of what truly mattered, life, love, and the future they would build together.

Evelyn lifted her gaze to Marcus and Emily, her expression raw with gratitude. "Thank you," she said, her voice trembling. "For keeping her safe when I couldn't."

Marcus shook his head, his voice steady yet gentle. "You're her mother, Evelyn. You gave her life. We just made sure she had the chance to live it."

Emily smiled, brushing away a tear. "She's going to grow up in a world where the light shines because of you. Because of all of us."

Evelyn nodded, her heart brimming with peace. The road ahead would not be easy. There were scars that would take time to heal, shadows that would linger at the edges of memory. But she was not alone. She had her child. She had her friends. And she had a community that had proven its strength, its resilience.

With the battle behind them and a new dawn breaking, the survivors turned to the task ahead, rebuilding their home and their lives. Scars of the conflict remained, crumbling walls, shattered homes, the silent weight of loss, but amid the ruins, a quiet determination took root.

The Savior remained among them, His presence a beacon of comfort and guidance. His light, steady, and unwavering, illuminated their path forward, both physically and spiritually. Under His watchful care, the sanctuary became more than a refuge; it became a symbol of hope, not just for those within its walls but for all who sought light in the wake of darkness.

As the sanctuary flourished, the light of their savior remained ever-present, a gentle yet unwavering reminder of the divine protection that had saved them. Once a battlefield, the city had become a haven of peace and prosperity, its radiance calling out to the world, offering hope to all who sought it.

Author Story:
Troy Eugene Biffath

Troy Eugene Biffath is a 56-year-old husband, father of five, and creator of songs and stories. For years, he kept creativity at a distance, uncertain it was his to hold. That shifted in 2023 when he began writing again, pouring love, struggle, and quiet grit into words. He brought songs to life, including "Lilith's Whisper" and "Trial by Fire," woven into his novel The Rise and Fall of Darkness. With more books on the way, he's found his stride.

I don't create for fame. I create because I finally can.